PLOTTING FOR MURDER

TAMRA BAUMANN

CHAPTER 1

As I stare into a pair of gorgeous green eyes, ones I should be smitten with, they're so attractive, all I can think is that whoever said life doesn't always turn out the way you planned wasn't kidding. I would've never guessed a few months ago that I'd be sitting across from an estate lawyer discussing my deceased mother's trust fund—one whose funds she couldn't access. Worse, I'd vowed I'd never live in the small town where I grew up, and six weeks later, I'm still here. A chef, trying to save my mom's failing mystery bookstore, Cloaks, Daggers, and Croissants. At least there's food in the store's name. That's something my culinary-loving heart can embrace.

A commotion near the front of the bookstore interrupts whatever Gage the lawyer was saying that I wasn't fully listening to, and we both turn to see what's going on.

"Is there a Sawyer Davis here?" a woman carrying a cute dog calls out.

I raise my hand so the older woman built like a linebacker can spot me. "Right here."

The woman skids to a stop at our table and tosses a big bag at my feet. The little dog she's holding looks like an adorable stuffed animal. Like a fluffy mini golden retriever, but with a white chin.

"You're a woman?" The lady with the dog tilts her head to the right, and so does the pup. Both seem confused about something. "Sawyer is a man's name, isn't it?"

If I had a dollar for every time I've heard that, I wouldn't be as broke as I am right now. "My parents were hoping for a boy, I guess. What can I help you with?"

"I'm here to deliver your mini goldendoodle. He's four months old today." The woman thrusts the pup my way. "Your mother already paid in full. Everything you'll need is in the bag."

This has to be some sort of joke. And not a funny one. "I'm sorry Ms...."

"Bertha, but everyone calls me Bert. On account of my overly large hands and feet for a woman."

It's tempting to point out that Bert is a man's name too, but I won't. And it'd be sort of rude to agree with her on her manly body parts. Besides, I'm too busy having a ministroke over the dog. "There has to be some sort of a mix-up. My mother passed away six weeks ago."

"Nope." Bert shakes her head as she thrusts the ball of fluff all the way into my arms. "Your mom ordered him three months ago. And I won't take no for an answer. Zoe said it was a deathbed wish, and I'm not messing with a witch and a promise."

My mother hadn't been a witch. She'd taught yoga and sold crystals in the back of her bookstore. Believed in the metaphysical and karma. Most called her an eccentric hippie. Hence the small mystery bookstore where everyone was always welcome to stop by, read a book in any of the cozy nooks she'd set up around the store, drink all the coffee, and eat all the croissants their hearts desired. All served on pretty china plates and cups. It's a welcoming little shop my mother ran with love, but it makes very little money.

Thinking of my mom chokes me up for the fifth time today, so I clear my throat and try to sound stern. "You don't understand, Bert." I try to give the dog back, but Bert has tucked her huge hands behind her back. "I can't take care of a puppy. Since my mom died, I've had my hands full with an old house in a constant state of disrepair and this mystery bookstore I inherited. I'm a chef who doesn't even read mysteries. I'm in so far over my head, I'm drowning in my own soup pot here."

Bert frowns. "But you read, right?"

"Of course, but I prefer happy romances, not whodunnits with dead bodies around every corner. They scare me."

"I kinda like to be scared out of my wits."

Of course, she does. And she is doing a fine job of scaring me too. No way can I add a dog to my already chaotic life.

Gage, the single blond lawyer sitting across from me adds ever so helpfully, "And Sawyer's a landlord now too."

I throw a hand out toward Gage in a *see what I mean* gesture that's falling on blind eyes and deaf ears. I hadn't noticed until now how large Bert's ears are too. No matter how big, they aren't hearing my plea.

The dog licks my chin, and I start to cave. Nope. Doesn't matter how cute the pooch is. My head will explode if I add one more problem to my life. "Please, Bert? You can keep the money. Sell him to someone else. It'd be the most humane thing for the dog. He doesn't need a person on the edge of a mental breakdown for an owner."

The little dog tucks his head under my chin and sighs. I think he already knows I'm practically a goner. I love all dogs. I just couldn't have one in my apartment back in Chicago.

Bert holds up her mitt of a hand like a traffic cop. "I'm not going against your mom. I need my muchachas all lined up just like they are, thank you very much." Bert turns and walks away.

I call out, "I'm pretty sure you mean chakras." Then I look into a pair of soulful brown eyes begging me to keep him.

3

Maybe my niece and nephew would want a dog? My sister could only kill me a little for giving the dog to the kids as a gift. How much trouble could a puppy be? "Does he have a name?"

Bert stops and turns around. "Cooper. Now that I know you're a female, I get it. Your mom told me the whole story about you and the sheriff. It's a doozy, that's for sure."

Of course, Mom named the dog after Dylan Cooper.

Real subtle, Mother.

Bert is almost out the door when she calls out, "There's some piddle pads in the bag, but he's due for a number two soon. Don't dally, or your customers are going to be stepping in a pile of fun. Have a great day!" She disappears out the door.

Gage is trying not to laugh, so I ask, "You knew about this, didn't you?"

He can't hold back his grin any longer. "Yeah." He reaches out and pats Cooper. "I told Zoe it might not be a good idea. That you'd be overwhelmed as it is. Then she told me why she ordered the dog knowing she wouldn't be here to meet him. I couldn't argue with her logic."

I lay a kiss on top of Cooper's fluffy head where there's a little white spot too. "My mother didn't have a logical bone in her body."

"Maybe, but she had a big heart. She needed to know you'd have someone who'd love you unconditionally. Like she did."

Oh, man. Mother's guilt—and love—are powerful things. Now I have no choice but to keep Cooper.

Tears fill my eyes as I hug my new little dog tighter. I miss my mom so much. She could be the biggest matchmaking nut sometimes, but she loved me and my sister, Megan.

"This is her way of telling me, again, to take Dylan back. But that is so not happening. Dylan's more of a dog than Cooper."

Gage smiles while staring into my eyes as if searching for something. Then he says quietly, "I was wondering how you still felt about the sheriff. But are you afraid your muchachas might get out of sync if you don't listen to your mom?"

"Not in the least." Is Gage flirting with me? I'm so rusty at dating, I'm oblivious sometimes. Probably not. He's built, blond, and handsome, and he'd never be interested in an average-looking brunette like me who's allergic to gyms. My workouts come from lifting pots with pork shoulders in them. Well, now maybe it'll be cases of mystery books, but not if I can help it. I'm still determined to own my own restaurant one day. And I have a plan to get around the stupid trust rules.

That's where Gage the smart lawyer is going to come in handy. "Is there any way to break the trust my grandparents set up for my mom?"

He shakes his head. "It was set up because your mom was so… To protect the money from her… You know what? Zoe was who she was, and it just didn't jibe with what her parents wanted for her. Unfortunately, you're going to be the one to pay the price. If you still want to keep the trust, that is?"

Um, let's think. Give up millions of dollars to go back to being broke trying to make it as a chef in Chicago? Or figure out how to outwit the trust? "I'll keep it for now. Thanks."

Mostly to give my mother the revenge she so deserves against her mean brother, my uncle and the mayor of our little town, who already got his half of the trust but wants my mother's too. My mother wasn't normal, but she was good, kind, and someone to emulate. I feel like she was depending on me to put my uncle in his place, and I'm up for the challenge.

On the other hand, I guess I can't blame my grandparents for putting so many restrictions on the money they left my mom. At the time, my mother was being nightly sawed in half as a traveling magician's assistant. And as a result of spending the rest of those nights in the same hotel room with said magician to save money, my sister and I came about. But they never married, which was probably a good thing.

Gage says, "You don't think you'll have any problems with your father wanting a share? Not that he's entitled, but it could cause some inconvenience if he decides to file suit."

"Oh, that's right." I lift a finger and finish off my fifth cup of coffee by ten fifteen in the morning. I really need to cut back. "You're new in town. You don't know the story."

Gage frowns. "I've been here eight years."

"Right. New in town. If you weren't born in Sunset Cove, you'll always be new. Anyway, my father once tried to get his share of the trust claiming a common law marriage. It was quite the fiasco. In the end, his bluff didn't work, and nothing ever came of it."

Gage leans closer. "Is your dad really a traveling magician? Still?"

I sigh inwardly. "Yep. Max the Magnificent. I'll introduce you the next time he shows up unexpectedly to sleep on my couch and before he magically makes himself disappear again. How long he stays usually depends on how much cash I have on me."

When I tell people what my father does, they always laugh and think I'm kidding. It wasn't any wonder why the kids of a hippie and a flaky magician never really fit in here. Sunset Cove, perched on the cliffs of Northern California, a bohemian tourist town just south of San Francisco, was meant to cater to those who loved art. And to the curious who couldn't afford it but appreciated it.

Digging through the bag Bert dropped at my feet I find a leash. "Mind if we continue this meeting at the park, Gage?" There's a roll of plastic poop bags inside, so I grab two, just in case.

"Sure." He stands and waits while I get the leash attached to Cooper's collar.

However, Cooper doesn't appear to be trained in the art of walking on a leash yet and thinks it's a tug game. And he's a better player than I am. He starts running for the door with the leash trailing behind. Seems I'm the untrained one here.

Gage is faster, though, and scoops up the puppy. "No, you don't, buddy." He expertly tucks Cooper under one arm and holds the bookshop's door open for me to pass through first. A gentleman and a lawyer.

Is that an oxymoron?

I call out to my emo goth girl assistant who I inherited along with the store. "I'll be back in a few, Brittany. Please be nice to the customers."

Brittany looks up from her phone long enough to say, "Whatever," then goes right back to what she was doing. Probably looking up how many shades of black her favorite lipstick comes in.

The two of us need to have a chat one of these days.

Gage and I walk across the street to the busy town square filled with tourists licking ice-cream cones in the warm July sunshine. He asks, "Why do you keep Brittany?"

I shrug. "She reminds me of me at that age. Doesn't fit in with the other kids at school. And she's being raised by a single mom who can't seem to hold down a job. She needs the money."

Gage puts Cooper down on the grass, and the dog wags his goofy long tail that sometimes curls at the end and starts sniffing. "You need the money too. I bet she puts off more customers than you keep."

Yeah. Brittany and I really need to have that talk. "Speaking of money. My understanding is that the trust can only be used for normal business expenses, for the upkeep of the commercial rental properties, and on my crumbling old house?" All the profits and rents collected go straight to the trust fund first. It's rarely enough to cover all the monthly bills.

"And for your health and education. Which prompts me to ask, how does a woman with an advanced engineering degree from MIT end up going back to school to become a chef?"

"Math was easy for me, and they wanted females in such a male-dominated field. I thought it'd be a great opportunity to really do something with my life while Dylan figured out his. Unfortunately, when I was done, Dylan was still *confused*, and I found out engineering bored me to tears. I went back to the one thing I knew made me happy. Cooking. So, what's to stop me from paying myself a million-dollar salary at the bookstore?"

The dog finds a tree and lifts his little leg as Gage says, "There are restrictions and limits in the trust. You'll find them near the end. So, what's the idea you wanted to discuss?"

I almost forgot this guy gets paid by the millisecond. Back to business. I'd fallen asleep from sheer boredom reading the complicated trust last night, but I have an idea to get my own restaurant. "It's all outlined right here." I hand him my plan to outwit my mean uncle.

As he reads the document, a slow smile forms on Gage's face. "So, the trust builds a restaurant. And I suppose this is all hush-hush so the mayor won't know the new tenant will be you?"

"See? That's why they pay you the big bucks. You catch on fast. And even better, I can keep all the profits from that business because I'll own it. As long as I pay the trust monthly rent to use the building and equipment." Cooper bounds back and then does his second order of business right at my feet. "Yuck. This is going to take some getting used to."

Gage grabs the plastic bag from my hand and gallantly handles the cleanup for me. "Your uncle has to approve any expenditure from the trust over five thousand dollars. I'd guess you'll need hundreds of thousands. It's why your newly acquired commercial properties are in disrepair. Your mom hated dealing with your uncle."

My Uncle Frank, my mom's only sibling, wants me to give up and go away so he gets all the money in the trust. It reverts to him if my sister or I don't want it. My sister already said she wants nothing to do with the trust because she's busy cutting open people's brains, making them better and getting paid more money than she can spend. I'm not letting the big bully win. "No problem. I'll just have all the contractors bill me in four thousand nine hundred and ninety-nine dollar increments."

Gage two-points the little bag into a nearby trash bin. "You still need the permits, and the mayor has a say in that."

"That's where you come in. If you can do all this for your very exclusive and private client, *moi*, who technically has millions in the bank but can't use them without being really sneaky, I think we can pull this off."

Cooper and I stare at Gage as his forehead crinkles in thought.

My stomach twists a little as I raise a hand and wave to my neighbor Bill, who's riding his bike on the path that leads to the cliffs.

Sunset Cove is a nice small town, with an idyllic square in the middle with a park. It includes all the typical touristy shops that sell art, ice cream, knickknacks, T-shirts, and more. It's perched on the cliffs overlooking the ocean. Recently, there has been an influx of young professionals from San Francisco who like their microbreweries, which we have our share of now, and who want to raise their kids in a place that has no real crime. Where the neighbors care about the kids and who'll tell you if little Jane or Johnny are doing something wrong. It feels plain nosy to the kids, but to their parents, it feels like raising their children in a loving village. And it's part of the same reason I keep Brittany employed. To help her.

Cooper and I wait patiently while Gage lifts a hand and rubs the back of his neck as he continues to read my plan.

Finally, he says, "I actually think this might work. It'd mean lots of meetings between us, though. My schedule is already pretty full, so it might have to be over dinner and drinks now and then." His smile makes his already handsome face even more attractive.

Okay. He's definitely flirting with me now.

My mother the amateur matchmaker is probably behind his attraction. I'm trying to decide if I'm annoyed at my mom or flattered that he'd be attracted. Maybe a bit of both. "How about we keep those dinners and drinks all about business? At least until the restaurant is open."

His smile fades as if I'd just hit his dimmer switch. "Sounds disappointing but reasonable. Luckily, I'm a patient man. See you in a few days with some papers to sign." He squats and pets Cooper. "You be good for Sawyer, little man." Cooper rolls on his back to alert Gage that there's a belly to be rubbed too.

"Thanks, Gage. I appreciate it." I hate to disappoint the guy, and maybe myself just a bit, because the man is incredibly good-looking, but I don't have time for anyone else right now. Maybe one day.

I return Gage's wave, and then my new puppy and I watch him walk away. Not a bad view from this side either. He's always dressed in sharp suits that fit his toned body well.

"New dog?" A deep voice that haunts me still even after so many years makes me cringe.

I turn around and have to lift my chin to meet the annoying sheriff's gaze. Dylan Cooper's blue eyes always twinkle like he has a secret. Because he does. He's seen me in my birthday suit. Luckily, I was way thinner back then. "Shouldn't you be harassing jaywalkers or something?"

He leans his body with way too many muscles closer. "I'd rather harass *you*." Then he crouches and pets Cooper. The dog clearly has no taste, because Cooper is practically sitting on Dylan's lap now. "This is a cute pooch. What's his name?"

Why can't the earth open right now and save me from having this embarrassing conversation? "Oh, look. I think someone is robbing Renee's store." I point across the park, to the ice-cream shop my only friend from high school runs.

Dylan ignores me as he lifts the little metal name tag

hanging from my dog's collar I had no idea was there. Then a big grin lights up Dylan's face. His shoulders shake as he laughs. "Is this your way of telling me you still love me?"

I want to taser myself with Dylan's weapon. "My mother's idea. Not mine. Obviously."

He stands, snuggles the pup against his chest, and scratches Cooper's ears. "Alexandra and Collin are going to love him."

Why my sister had to go and marry Dylan's brother, ruining family Christmas gatherings for the rest of my life, is a mystery I'll never solve. Yet, Dylan and I both love our niece and nephew more than we enjoy fighting, so we tolerate each other. At least in front of the kids.

"Yeah. Well, gotta run." I hold my hands out for the dog, but Dylan makes no move to hand Cooper over. It's doggie blackmail.

He says, "Heard you were resuming book club tonight. And that you're cooking. Need another member?"

Brittany must've tattled. She doesn't say a word to paying customers all day, but Dylan comes in with his wavy dark hair, pretty smile, and dazzling blue eyes and the kid sings like the fat lady at the opera. My plan is to try out some recipes I'm considering for my new restaurant on the book group.

"Didn't make enough. You eat like a starving pack of wolves. Dog, please." I hold out my hands again, and this time, he passes Cooper over.

"How're you holding up? Anything I can do to help?" Sincerity beams from within his gorgeous eyes.

I don't want him to be nice to me right now. I might cry. And he's the last person I'd want to see my tears. Ever again. "I'm okay. Thanks, though." I have to blink hard to stop the burning in the back of my eyes.

I put Cooper on all fours, and we head back toward the bookstore. "If we have any leftovers tonight, I'll have Brittany run them by your office tomorrow."

11

Dylan, a self-proclaimed foodie, has a better palate than even my highly trained one, having traveled the world during his time in the military. Not that I'd ever tell him that. Still, I'd like to know what he thinks of my new crab cake recipe because he never holds back. He's always brutally honest.

He calls out from behind, "See? You do still love me."

Brother. Moving back to Chicago is looking better and better. On the other hand, my mom only ever asked one thing of me. Right before she died, she asked me to *try* living here again. So, I'm trying.

Dylan living here again isn't going to make things any easier. He and I dated in high school and through my years at MIT, after which we planned to be married. Unfortunately, then his father left his mother after thirty-five years of marriage. Shortly after, his mom died in a car crash. Some say running her car over a cliff wasn't an accident. She'd done it on purpose because of her grief. As a result, Dylan lost faith in his father and in the institution of marriage, and it left him questioning his love for me.

We're both thirty-two now, haven't been together for almost eight years, and because our sibs fell in love, we've found a way to be around each other at holidays that seems to work.

Besides, I can't leave and let my uncle win. He disrespected my mom every chance he got, and if I don't accept the terms of the trust my grandparents set up, it all goes to him. I'll just have to learn to live in the same small town along with Dylan Cooper. And Gage. And any other men my mother probably guilted or cajoled into asking me out after she'd passed, in case I don't take Dylan back.

Dylan will be the toughest. The man broke my heart so badly, it's never been the same.

CHAPTER 2

*C*ooper and Brittany watch as I shove around a few tables and chairs in the small dining area in the bookstore to prepare for the Thursday-evening book club. I ask my black-clad employee, "Do we have enough coffee left for everyone?" Our daily delivery doesn't always last the whole day, what with all the people who stop by because the croissants and coffee are always free. Hearing the latest gossip is fun, but it'd be nice if a few actually bought a book now and then too.

Brittany shrugs. "Don't know."

I close my eyes and count to five. "Perhaps you could go check for me?"

"Dude. This is a *book club*. They drink alcohol."

I stop my arranging. "We can serve alcohol in the store?"

"Not legally." Brittany rolls her eyes. "There's a bunch of cases of wine in the back by the heater, and that old fridge in the other corner is filled with beer. I put the glasses out by the front door like I always do. Zoe never let me handle the booze. That's your job."

"Good. Because I could use some wine right now myself." I hadn't noticed the wine because I haven't begun to tackle the messy storage room. I've been too busy trying to make the storefront look organized and neat the past few weeks. Just like my mom always did.

She'd arranged little reading nooks scattered about, themed and organized by author. The Black Crow nook consists of two comfy chairs behind some bookcases surrounded by works of Poe. Around another set of bookshelves is the Agatha Christie Parlor, with its wingback chairs near the fireplace surrounded by the works of the grand dame of mystery. And in the rear, the more modern J. D. Robb futuristic futon and chairs beckoned for relaxed reading comforts. My mother wanted people to come and stay for a while, and I want to keep that tradition going.

Before I go into the back room, I look around to see if the two customers in the store need anything. One, a middle-aged, dark-haired man I don't know, is busy reading the back cover of a book, and the other person had been my nemesis in high school, red-haired bombshell Crystal Meyers. She'd always had a crush on Dylan and therefore hated me. Why she's been hanging around so much lately was another mystery. Probably scouting the place to see if Dylan ever comes to visit me now that I'm back. Well, he doesn't, so Crystal can have Dylan Cooper all to herself.

I go into the dusty back room, stacked to the roof with old books, pass the bathroom, and find the many cases of wine. My mom must've found a sale or something, because there must be twenty cases of the inexpensive California vintage.

We're having crab cakes, truffle mac and cheese, and spicy corn on the cob, so I grab two bottles of white wine. There's a cooler by the fridge, and I load that up with ice and throw the beer and wine inside. Then I haul it all out to the dining area with Cooper on my heels.

He hasn't let me out of his sight all afternoon, poor guy. His life is in upheaval too, being torn from his mom and siblings.

And now all we have is each other. My sneaky mother might have done me a huge favor by giving me Cooper after all, because her matchmaking attempts from the grave certainly aren't going to work.

While I was busy being a barback, Brittany has been busy arranging the appetizers I brought from home. She says, "These look pretty good."

I quickly make plates for her and her mother, then wrap them up in cellophane. As I hand over their food, I ask, "How many do we usually have for book club?"

Brittany looks at her phone and then starts packing up her things. "Five regulars plus a few randoms sometimes. Wade and Chad only showed up because Julie wanted to get a night off from her kid. The googly eyes they make at her makes me want to barf. Admiral Wright is the one who runs it mostly."

It's surprising that the Admiral runs the book club. He has a screw loose. And no one actually knows if he was really ever in the navy or not.

Julie Boyle steps inside the front door along with Chad Fellows and Wade Peters. All three went to school with me, although the guys were a few years ahead. Wade and Chad were always competitive with each other and got into all kinds of trouble because of their stupid dares. I've heard nothing has changed, and Dylan had to throw them both in jail last weekend for being drunk and disorderly when they got in a fight about a pool game at Skippy's, our local dive bar.

My mom paid Chad, our top local gardener, through the rest of the year to care for the massive flower beds at my house. He and his cute smile had been by earlier to spray. No way my mom the matchmaker would hire a wrinkly old man to tend her gardens. That wouldn't work into her bombard-Sawyer-with-choices-in-men plan.

Chad's a nice guy, though. And mom hired Wade to tackle a huge carpentry project at our crumbling Victorian before she died. I'm afraid the termites are winning the war, but Wade assures me he can fix all the bad woodwork. I think my handsome blond carpenter might still be there by Christmas at the rate he's moving. I suspect my mother has implanted Wade in my home as a dating option as well. Like give me a buffet to choose from, and maybe I'll end up with one choice. "Hi, guys."

Chad lifts a hand, and before Julie can say anything, Crystal grabs his arm and drags him to the other side of the store for a hushed conversation. Like she'd been waiting for him because she knew he came to book club. Maybe that's why she's been hanging around so much?

Chad's gardening gloves still stick out of the back pocket of his jeans as his hands wave with expression at whatever they're arguing about.

Wade smiles. "I've been looking forward to this all day. You're an amazing cook, Sawyer."

"Thanks." My mother probably told him to say that to get on my good side.

As Julie, who always reminded me of a delicate pixie, lifts her perfect chin in greeting my way, Wade grabs an empty beer mug from the front counter, hands a wineglass to Julie, and then they both head to the dining area toward the food and liquor. Since Wade is practically a fixture at my house lately, I'll let him serve himself. Like he does with the leftovers in my fridge at home on a regular basis. The guy is always hungry. Speaking of which, I need to refill the mac and cheese already.

By the time I'm done, the tables are filling with the members of the club. Chad has finished his fight with Crystal, and she's left and so has the lone man who was browsing. Chad pulls out a chair and sits with Julie and Wade. Looks like the food is holding up, but we might need more wine. Mostly for me.

Brittany mumbles, "I'm out," and then says something that might have actually been a "thanks for the food."

I'm busy watching Madge Wallace, the dispatcher at the

police station who wears ugly Christmas sweaters year-round, trip through the front door spilling her bag full of yarn and needles everywhere. Luckily, the Admiral, who is tall, white-haired, and still spry is right behind and catches her before the middle-aged woman falls. He has to be in his seventies. I'm impressed he can still move that fast. He calls out, "Hello, Sailor."

He's always called me that instead of Sawyer. I've never figured out if he does it on purpose or actually thinks that's my name. "Hi, Admiral. Nice catch."

He blinks at me like he's confused. "Catch?"

"You know, Madge? Never mind. Nice to see you guys."

Cooper sees the yarn on the floor and yelps with glee. Before I can stop him, he's across the store. He grabs a mouthful of purple yarn and takes off. He's running circles around people's feet, hog-tying everyone with yarn. The ones sitting down have their legs tied to their chairs.

Amid all the confusion, I yell, "Nobody move. I'll get some scissors."

Wade leans down and catches Cooper. Then he gets in his face and growls, "Stop it! You could've hurt someone!"

Cooper is whining and shaking with fear. Before I can inter- vene, Brittany sets her things on the counter and snatches Cooper from Wade. "He's just a puppy, bro. Calm down."

Okay. Brittany is all right after all. Maybe I can teach her and the dog some manners at the same time.

After I cut everyone loose, I tie Cooper's leash to the front door handle and flip the CLOSED sign over as Brittany leaves.

"Nite." I wave to Brittany as she passes by, and then I lock the door behind her. I'm starving, so I grab a plate and pour myself a jumbo glass of wine. I sit with Wade, Julie, and Chad and then dig in too.

The baked crab cake is light and flaky with just the right amount of bay seasoning. Might need a little more salt next time, but pretty close to perfect. The truffle mac and cheese makes Julie moan with pleasure every time she puts a forkful into her mouth, and I see that Chad and Wade have had three servings of the corn each, judging by the empty cobs. I glance at the Admiral's and Madge's empty plates at the next table, and I declare it a winner, winner chicken dinner. The crab cakes and spicy corn on the cob are going on my menu for sure. The truffle mac and cheese will be a signature side offering. It's a good start.

As I clear the plates from our table, Chad, who's looking a little red-faced, says, "Be right back." Then he heads for the bathroom in the back room while holding his stomach.

I hope he isn't allergic to the crab. The rest of the group looks happy and full as they stand and make their way to the couches and chairs set up as a little reading area in the corner to start their meeting.

I get busy stacking the dishes I have to wash by hand in the little sink in the corner. After things are tidy again, I check on Cooper. He's nowhere to be found, but his collar is hanging from the leash still tied to the front door. Where has he gone off to?

"Cooper?" I call out, and after a moment, my little dog appears, weaving around the bookcases and holding some cloth object in his mouth. I lean down and take it from him. It's a glove. Like the ones Chad had in his back pocket. I lift my head to see if Chad has rejoined the group, but he hasn't.

My stomach drops. I hope he didn't get sick from my food. If that news gets out, my restaurant might never get off the ground without local support. That is after it's built and I spring the news on my uncle that I own the restaurant.

Julie, as blonde and blue-eyed as Wade, walks my way with her empty wineglass. "Need a refill. Thanks for the awesome food, Sawyer."

"My pleasure." I grab an almost empty wine bottle and pour

the rest into her glass. It's only a half pour. "I'll grab another bottle from the back."

Julie points to the glove I'd laid on the counter. "Chad must've dropped that. Is he still in the back?" She puts her glass down and heads for the rear. "I'll get another bottle while I go check on him."

Dropping to Cooper's level, I whisper, "I guess everyone knows where the liquor stash is around here. Or maybe that was a ploy for some alone time to make googly eyes at each other. You need to go outside, Coop?"

A loud scream from the back startles me. Was that Julie?

I run to investigate. Julie is at the other end of the stock-room, leaning over Chad's prone body. He's facedown on the floor and not moving. My stomach lurches before I squeak out, "I'll dial 9-1-1. Does he have a shellfish allergy, Julie?"

She shakes her head. "We eat crab all the time." Tears stream down her cheeks as she shakes Chad's shoulder to wake him.

I head to the kitchen to find my cell, but dispatcher Madge has beat me to it. She's already talking to the rescue crew. After she disconnects, she calls out in a take-charge voice, "Help's on the way. Does anyone know CPR?"

Wade and the Admiral both nod and then head back to help. A few moments later, Julie reappears, white as a ghost and shaking. "He's having trouble breathing."

Madge and I each take one of Julie's arms and lead her to a couch. "Help will be here any second." Then I glance at Madge. "Should we call Dylan too?"

"Just texted him."

The front door is still locked, so I jog across the store and turn the bolt to let the emergency crew in when they arrive. My mind is racing for what we should do next. Cooper barking at all the excitement isn't helping me think.

Madge sits next to Julie on the couch and rubs her back in comfort. Madge is used to taking emergency calls for her job at the station and is the only calm person. I'm totally freaking out inside, but I'm trying to stay calm too.

Thankfully, the fire station is right down the street, and two paramedics arrive. One of the men asks, "Where is he?"

I point to the storage area. "In the back. Right through there."

Dylan arrives next and runs past me to the storage room too. Moments later, the Admiral and Wade return to the couches. Wade puts an arm around Julie's shoulders and lets her cry on his shirt. I don't know what to do except hug my dog and hope Chad is going to be okay.

Dylan reemerges and stands close to me by the door. He whispers, "They're working on him. It doesn't look good. Chad might have been poisoned. Don't let anyone leave without talking to me first."

"Poisoned? How do you know?" I was the one who fed him. There's no way it was something I made.

"You don't want to know. You're squeamish."

That's true. Spider guts make me want to puke. I didn't do so well in my butchering classes at school. I whisper-scream, "You know I didn't poison him, right?"

Dylan leans even closer. "I know there's only one person in this town you'd like to poison. And it's me."

I lift a shoulder. "Nothing as extreme as that. Slow torture, maybe."

"You're doing a good job. Guard the door. Two of my men are on the way." He starts walking back to the storage room again, and my mind races for ideas about how Chad could have been poisoned. Could it have to do with the fight Chad and Crystal had? But how would Crystal poison him? Was there a needle mark? A chemical absorbed through the skin like those people did to that guy in Malaysia at the airport just by touching his face and then washing their hands? No. I watch too much TV, and my imagination can get way out of hand.

Who in the group would want to hurt Chad?

There are too many unknowns.

Two deputies arrive in plain clothes with their badges tucked into their jeans' waistbands. One sits with the four book club people gathered on the couches and takes notes, while the other joins the men in the storage room.

Hugging Cooper closer, I stand guard like I've been told to do. Moments later, the paramedics come back out with their kits, their faces solemn. Dylan's eyes connect with mine, and I know.

Chad's dead.

My knees grow weak, and I have to grab the door handle to stay upright. Dylan is instantly by my side and leads me to one of the chairs in the dining area. "You okay?"

I shake my head. I can't take any more death. My Mom's was devastating, and now Chad? It's too much.

Dylan crouches in front of me. "This is a crime scene now, and you're a witness. Maybe my best witness because I know you're logical and astute. You don't miss details." He stands and finds a pad of paper and a pen at the register. "Write down everything that happened here tonight. Every detail. Nothing's too small or insignificant. Can you do that for me?"

I blink at Dylan through my tears. I know him better than anyone else, and he knows me the same. "This is busy work until I can stop freaking out, right?"

"See?" He grins. "You never miss a detail. I have to go talk to the others now, but I'm serious. I want you to write down everything. Please?"

"Okay." I draw a deep breath and try to put all the events of the night in order in my head before I write them down, but I can't concentrate.

Death is a strange thing. One minute you can be talking to someone like we were with Chad, and the next moment, they're gone. It was that way with my mom too. I'd flown in from

Chicago, dropped my bags at the front door, and run up the stairs to see her. After she'd asked me to try to live here, I didn't want to disappoint her and say no. Instead, I tried to distract her.

I'd been holding her hand and telling her a story about what my sister, who was at the hospital operating but due later, had said my niece and nephew had done the day before. Mom smiled at their antics. Then her grip got a little tighter, and she whispered, "You know I love you, right, Sawyer?"

I'd said, "Of course. And I love you too. Need anything?"

She nodded and said, "A chocolate milkshake, please."

This was odd because the hospice nurse told me Mom hadn't eaten much the few days before, but how could I say no? I told her I'd run to the diner and be right back. By the time I got back, she'd died.

The hospice nurse said this was typical behavior. That patients hold out until all their loved ones get there if they can.

I hate that I wasn't with my mom during her final moments. In the end, though, now that I've thought about it some more, Mom probably let go while I was gone because she knew me so well. That it would've haunted me forever to see her die, because she *was* the only person in the world, who loved me unconditionally.

When I finally went to my old bedroom to try to sleep that night, I found my mother had left a sealed envelope for me. Tucked under my pillow. I haven't opened it yet. It's like I still have one last chance to talk to her, to hear her words, so I keep putting it off. I probably need to open it soon in case it's important, but I can't seem to do it.

But I'll never drink another chocolate milkshake as long as I live.

CHAPTER 3

I'm dreaming I'm dancing with a tall, faceless man who has just leaned down and placed a soft kiss on my cheek. Then the kiss turns more into a slurp, and I'm pretty sure it's not my Prince Charming with poor kissing skills anymore. I blink my eyes open. It's morning and a cute set of brown eyes are staring into mine. "Hi, Cooper."

I'd fallen asleep at the shop on a couch while a crime lab from San Francisco did their thing all night long. The shop is quiet now, so everyone must've finally left.

I reach out to pet Cooper. "You probably need to go out." While wiping Cooper's drool from my face, I sit up and see Dylan.

He hands me Cooper's leash. "He just went. Found his food earlier, so he's all set. Did you know you snore?" His grin tells me he's teasing me as usual.

"No, I don't." I rub the sleep from my eyes.

I have a stress headache and need coffee. As I stumble to the pot that's full and ready to go, I realize it must be later than I think. The coffee and croissants get delivered every morning at ten. I find my cell that's almost dead. It's eleven thirty.

"Wow. I can't believe I slept so long." I glance toward the storage room, and the yellow crime tape is still there. "Has Brittany shown up yet? She's supposed to be here by ten." I take a long slug of coffee and nearly sigh as the warm mocha blend slides down my throat.

Dylan nods. "She got here a half hour ago. I talked to her and then sent her home. I need to talk to you about her."

This perks me right up. Or maybe it's the coffee. "You don't think she has anything to do with this, do you? She left before everyone ate."

"Can't discuss that. You're technically a suspect too."

"Really? And what would my motive be to kill Chad? I'm mad because he sprayed my mother's gardens wrong? I just moved here. I have no beef with anyone. And you know it."

The corners of his lips tilt. "You're not high on my list, but you're still on it. So don't ask me about suspects or evidence."

I pour Dylan a cup of coffee with one cream and a touch of sugar, just the way he likes it. Sucking up will hopefully get me the information I'm dying to know. I need to clear my name and my food as soon as possible.

I hand him a steaming to-go mug and pick up mine. "Why don't we walk and talk? I need to go home and get cleaned up before I open the store for the day. Assuming I can do that?"

He shakes his head. "I need the rest of the day. We'll clear out by this afternoon."

"Okay. I made two batches of food yesterday. One for the store last night, and the other is still home in my fridge. You're welcome to join me for lunch if you're not afraid I'll poison you too." Crab cakes are one of Dylan's favorite things. It pays to know way too much about people.

Dylan smiles as he accepts the coffee. "I should arrest you for attempted bribery. But since I had to send all the leftovers to the lab last night and I didn't get to taste the crab cakes, let's go."

I pick up Cooper's bag, find my purse, and lock the doors

behind us. Then I hand Dylan my key so he can come back later. "I have an extra at home."

Cooper, Dylan and I start for my house, which is only a few blocks up the hill. I draw in a deep breath of the salty breeze as we climb the steep sidewalks. The fresh, cool ocean air here always relaxes me. I'd forgotten that part. "What do you want to know about Brittany?"

"Do you recall who was with her in the showroom right before you closed? Just before the club members arrived?"

"Yeah." I chase behind Cooper, who is a terrible leash walker. "A man I didn't recognize, dark hair, average height, wearing khakis and a green polo shirt, and Crystal. Chad and Crystal were having some sort of disagreement, and then she left. I didn't see the man leave."

"And Brittany put the entirety of the food out for you while you were in the back?"

The coffee in my gut turns on me a bit. "Yes." And that had been unusual. For her to pitch in like that went against the norm. She's a pain sometimes, but I know in my heart she's a good kid. "We all served ourselves, and as far as I know, no one else got sick. And I was the one who dished up a plate for her and her mother. It doesn't make sense she'd do anything to the food, then leave and hope the right person ate it. If that's your theory."

"It's not, Sherlock." Dylan takes the leash from my hand and tightens up the length. Amazingly, Cooper steps right in line for him. Traitor dog.

He says, "I watched the security camera footage last night, and I can't see when the unknown customer left either. You need to upgrade your ancient equipment and your wireless speed. The picture freezes for huge gaps in time. And put cameras in the stockroom. Employee theft is common."

I laugh. "Somehow I don't think Brittany is going to steal

one of the books back there. She reads comic books about half-dressed aliens."

"Upgrade them anyway. Might be something valuable back there."

"Wait. What?" I stop in my tracks. "Why do you think that?"

"You'll find this part out soon enough, but Chad wasn't anywhere near the bathroom when he died. The Admiral has an interesting theory about that."

"The Admiral is delusional. As far as I can see, it's all just old books." I'm asking Brittany if she's heard this rumor first thing tomorrow, though.

We start walking again toward my old Victorian money pit. As much of a pain as it is to maintain it, I've come to appreciate its old bones and classic lines. I'd like it better if everything worked, but I can only handle one challenge at a time. When we arrive at my house, we climb the wooden steps that badly need paint and find the front door is slightly ajar.

Dylan throws an arm out to stop me. "Did you leave this unlocked?" He leans closer, probably looking for jimmy marks.

"No." I push his arm aside and open the door the rest of the way. "Wade is here most days working on the rotting wood and staircase. He might have eaten your crab cakes by now too. He tends to make himself right at home."

Dylan frowns at this news but grabs my arm to stop me so he can enter first. "Stay behind me."

I roll my eyes. "Such a drama queen. This is Sunset Cove, not Chicago."

"And you had a dead body in your bookstore last night."

The man makes a good point. I call out, "Wade? Are you here?"

Dylan shoots me another frown. I suppose he hoped to catch an intruder red-handed for a change. It *is* Sunset Cove, and those types don't come along often. Must get boring for a former army sniper turned sheriff at times.

"Be right there." Sounds of Wade descending his creaky ladder confirm my theory. The guy can't shut a door behind him to save his life.

When Wade meets us in the foyer, Cooper yelps and moves behind me.

Wade kneels and says, "Hi, buddy. Sorry, I yelled at you last night." Then he looks up at me and grins. Wade reminds me of a blond surf bum I once knew. "I didn't realize it was *your* dog, Sawyer. I thought it was a stray who'd wandered in. I apologize for scaring him."

Cooper isn't accepting the apology—he'd been terrified last night—but I will. Wade has been nothing but kind to me. "No worries. Want some lunch? I was going to heat some crab cakes for the sheriff."

"Um. No, thanks. I'm good." Wade's sheepish smile tells me he's already been in my fridge today. Or is afraid of my crab cakes.

Wade's grin fades as he turns to Dylan. "Any more news?"

"Not yet. Have to wait for lab results. You and Chad have been friends forever. Any idea what he might have been looking for in the storeroom?"

Wade shrugs. "He was sort of near the fridge area, so maybe another beer? If I think of anything else, I'll let you know. Enjoy your lunch, guys." He winks at me before he leaves like it's going to be something more than lunch.

Which it's not.

I shake my head and walk down the long hallway to the back, where the one nice room of the house is. My mother had the kitchen gutted and remodeled last year. She'd asked me for a ton of advice about appliances, cabinets, countertops, and pantry space before she told me she was dying of cancer. Probably wanted to give me one more reason to stay here after she was gone.

I say to Dylan, who's trailing behind, "You might as well just tell me what everyone said last night. They'll all stop in tomorrow out of sheer curiosity anyway. It is a murder mystery book club. It's what they live for."

Dylan sits down in the built-in nook to take off Cooper's leash. "Nope. Not happening."

Stubborn. However, my crab cakes might still do the trick.

I open the big stainless-steel fridge and hope they're still there. "Oh, look. Wade ate the leftover fajitas. You're in luck." I pull out the tray of crab cakes and sides. Then I set them on the stone countertop.

"Probably didn't want to risk dying too. Have you been through all your mother's paperwork from the store? And her personal papers too?" Dylan plays with the salt and pepper shakers on the table. He has a habit of fiddling with whatever is nearby when something is bothering him. Or when he's about to break up with me. Too late for the latter. Been there done that.

"Yes. That's part of what I was talking to Gage about yesterday, why?" Well, there was the envelope my mom left me, but that's private, between her and me. And I'd only gotten three-quarters through the trust before it bored me to sleep. But Gage has filled me in now.

"Mind if I look through her study? See if I find anything you might have missed?"

"Actually, I do mind." I turn on the heating drawer on my commercial-grade oven and place the leftovers packed in an aluminum tray inside. "Unless you'd like to tell me what you're looking for."

Dylan's lips thin. "I can get a search warrant if I have to. Can't we do this the easy way? For a change?"

I didn't miss the last part. He thinks I'm difficult for refusing to have a romantic relationship with him again. I think I'm a saint for even speaking to Mr. Tall, Dark, and Handsome at all. However, a search warrant means he has a real reason to look. Maybe my crab cakes aren't going to do the trick after all.

"I'm not trying to be difficult." I slide in the nook across from Dylan. "You work for the mayor's office. And there are papers in the study that are none of the mayor's business. You know Uncle Frank wants me and the bookstore to fail so I'll leave and then he'll get the trust money."

My new dog jumps up on Dylan's leg and lays his teddy bear face on Dylan's knee. Then Cooper bats his eyes in a coquettish way.

Dylan falls for the act and sets the dog in his lap. "Are you suggesting your uncle had something to do with staging a murder at your store?"

I wouldn't entirely put it past the guy. "No. I don't want to give my uncle any more ammunition. You knew Mom. She wasn't good about following rules, and she hated any interaction with Uncle Frank. Which she'd have to have done to keep her properties up to code."

Dylan opens his mouth, but I raise a hand to stop him. "I'm taking steps to rectify the health and safety stuff, I promise. It'll all be fixed soon. I'm asking what you're looking for so you don't see something you can't unsee. And feel compelled to be your rule-following self and report it."

He runs a hand down his face. "How long before the repairs to the commercial properties are done?"

"Three weeks. Maybe four. I promise, no one is going to die from what's left to fix. It's mostly plumbing and sewer stuff." Mostly. I won't talk about the leaking roofs right now. Hopefully, it won't rain anytime soon.

Dylan's phone rings, and he takes the call while I ponder all the events from the night before. I still don't see how someone could have poisoned Chad. Unless it'd happened during the commotion with Cooper wrapping everyone up in yarn. I was pretty busy cutting people loose, so I wouldn't have noticed.

After a series of "yeahs" and grunts, Dylan finally hangs up and puts his cell away. "Sorry. That was the lab making excuses for why they can't get the results back any faster. Where were we?"

"I was reassuring you that all my buildings will be up to code in no time, and you were about to tell me what everyone said about last night."

"Nice try." He runs the salt and pepper shakers that look like sumo wrestlers around in circles again. My mother's taste in knickknacks had never been the best. Finally, he says, "Did you tell your mom you'd never move back here?"

"Yes. However, she asked me to try to live here the day she died. So here I am."

He nods. "That makes more sense of what the Admiral told me about something valuable in your storage room. I'll hold off on her office for now. No promises for later."

"Thank you." I take the food out of the oven and make us both a plate of crab cakes, truffle mac and cheese, and spicy corn on the cob. I slide his meal in front of him while I plug in my cell that's about to die, and then join him. "You know this is going to make me go ransack my mom's office the second you leave."

Dylan switches his plate with mine as he says, "I'm counting on it." He digs into my former meal with a grin.

"Clever." I take a big bite as well to prove my food isn't tainted. The truffle mac and cheese has gotten even better overnight. "I read once that poisoning is more commonly a woman's crime. Do you think that's true?"

Dylan lifts a shoulder. "Not necessarily. Women do tend toward less violent crime in general, but there are always exceptions to the rules. Sneaky way to ask me if I think a man or woman killed Chad, though."

Busted.

"My chef's reputation is on the line here. I'm in a hurry to clear my name. So, have you ruled anyone out yet?"

"I can't discuss that. I promise, you'll be the first to know after I arrest the person who did it."

"'Kay." Silently chewing and thinking at the same time, I finally ask, "If I guess what you're looking for in my mom's office, will you blink twice?"

"Nope." He throws his napkin at me and then puts his plate in the dishwasher. "The crab cakes needed more salt."

That I knew. "How about the rest?"

He picks up my cell phone. "Perfect."

My happy chef's heart swells a little at that.

He sets the phone down and says, "I put my numbers in for the station and my cell. Call me if you need anything. Day or night. Even if you'd just like some company." His brows hitch.

"Luckily, I have a *new* dog for company. Keep me posted on the investigation, please."

"Will do."

As he's walking down the hall, I say, "Hey. How did you know my phone's unlock code?"

"Some things never change. See ya, Sawyer."

I hate that he's right. I'm changing the code right now. But then I might forget it. He's a sheriff. I guess I can trust him not to spread that piece of information around.

After I clean the kitchen, Cooper and I head upstairs to my mom's study. It's a big room with lots of built-in wooden bookcases, a large old desk where my grandfather made his millions developing real estate, and some nice windows whose views extend to the ocean. And it's as messy as the storeroom in the bookstore.

I open the top desk drawer and start in.

A few moments later, Wade flops into one of the torn leather guest chairs in front of the scarred desk. "Hey, Sawyer? Got a second?"

Shoving the papers that want to escape back into place, I

shut the drawer and give my carpenter my full attention. "Sure. What's up?"

Wade's forehead crumples like he's struggling with something. I hope he's not going to ask for a raise.

He clears his throat. "I need a woman's advice about something."

Oh. That I can do. I instantly relax. "What can I help with?"

"Before we get to that, what do you think of this molding pattern? It's as close as I can find to the original." He sets a piece of wood on my desk.

I pick up the little sample and shake my head. "I'd really like to find something closer than this. I don't want to have to replace the molding throughout the *whole* house. Can you keep looking?"

"Okay." He slips the sample back into his pocket. "I'll see how much it'd be to have it custom-made to match."

"That'd be great. Thanks." I fold my hands and wait for whatever else he wants to discuss.

He chews his bottom lip for a few moments like he's gathering his thoughts before he finally says, "I didn't tell the sheriff something about Chad and Crystal last night. I'm sure it doesn't have anything to do with what happened to Chad. So, do I keep a secret Chad shared with me in confidence? Or do I tell? Chad was my best friend, you know?"

This makes me sit up taller. "Do you think you know what they were fighting about?"

Wade cringes while he nods. "I figured Crystal would tell Dylan when he spoke to her, but she didn't. She told me this morning it wasn't anyone's business. I'm afraid it might affect Julie too if the sheriff figures out that Chad and Julie have been dating secretly so Crystal won't find out. It'll make Julie look guilty."

Oh boy. Things are heating up now. A love triangle? What

was it I'd read people typically kill for? Love, greed, and money? "Were you helping Julie and Chad cover up their relationship?"

"No. They've been sneaking around for a while, but Crystal was just asking Chad to do the right thing."

Do the right thing? I could take a few guesses here, but the one at the top of my list was "So Crystal's pregnant? And wanted Chad to support the child?"

Wade blinks rapidly. "I don't want to say, but Chad and Crystal were broken up when he started dating Julie. They've tried to keep their new relationship on the down low because of Crystal. You know what a psycho Crystal can be when she has her sights on a guy, right? From back in high school with Dylan? Borderline stalker."

"Yeah. I know very well." What was I going to do with this information? "I think you should tell Crystal to tell Dylan, or you will. It's the right thing to do."

Wade's brows scrunched together. "Would it be okay to tell Crystal that I confided in you for advice? I bet then she'd cave and tell Dylan before you could. She'd hate to see you appear to know more than she does."

Too true that.

I smile and nod. "I think that's an amazing plan. Any idea when my staircase will be done?"

Wade smiles as he stands. "Maybe when the amazing food runs out." He winks at me again before he walks out the door.

I lay my head on the desk and moan. My mother knew our hungry carpenter was going to be practically living with me after she was gone. Had she hired Wade as a backup in case I didn't get back together with Dylan? Or fall for her handsome lawyer, Gage? Who knows what crazy things my mother cooked up, but she was famous for her fall-in-love schemes.

As I ponder my life for a few minutes, I think about that envelope again. Maybe it's time to pull the trigger. It might shed some light on how my mother planned to meddle in my love life, so I can make it stop.

I walk down the hall with Cooper right on my heels, to my old bedroom that's the same as I left it fourteen years ago. Purple walls, bedspread, and curtains. A white desk and a corkboard filled with blue ribbons from math competitions across the country. My acceptance letter to MIT is still pinned underneath my acceptance letter to culinary school in Chicago. I smile as I open my desk drawer and pull out the sealed envelope my mom left for me. My life was so simple back when I was in school, but I didn't know it. Everything had seemed so dramatic.

I hold the envelope in my hand, stalling and thinking maybe not much has changed. I have a murder to solve to save my chef's reputation, and a tricky trust game to play to beat my uncle. Two men are giving my hormones a headache, and I have a dog now to care for twenty-four seven.

I work up the courage to run my finger under the flap and pull out the folded paper inside. It's been printed out from the computer because my mother's handwriting is sometimes impossible to read. As tears form in my eyes, I begin to read her heartfelt note. When I turn the page, my bruised heart nearly stops.

Stunned, I blink away the tears and reread the whole letter just to be sure I'm comprehending the words. My mother was a heck of a lot smarter than I ever gave her credit for. And the Admiral might not be as crazy as I thought. Though if he has a big mouth, it might have something to do with why Chad is dead.

I pick up my cell and look for the number Dylan just input.

When Dylan answers, I say, "I think I just found what you were looking for."

CHAPTER 4

ith Dylan due back at my house any minute to see the letter, I grab a quick shower. The small bathroom attached to my mom's bedroom where I sleep now is so steamy, I crack the door open to let the hot air out. I really need to see about fixing the exhaust fan.

After wrangling my thick hair into a ponytail, I wipe a circle of steam off the mirror with the sleeve of my robe. Then I dial my sister's cell and hit the speaker button, so I can put my makeup on and talk at the same time.

Megan answers with "You've got three minutes. I'm heading into surgery."

It seems my sister is always in the middle of an emergency of some sort, be it at the hospital or home. I'm lucky she answers my calls at all, but since Mom died, she always picks up. She worries about me here in this big lonely house by myself.

I quickly say, "This is going to take more than three minutes. Mom left me a letter that says she hid some valuable things for us to find. Something here at the house and another thing at the bookstore. And of course, she wants me to reconsider being with Dylan again."

"We all want you to reconsider being with Dylan again. But what could she have hidden of value for us? She had no money beyond the pittance the trust allowed."

I'm going to ignore the Dylan comments. "I don't know. She said they're worth enough to start any kind of restaurant I want. It might change your mind about giving up your share of the trust. Can you guys all come to dinner tonight?"

"I'm not changing my mind about the trust. It's been nothing but a carrot dangled in our faces that we'll never get. I'm not playing the game anymore. It's all yours. Especially if you'll make a succulent pot roast with those caramelized potatoes, baby onions, and carrots that suck up the juices in the same pan, and then your famous blueberry crumble for dessert, you got a deal."

Succulent? Caramelized? My sister never talks like that unless she's dieting. Usually, she talks about gross stuff like cranial hemorrhages. "You've been drinking protein shakes instead of eating real food again, haven't you?"

"Been busy. Don't nag. Just feed me. Please?"

How can my chef's heart refuse? "Only because now I'm concerned for my niece's and nephew's eating habits too. Six o'clock work?"

"Probably can't round Lance and the kids up until six thirty. And FYI, Alexandra has decided she needs to be called Alex. And she's a vegetarian this week. Gotta run. Love you." Megan hangs up.

"Love you too." I tap my phone to disconnect the call and shake my head as I lean closer to the mirror to apply my mascara. Guess I'm making "Alex" a vegetarian meal along with my sister's caveman cuisine.

Dylan's deep voice calls out from far away, "I *love* succulent pot roast. And I haven't seen Lance and the kids in weeks. Can I come to dinner too?"

Great. If my sister only knew I'm rarely alone in my house

anymore, she could stop her worrying. Lately, my home has been crawling with men. And so much for my watchdog. Cooper didn't even bark.

I cap my mascara and go for the lip gloss. "Knocking would have been nice. What if I hadn't been decent?"

A slightly muffled response says, "Then my day would've been complete?"

"Or you'd have to arrest yourself for breaking and entering along with being a Peeping Tom."

Dylan laughs. "Wade let me in on his way out to get more wood and said you were up here. And I did knock, but then I heard you talking to Megan from out here in the hall, so I was waiting until you finished. Can I stop screaming through the door now? *Are* you decent?"

"Mostly." I wipe the rest of the fog from the mirror. "Come in. The letter is on the bed. I'll be out in a second."

"So, is that a yes or a no? For dinner. Hi, Cooper." The bed creaks, so I assume he sat on the edge to read the letter and to pet my dog. He says, "Why would Alexandra decide to be a vegetarian all of a sudden? Used to be all she'd eat were hot dogs and hamburgers when she and Collin spent the night. I've been trying to get them to try real food for years."

My lip gloss stops midswipe. "They spend the night with you sometimes too?" My sister and brother-in-law live in a cool restored Victorian on a hill in San Francisco. It's a forty-five-minute drive from there to Sunset Cove. I assumed he'd go there to see them. And that I was the one the kids loved to have sleepovers with. "And you cook for them?"

"Sometimes. Or we go out. They love to stay with me when Lance and Megan go away. I'm a fun guy. Remember?"

We did have some fun times way back when. "I've blocked all memories of you, so I wouldn't know." I shut the bathroom door all the way and then slip into my jeans and pull a T-shirt over my head. I suddenly have the day off, so it's casual for me today.

I join Dylan on the side of the bed and tie my sneakers while he reads the letter. Cooper is snoozing with his white chin on Dylan's boot. "The letter says the Admiral knew about the things my mother hid. Do you think he told anyone else? Like Chad? Not to be rude, but he's a few cards short of a full deck."

"He said last night he hasn't told anyone else, yet clearly he helped your mom orchestrate all this." Dylan's rubbing the back of his neck like it hurts.

He's probably at the part of the letter where my mom said men could be immature boneheads sometimes, and Dylan had been young, so I should forgive him for leaving me at the altar after he'd developed cold feet. Later, I'd found out he'd chosen the army over a life with me. Mom says he left as a confused boy and then returned to Sunset Cove a changed man.

I changed in all those years too. Into someone who will think long and hard before giving my heart to anyone else again. It can take a long time to heal.

Dylan hands me the letter and frowns. "You just left this on your bed? Wade could've found it."

"If that's your sneaky way of asking if Wade is allowed in my bedroom, the answer is no. I'm just stuck with him in my hallways until my termite-infested woodwork can be replaced. All over the house." I fold the letter and stick it in my pocket to show my sister later. "So, what do you think? Was Chad looking for whatever my mom hid at the store? Could he have found out somehow before I did? And if so, maybe he told someone else, who killed him before he could find it? Like Crystal, who he was arguing with?"

Dylan's eyes cut my way, and I can almost see the wheels turning in his head. He's deciding how much to tell me. It's annoying.

Finally, he says, "It's possible. Your mom hid something here too, though, so start locking your doors at all times until we figure out who else knows."

"Tell that to my new roommate, Wade, who clearly grew up in a barn." I chew my thumbnail as I think about the letter. "Gage told me yesterday that Uncle Frank has to approve any spending over five grand. So, maybe the Admiral bought whatever is hidden and my mom paid him back in little chunks, so my uncle wouldn't find out?" The money to buy them had to have come from the trust somehow. I've been through all her banking records, and she's never had more than a few hundred bucks at a time, as was my grandparents' plan evidently. I can't figure out how she could buy such expensive things without my uncle finding out.

Dylan nods. "Maybe. Or she disguised it as something for the business or house expenses. She did that expensive kitchen remodel last year with a firm out of San Francisco, so maybe look at those bills."

"I will. I found some in a file last month."

"The Admiral says he left instructions in his will regarding the items in case he dies. Your mom told him to tell you where the hidden pieces are only if you declined to live here and thereby officially surrender the trust to your uncle. So you'd find whatever they are before he got the property. The Admiral says your mother hid the items well so you'd stick around for a while."

Of course she had. "I'll either have to actually move away for the Admiral to tell me where to look or stay and find the mystery things myself? And let me guess. Gage is the Admiral's lawyer too?"

Dylan taps his nose.

"So, Gage knows what and where the things are hidden too if it's in the will. Could he or a paralegal have told someone?" And is Gage interested in me because whatever my mother hid for me is worth a ton of money? Enough to open the most elegant restaurant I can imagine, according to my mom. But my sister should have half when I find whatever these mystery items are.

"I'm going to go ask Gage that question right now." Dylan pats Cooper goodbye. "What was the verdict on dinner? Am I invited or not?"

He loves being with Megan, Lance, and the kids as much as I do. And I'm stuck with him until this mystery is solved anyway. "Fine. If you'll tell me what Gage says, I'll double the size of the pot roast to accommodate your appetite."

Dylan smiles. "We'll see."

So irritating. "If you don't spill, you'll get whatever vegetarian thing I make for Alexandra."

"I'm sure that'll be incredible too." He pulls out his wallet and hands me eighty bucks. "After reading that letter from your mom, I think I should pay for dinner tonight. I really am sorry I hurt you, Sawyer. Your mom is right. I *was* an immature bonehead back then. See you later."

I stand in my bedroom with the money in my hand and a big lump in my throat as I watch him walk away. Mom's letter must've gotten to him.

I should run after him and give him the money back, tell him he can't fix what he did with cash. Yet I know deep down he also gave me the money because he knows I'm basically broke right now. It was a nice thing to do, to apologize and save my pride at the same time.

I guess I'll get enough pot roast for him too.

AFTER I'VE GOT Cooper settled in the laundry room with a treat and some chew toys Bert sent along, I head down the hill to the grocery store. First, though, I want to check in with my bestie Renee at her ice-cream shop. She'd been away all week at a confectioner's conference but is due back today. Who knew they even had those kinds of things, but man, I bet it'd be fun to tag along and sample the goods.

I pick up the pace when I hit the town square because everyone will want to know about the events of last night if I give them a chance to stop me. As I pass by Bang Bangs, the beauty parlor, I'm relieved to see Pattie Smith's hands buried deep in a head full of shampoo. She lifts her chin in greeting so I wave and keep moving. Mr. Martinez, who runs one of many art galleries on the square, holds up a finger to stop me but I smile and tap my wrist to indicate I'm late. Thankfully, The Daily Scoop, Renee's ice-cream shop that sells amazing sweets too is next door. I duck inside and draw the lovely familiar aroma of sugar, cinnamon, and chocolate deep into my lungs. I used to work here in high school for Renee's parents, who've since moved to Hawaii to retire. The unique mixture of sweetness never gets old.

I weave my way around the empty little tables and lift a hand in greeting to Zelda behind the counter. "Hi, Z. Is Renee here?"

"Yep. You can go on back."

Zelda's hair is orange today. Probably on purpose but it could be a dye job gone bad. She's in her forties, but her fashion always screams sixties bohemian. She's a free spirit who's married to an insanely wealthy artist. Why she works in the ice-cream shop is a mystery no one seems to be able to solve.

I poke the swinging door and make my way past the walk-in freezer and head for the small office in the rear. Before I get there, I spot my pal on a ladder yanking a huge box of sprinkles from a shelf. Renee is one of those people who couldn't care less what people think of her, and she does what she pleases. She's tall, tattooed, olive skinned, dark haired, and gorgeous. Today she's wearing a sexy gauzy shirt, designer jeans, and cute boots that have no business in an ice-cream shop.

"Hey. How'd the trip go?"

"Amazing!" Renee swivels her chin over her shoulder and grins. "Found some new candy. Of the man variety. I'm meeting him tonight in the city."

"What do we know about this guy? Have you googled him?"

Renee shakes her head. "He's the heir to a chocolate bar fortune, and I've known his parents for years, but I'd never met their hunky son. I'll forward you all his deets if that'll make you feel better, Mother."

"It will, thanks."

Renee hands me the box of sprinkles. "Then I'll also forward the same info for Saturday night's date too."

I place the box on a counter. "Did you find any actual new candy at this convention, or were you too busy flirting with guys?"

She starts down the ladder. "All work and no play, as they say."

"And knowing you, you told them both right up front that you aren't looking for anything serious in a relationship, right?"

"Why constrain myself to one flavor when there are so many to sample?" She climbs down the rest of the way. "Anyway, enough about me. I heard about poor Chad." Renee grabs two cinnamon rolls from a rack and hands me one. "What happened?"

Before I can answer, Zelda calls out, "Speak up or get out here so I can hear too!"

I want to tell Renee about the note my mother left, but it'll have to wait. Not that I don't trust Zelda, but the fewer who know about the hidden things, the better.

Once we're all assembled out front, I finish my cinnamon-and-icing treat while I fill the women in on the events of Thursday night.

When I'm done, Renee frowns. "Do you think it was that customer who was browsing? I've known all the others forever. I can't see any of them committing murder."

"I don't know. And Dylan won't tell me what he knows."

"Crystal could've done it." Zelda crosses her arms. "And here she comes now to pick up her special-order truffles." Zelda rounds the counter to pack up the order.

This is my chance to find out what Crystal and Chad were arguing about, so I cross the store to confront her.

Crystal, with her long curly red hair flowing behind her and her bombshell body barely squeezed into a white shirt and tight jeans, breezes past me as if I don't exist.

"Crystal? Can I ask you something about last night?"

My nemesis stops and huffs out a breath. "Not now." She turns to Zelda and barks, "Is my order ready? I'm late!"

"All set, Crystal." Renee rounds the candy counter and accepts the truffle box from Zelda. As she rings up the sale, she says, "But you snap at one of my employees ever again and you won't be welcome back. That'll be twenty-two dollars and fifty-seven cents."

"At these prices, I won't be back!" Crystal throws two twenties and a five on the counter and then glances at me. "What do you want to know, Sawyer?"

While Renee makes change, I slip beside Crystal. "What were you and Chad arguing about last night? Wade said you wanted him to do the right thing. Are you preg—"

"It's none of your business." Crystal accepts her change, picks up the box, and then pokes me in the shoulder. "Tell your boyfriend it had nothing to do with Chad's death. And then keep your face out of my business."

"Dylan's not—"

Crystal bumps me so hard on her way to the front door, I have to take a step back.

After the door swings closed behind Crystal, Zelda says, "See? Something's not right with that woman."

I have to agree.

~

AFTER THE LAST of the dinner dishes are cleared and Wade, who'd decided to join us, has finally left, I grab my sister to talk. "Come with me to the kitchen, please." Dylan warned me earlier to speak about the details of our weird mystery with only my family, so I've been dying to talk to Megan all night. Lance and Dylan are playing cards with the kids, so this is my chance for some privacy.

My sister smiles. "You and Dylan seem to be getting along better."

"That's only because of the murder at the bookstore last night."

My sister blinks rapidly as she sinks into the kitchen nook. "What are you talking about?"

As I recount the events, my sister slowly drinks her coffee. After I'm finished, she sets her cup down and shivers. "I hope Chad's death doesn't have anything to do with what Mom hid."

I nod and hand her the letter from my back pocket I'd forgotten was there. "You should read it yourself. And claim half of whatever it is she hid."

"Nope." She shakes her head and quickly reads the letter. After she's done, she hands it back. "I want you to have your restaurant. Lance and I are fine. Why don't you tell the Admiral you've decided to move away so he'll tell you where the things are? Then you can move to San Francisco with us and start your restaurant there?"

"Because then Uncle Frank wins. The trust will go to him, and he'll get millions that he'll actually be able to spend, unlike us. Besides, I think I've figured out a way for the trust to build me a restaurant without Uncle Frank knowing. And we need a nice dining option in Sunset Cove much more than another in San Francisco."

"You're the smart one in the family. I have no doubt you'll

figure it all out." My sister, who's really the smart one in the family, looks more like my dad, with her deep blue eyes and contrasting black hair.

Her pretty eyes look droopy after her long day at the hospital as she reaches out and takes my hand. "I'll support whatever you'd like to do, but I'm worried this could become dangerous if others find out about the mystery items. Please think about my offer to live with us. Okay?"

"I will." However, not seriously. I'm thirty-two. I'm not going to go live in a spare bedroom at my big sister's house.

Lance comes inside the kitchen to refill his coffee cup. "You're up, Auntie Sawyer. You taught them to play poker, so you let them take your money for a while. They triple their allowance every time I play them."

"That's because you're bad at bluffing. Help yourself to dessert, you two, while I go win some of Lance's losses for myself."

Lance smiles and heads for the blueberry crumble. "I'm going to have to double my workout tomorrow. It'll be worth it." He and Dylan both have the same great smiles and dark hair, and both like to stay fit, but Lance has forgiven their father, while Dylan has hung on to his deep resentment over their father's so-called part in their mother's death. Lance always has a smile on his face, while Dylan often seems troubled. I wish Dylan could come to terms with his pain like his brother has.

I wander into the living room, with its old overstuffed red couches and faded tapestry chairs that belonged to our grandparents. Dylan, Cooper, and the kids sit around a beat-up coffee table on the floor. Alexandra's coins are stacked the highest, then Dylan's. So I scoop up a handful of change from the sheriff's pile. "Thank you very much. Deal me in, Collin."

Collin, eight, a dark-haired blue-eyed clone of Dylan except for his missing front teeth, grins. "You're going down, Aunt Sawyer."

Alexandra, ten and a brunette like me, rolls her brown eyes at her brother. "You've never beat anyone but Dad. And *everyone* can beat him."

While the kids bicker and the cards are passed out, I turn to Dylan. "What did Gage say when you talked to him about the Admiral?"

Dylan checks to see that the kids aren't listening. "He said there are instructions in the Admiral's will to find a sealed envelope in his safe deposit box upon his death, but he doesn't know what's in the envelope. His instructions were that only Zoe's heirs should open it."

Huh. So maybe the secret is still safe after all. "Can we really trust that the Admiral has kept the secret? It's not like we can ask the others in the book club without giving the secret away, right?"

Dylan finishes passing out the cards. "There might be a way to ask, but it's early yet for that. Chad might simply have been getting another beer."

Maybe, but there was a cooler out front filled with beer, and he was holding his stomach as if it hurt. "Did Crystal call you this afternoon? Wade told me she was holding something back from you about her fight with Chad."

Dylan's right brow pops as he picks up his cards. "Do you know what the argument was about?"

I shake my head. "I tried to ask, and all I learned was that Crystal pokes really hard."

"That's why you need to let me do the police work." Dylan folds. "Sorry, guys. Duty calls." He pushes his pile of change in front of Collin and then glances at me. "Did Wade mention where he was heading tonight after we ate?"

I nod and rearrange my two pairs. "Skippy's to play pool. Ten bucks says you'll find Crystal there too."

While shaking his head, he stands. "I never win when I bet with you. Thanks for dinner. It was amazing."

"You're welcome. And instead of ten bucks when you find Crystal and Wade, will you stay away from my store tomorrow so people will come to fill me in on the gossip? Then we'll call it even."

"Bye, guys." Dylan kisses the kids on the top of their heads and then turns to me. "If only that were all it'd take to call it even between us." He walks to the kitchen to say his good-byes.

I'm not sure Dylan and I could ever go back to what we were. Being friends again is a start.

Collin says, "How come Uncle Dylan didn't kiss you on the head too, Aunt Sawyer? Is he mad at you?"

Alex pokes an elbow into her brother's side. "Because Aunt Sawyer's not a kid. That's why." Then she turns to me. "Can we spend the night tonight? Please?"

Collin throws his cards down and jumps into my lap. He bats his eyes as cute as Cooper does. "Yeah. Please? Maybe even the whole weekend? Please?" Cooper can't stand being excluded and jumps into Collin's lap.

My heart melts into a puddle of goo at their sweet request. But then Dylan's words earlier about locking my doors here until we figure things out makes me reconsider. I can't risk even the slightest chance of harm coming their way. "Not this weekend, guys, but soon. I promise. Better run to the kitchen now before your dad eats all the blueberry crumble."

As the kids and Cooper scamper down the hall, I clean up the cards.

Am I in danger? Is that why my mom got me a dog? To alert me of intruders?

A shiver runs up my spine, but I shake it off. I'm newly back home. No one would have any problems with me. Still, I won't have the kids sleep over until this mess is cleaned up, just to be safe.

CHAPTER 5

On Saturday morning, as Cooper and I walk to my store, I dial Renee's number. She picks up on the third ring. "Hi, Mom."

It makes me laugh. "You didn't check in with me last night."

"Because I didn't get in until late. Didn't want to wake you."

"A text would've worked."

"You'd hear the chime. Then you'd wake up to read the text and be mad because you couldn't go back to sleep."

"True. How was your date?"

"Wonderful. We took his PJ to Napa."

"What's a PJ?"

"A private jet. He's a candy bar heir, remember? Now I'm in the middle of getting a massage, though, so I have to let you go. I'll call you later."

"How do I know your date hasn't taken you hostage and is making you say that?"

Renee groans.

I love how exasperated she gets with me and my overly protective nature.

Finally, my aggravated pal says, "We should have a code. How about 'Goodbye, Sawyer. Have a nice day.'" She hangs up.

I'm still smiling as I take out my key to open my store's front door. The lock won't turn. I wiggle the key and jiggle it back and forth. Nothing. Maybe I picked up the wrong set of keys? The label scribbled in my mom's lousy handwriting confirms it's the spare key for the bookstore. Probably.

Maybe the key will work in the back door. When I turn to go around the block, I spot a round hole in the farthest pane of glass on my storefront. The hole is bigger than a bullet would leave, thank goodness, but smaller than my fist. The safety glass has held everything in place around the damage.

When I kneel down to peer inside, I see the offender. It's a golf ball sitting by the dining area. Maybe some kids were goofing off in the park, but after Chad's murder, I better take this seriously.

I say to my dog, who is sitting beside me, "Now we're going to have to track Dylan down to get my other key back and to report this. And we're supposed to open in twenty minutes. Who knows if he even works on Saturdays?"

Cooper's brows lift as if asking a question.

"I know. I don't want to go to his house either. Too many memories there, right? Let's hope he's in his office this morning." I hear that Dylan lives in his parents' former house. The same house where that birthday-suit situation first happened.

I spin around and head across the park toward the municipal building that houses all the essential city offices. When Cooper spots a tree with his name on it, he nearly yanks my arm out of its socket.

"Really? After piddling in my bedroom while I was getting ready and then leaving a deposit right inside the front door before we left too?" Potty training is going to be my number one priority as soon as Chad's murder is solved. "If you'd do this kind of business when you're in the backyard rather than dig in my mother's flower beds, we'd get along just fine."

"Hi, Sawyer. I bet you're looking for these," Gage says behind me.

I turn, and he's holding a shiny set of keys. He smiles like a kid who just got an A on his report card and says, "I took the liberty of having your locks changed this morning. I sent Ed to your house a few minutes ago too."

Wait. What? "Why did you do that?"

"I was worried about you." He frowns as he drops three sets of keys into my hand. "I thought after what happened, you should have the locks changed. I paid for it all out of the trust fund. Just in case you didn't have the..." He clears his throat and cuts himself off. "I apologize. I asked the sheriff if he thought it'd be a good idea to change the locks yesterday. When he agreed and said to upgrade the cameras too, I arranged for it as I would have with your mother. Have I upset you?"

"No, I'm not upset. You just surprised me."

He nods. "I'll be sure to call you first in the future."

"Thank you." Gage took terrific care of my mom. He arranged for her hospice nurse and always looked out for her interests when it came to my bully of an uncle.

"My pleasure." Gage's smile returns. "Should I call Ed and tell him to stop working on the locks at your house?"

"No. It's a good idea. Wade is there working today anyway. And the locks are so old, a ten-year-old with a bobby pin could pick them. New cameras at the shop make sense too. Would you arrange for all my commercial properties to have better locks and cameras as well?"

"First thing on Monday morning." Gage bends down to pet Cooper but keeps his eyes locked onto mine. "How are you? After what happened?"

I'm still a little surprised about Gage changing the locks without even talking to me first. However, Mom had given him power of attorney to make those kinds of decisions, and I've never changed that.

Yet, did he really not know what was in the Admiral's will or was he using that attorney-client rule thing? Was Gage obligated to tell Dylan the truth? If the Admiral had kept quiet, how would Chad have known something was hidden in the storeroom otherwise? I hate to question Gage's motives, but things still aren't adding up.

"Oh, I'm sorry." I realize I've been so deep in thought, I still haven't answered Gage's question. "I'm fine. It's just a strange thing to have happened to such a nice guy like Chad. You know?"

Gage's brows shoot up. "I hate to speak poorly of the dead, but Chad's reputation wasn't all that great. Apparently, he wasn't only providing gardening services during many of his house calls. Maybe a jealous husband or boyfriend was behind his death?"

There *had* been that unknown customer who quietly slipped out without buying anything. Could he have been a jealous husband? Or could my mom and Chad have had a fling? During which she told him about the things she hid? No. That doesn't make sense.

Shaking my head at all the possibilities, I say, "I was there and still can't figure out how it could have happened." I start walking back to my store again, and Gage falls in step.

He says, "I filed all the paperwork for your restaurant permits yesterday. Guess who showed up in my office two hours later?"

My stomach clenches. "Uncle Frank?"

"Yep. He thought one of his properties would be a better fit than yours. He wanted me to present the idea to the restaurant owner. So, I'm presenting it."

What an underhanded move. No wonder most of my newly

inherited properties sit empty. "Tell Uncle Frank that when pigs fly, he'll have a deal."

"Got it." Gage clears his throat again. "Want to have dinner with me tonight? There's a new Thai place in the city I've wanted to try."

As much as I love Thai food and going into San Francisco for dinner, I'm determined to stay off the man train for the time being. "I can't. I already have plans." To hunt for whatever my mother left me. But he doesn't need to know that.

Gage jams his hands into his pockets. "Okay. Maybe some other time."

"Sure." I slip the key into the new lock at the bookstore, and it turns nice and smooth. "Have a good day."

"You too." Gage lifts a hand and walks away as Cooper and I enter the store.

I take off Cooper's leash, then hit the alarm and the lights. I'll not touch anything regarding the golf ball until Dylan has a chance to check it all out. In the meantime, I head for the storage room to stash my lunch in the refrigerator. My imagination still in overdrive wonders if I'll see a chalk outline on the floor like in the movies, but I don't. All I see are stains on the concrete floor that I'm sure I don't want to know the specifics of. I tug open the fridge and toss the brown bag lunches inside. And then a thought hits me, so I open the freezer. Isn't that where everyone hides things?

I stick my head inside. There're ice cubes in the plastic bin, and an old single-serving frozen lasagna covered in crystals. Well, it couldn't be that easy. Could it?

At the sound of the buzzer, I hurry to the back door to let in Wilma, the croissant baker and world's best maker of coffee, to fill us up for the day. "Good morning."

Wilma, who's dark-haired and in her late fifties, never seems to age in an almost vampire-like way and is willow thin some-how, even surrounded by amazing baked goods all day. She says, "Morning, Sawyer. Sorry to hear about Chad." She passes by with her rolling cart filled with goodies and sets out toward the showroom.

"Me too." I grab a box of croissants to help my mom's best friend haul in the goods and so I can make my stomach stop growling at the same time. After we get to the dining area and I take a bite, I mumble, "Can I ask you something?"

"Anything, sweetheart." Wilma swaps out the insulated coffee carafes she refills daily. She's had to bring two more a day since I've been here. I really need to cut back.

"My mom and Chad never had anything more than a …business relationship. Did they?"

Wilma smiles. "Your mom wasn't a nun when it came to men, but she drew the line at men young enough to be her children." Wilma puts the last empty carafe on her cart and is all packed up. "Zoe hired Chad's father because he was the best gardener in the area. Chad inherited the business and his father's skills, so she kept Chad on after his dad died. Your mom took great pride in her flowers. Nothing more."

Phew. That's a relief. "Thanks, Wilma. Have a great day."

"You too." Wilma surprises me when she wraps me up in a hug. "I'm glad you've decided to stay, Sawyer. Your mom always thought you belonged here. So get busy looking for what your mom left for you so that you can open that restaurant and we can have more than simple diner food around here."

The air whooshes from my lungs. "You know about what she left me?"

"Not the specifics." Wilma gives me one last squeeze and then releases me. "Just that your mom found a way to stick it to your Uncle Frank and help you at the same time."

My croissant grows heavy in my gut. "Who else knows?"

"Just me and the Admiral before Thursday night. He called and said he felt he'd better tell Dylan just in case Chad had found out somehow. See you on Monday."

"Bye." I lift a hand and watch her leave through the back room. The more people who know the secret, the more chances of a leak. I wish I knew for sure what Chad had been doing in the storeroom.

As I consider the possibilities, it occurs to me that I own a dog now, and where the heck is he?

Searching for my pup, I turn in a circle in the middle of the store filled with little reading nooks that make things cozy but are a shoplifter's dream. Not that anyone would steal a book these days. They just pirate them online.

Stretched out on his back, four paws in the air, sound asleep, Cooper is snoozing on the love seat in the front. A perfect spot to people-watch and sunbathe. Perhaps he didn't get enough sleep last night for all the crying he did when I wouldn't let him up on my bed. Or on any of the furniture at home.

My sleep-deprived brain tells me to scold him for being on the couch, but he's so darn cute and always ready for a cuddle that I'm going to have to fight the battles I can win. I can't watch him all day at the store and work too. So I'll enforce the rules at home and be happy with that.

Cooper opens one eye, sends me a knowing doggy grin, then goes right back to sleep. That's when I spot the golf ball in his mouth. Should've known he'd find that.

On closer inspection, there's something written on the ball. Cooper's drool has made some of the letters run. It looks like the first word might have been my name. I can't read the middle part of the message, but it ends in OME. Like Sawyer go home?

Yikes. Someone did this on purpose.

I grab my cell and text Dylan. Then I take a picture of the golf ball, making sure I get the brand and the partial message. I grab a tissue and wrap the ball for safekeeping.

Feeling shaky all over at the direct threat, I go back to the register and grab the money from the safe under the front counter to load up the cash drawer. When I'm done, I unlock the front door to open for the day, refusing to be intimidated, because that's clearly what the golf ball was intended to do.

Could my uncle have something to do with this? Maybe he's trying to scare me off, so I'll leave and he can cash in on the trust? That's probably it. If someone really wanted to send a threat, wouldn't they do more damage than throw a little golf ball through the glass? Or did someone do that because they could stand across the street at the park to launch it, out of range of any security cameras? I had had a bit of a disagreement with the town council not long ago about changing the lettering on the bookshop's windows. They want everyone on the square to match, but I think that's silly and said so. Maybe this was the president Joe Kingsley's way of reminding me I'm out of compliance?

I should stop freaking out and wait to see what Dylan thinks before I lose it.

Pushing down my fear, I pour coffee into my jumbo insulated metal cup and start in on my second croissant of the morning. Stress eating always helps what ails me.

When the door opens and Brittany strolls in, I nearly choke on my coffee. "Thank you for being on time today." Almost. I'll take it.

She shrugs. "Least I could do after getting paid for not working yesterday. I *do* get paid still, right?"

I withhold my sigh, remembering what it'd been like to grow up surrounded by friends who had everything while I had very little. My mom was rich in real estate she couldn't sell, but never in cash. "Of course. How about straightening up the shelves this morning to start?"

Brittany pops her gum. "Fine."

I'm going to keep the golf ball incident quiet until I can speak to Dylan.

The door opens, and in flies Madge, the always-in-a-hurry police dispatcher. She wears the sweaters she knits no matter the temperature. Today's creation has a big yellow cat on an orange background. "Sawyer, I only have a few minutes, but I wanted to ask you something." She pours herself a cup of coffee and grabs a croissant. She finds a seat in the little dining area and pats a chair beside her.

I join the dark, short-haired, middle-aged whirling dervish, and then Brittany pulls out a chair too and sits. She props her hand on her chin and asks, "What have you overheard?" Like this is a routine they have I don't know about.

Madge leans closer and glances around the otherwise empty store once before she says. "That's what I'm here to ask you guys." She turns to me. "You and Dylan go way back. What has he told you?"

"Nada. Even my crab cakes yesterday couldn't make him talk."

Brittany rolls her eyes. "He's at your house and you feed him, probably flirt with him a little too because you always do, and you still got nothing? You got no game, sister." Brittany's little grin tells me she's just pushing my buttons.

"I don't flirt with Dylan." Spar with him? Absolutely. I can't seem to help it.

"Sawyer's new to the club, Brittany." Madge chuckles into her coffee. "Give her a break."

That and I don't read mystery novels like they do. Maybe I should start. "Dylan operates by the book. Keeps everything on a need-to-know. It's super frustrating."

Madge nods. "He does. The deputies aren't as tight-lipped though. Greg asked me this morning what I use to keep pests away from my gardens. Bet that has something to do with the flurry of activity after they got back from searching Chad's place for clues yesterday. I saw a big container filled with something liquid. Next thing you know, a lab guy from San Francisco comes and picks it up."

Brittany lifts her phone and starts tapping. "So maybe Chad

poisoned himself with bug spray? And the chemicals just happened to kick in during book club?"

I add, "He *had* sprayed my gardens earlier in the day."

"Was that *all* he took care of, Sawyer?" Brittany's grin turns full-out mischievous now.

"Yes." I take another slug of coffee to help my brain keep up with these two. "I'm off men, for now, remember? Gage just told me about Chad's extracurricular activities. If everyone in town knows, why would Julie date him?"

Madge's eyes widen. "I didn't know they'd been dating. This does thicken the plot. I've been sure it has to be Crystal who did it this whole time. How do you know this?"

"Wade told me yesterday." Cooper trots over, gets rubs from Brittany and Madge, and then curls up at my feet.

Madge finishes up her coffee. "Maybe Chad cheated on Julie too? And she wanted revenge? She was sitting right next to him, eating during the puppy-and-yarn confusion." Madge smiles and pats Cooper again. "You're almost too cute to get mad at, though. Aren't you?"

I've come close but can't disagree.

"Wait." Brittany holds up a finger. "I just looked up chemicals used in gardening. Did Chad wear protective gear while he sprayed your garden, Sawyer?"

I nod. "I was getting coffee and saw him out the back window. He wore a jumpsuit and a mask but he always said he was using safe, all-organic ingredients. My mom had insisted on that for the environment."

Brittany frowns. "Herbicides, most likely. Hard to tell from this, but most of the effects of common natural pesticides are more long-term rather than instant. It does say pesticides can be dangerous if absorbed through the skin or if rubbed near the mouth or in the eyes. In large doses, it can be fatal. Maybe he accidentally ingested it before he got here. Maybe the biggest mystery here is why Julie would ever date a cheater like him."

So what was "the right thing" Crystal wanted Chad to do during their fight?

I won't share my question with the gals because maybe it didn't have to do with being pregnant at all. I don't want to spread false rumors. I hated when kids did that to me back in my school days here. News travels at the speed of light in small towns whether it's true or not. That I remember painfully well.

"Gotta get back." Madge hops up from her chair. "Keep your ears open and your eyes peeled, ladies. There might be a murderer on the loose!"

Brittany smirks. "Or a careless, cheating gardener has finally gotten bitten in the butt by karma."

"See you soon." I wave to Madge's back and then turn to Brittany to ask the question that's been bugging me since yesterday. "Is there anything about this bookstore that I need to know? Like something my mom would've wanted me to take care of that I haven't?" This is the only way I can think of to ask my question about the hidden things in my mom's letter without raising a question in Brittany's mind.

"Yeah. One huge thing." Brittany's right brow arches as she stands.

My heartbeat speeds up in anticipation. "What is it?"

"She probably wished you'd read a mystery in the last ten years. You're pretty useless when customers ask for recommendations. That must be why she begged me to stay on here after she died. To help you out."

"Ha. Ha. Go straighten, please." I'm still not sure who's helping who here, but it doesn't matter. And I've been studying the top one hundred lists that come in the mags each month. I've almost memorized the top one hundred classics. Almost. Well, maybe I know the top twenty-five or ten for sure, but it's on my to-do list.

Just as I start for the storeroom to begin my search for whatever my mom hid, the front door opens, and a familiar booming voice calls out, "Sawyer?"

Uncle Frank's voice sends a rod of steel up my spine. I will not be intimidated. Hopefully he hasn't figured out my sneaky plan to make the trust build me a restaurant. Or maybe he's come to add to the intimidation of the golf ball? A one-two punch?

I have to lift my chin to face him because my uncle is tall, mostly bald, and built like Mr. Clean, the exact opposite of my calm, pixie-sized mother in almost every way. His forehead has frown lines permanently etched, and his suspicious squinty eyes are searching mine. Then when he smiles with his blazingly white capped teeth, the charming and persuasive parts of him shine through. It's how he's the mayor.

However, I'm not falling for it. I stand in the way of lots of money he thinks he deserves, and I can't afford to forget that.

I plaster on a smile too. "Hi, Uncle Frank. How are you?" I refuse to look as rattled about the golf ball as I feel.

His grin dims. "Not so hot. Having a murder is never good for a tourist town. What do you know? Dylan says it's too soon to talk about, but you were here Thursday night, right?" He walks to the dining area and pours himself a cup of vanilla roast and then grabs a croissant.

Relief that this visit isn't about my secret restaurant allows me to let out the breath I'd been holding as I join him and refill my mug. "Not much. We're waiting on lab results. I didn't see anyone poison Chad, if that's what you're asking."

His frown lines deepen. "This isn't going to help your sales. And neither is giving away expensive croissants and gourmet coffee for free. If you're going to make this sinking ship flounder much longer, you'd be smart to quit giving all this food away as your hippie mother did. At least charge for it."

I set my mug down and cross my arms. He isn't wrong, but the free coffee and croissants add that extra touch of charm to the shop my mother wanted. I plan to do the same at my restaurant. "I'll consider your ideas, thanks. Now if you'll excuse me—"

"You must be running out of savings by now. I saw the numbers last week. You're only doing slightly better than your mother ever did here, and that's still dismal. You're a chef, not a bookstore owner, and it shows."

My heart pounds, but I'm determined to hold it together. "I'm learning to be both. I have to get back to work, so I'll let you see yourself out." Pivoting on my toes, I start for the storeroom again and hope he leaves.

"How much will it take, Sawyer? Name your price to go back to Chicago and let me make my parents' legacy a proud one again."

He has never offered to buy me out before, so he must be at the end of his rope. Well, so am I.

My eyes cut to the left, and I see Brittany watching with concern in her eyes and holding an upset Cooper, alarmed by the raised voices. Her job is on the line too here. So, I give her a confident "watch this" nod.

Slowly, I turn around and face him again. My hands are shaking, so I fold them. "I'm not here for money, Uncle Frank. I'm here because of my mother. Over the years, you've tried to take her home away, run her out of town, and steal what was rightfully hers. In the end, she was smarter and tougher than you ever gave her credit for. And so am I. I've got a tenant moving in next door who will keep me afloat for many years to come. Despite your best efforts to block renting my buildings."

His eyes narrow. "You'd be smart to watch your tone, young lady. Because I won't offer you this kind of money ever again. Now, how much?"

I narrow my eyes right back. "I don't need your money." Liar, liar, pants on fire. I cross my fingers behind my back so that I won't be struck by lightning on the spot. Yet according to my mom, I won't need money after I find the hidden things.

"Oh, really?" He laughs. "I saw the lease for next door. They aren't paying rent until the restaurant opens. That could take months. You had your chance to go back home with a fistful of cash, but now you blew it." He turns and stomps toward the door. "I will crush you at whatever game you think you're playing, Sawyer!"

I call out, "Challenge accepted. Have a great day!" ever so sarcastically. What is he, a comic book villain? Crush me? Go ahead and try.

After the adrenaline pumping through me eases a bit, I realize I might have just lit a fire under my uncle to mess up my restaurant plans.

Had my quick temper just driven the last nails in my coffin?

I better find whatever my mom left for me ASAP!

CHAPTER 6

$\mathcal{J}$'m up to my elbows in dusty books in the storeroom, searching for whatever the heck I'm supposed to find, when Brittany clears her throat behind me. "What're you doing? You've been back here for hours."

I glance over my shoulder. Cooper is right at her feet. He loves Brittany as much as he loves me. "Nothing. Just trying to figure out how to organize all this." Once again, a lie. A necessary one, though, on so many levels.

"The Admiral's here. You said I should get you when he came in." Brittany's frown deepens. "Dylan asked me to tell him if I observed any strange behavior. You talking to the crazy guy on purpose and spending all morning playing with these books qualifies." She lifts her cell and waggles it. "Spill or you're busted."

"Go ahead." I dust off my hands and then climb down from the stepstool I'm on. "Call him if you'd like." Dylan just called, and when I filled him in about the golf ball, said he'd be over soon anyway.

"Nah." Brittany tucks her phone away. "Then he'd just come over here, and the two of you will do your weird we-don't-like-each-other-but-really-we-do dance. It'll make me lose my appetite. And it's lunchtime."

I suppress the urge to engage about my feelings for Dylan. "I packed turkey sandwiches for us today. Why don't you grab one and take it to the park?" Brittany never eats lunch unless I bring it for her. I don't like to see her go hungry.

She crosses her arms. "Oh, so now you're trying to get rid of me while you talk to Admiral Crazy?"

"Yep. You could report me to Dylan while you eat. Now scram, please. And take Cooper with you."

Brittany lets out a long sigh but heads to the fridge. I hurry out front to talk to Admiral Wright.

He's sitting in the dining area with a book, some coffee, and a croissant. He's a regal-looking older gentleman, tall, thin, with chiseled cheekbones. He wears button-down shirts, cardigans, and khakis, along with highly polished leather shoes every day. His bushy white eyebrows hop up when he sees me.

"Hello, Sailor. Before you ask, I need to inform you that I'm a trained former military officer, so no form of torture will make me crack. It's why your mom chose me to be the keeper of your fate."

Brittany stops eating her sandwich midbite and stands beside me. "Keeper of her fate?"

"Out." I point toward the front door and return my employee's stare until she grumpily caves and heads outside.

She says, "Come on, Cooper. You need to go out anyway."

Cooper looks back and forth between us and then decides to join Brittany at the park to do his thing.

That the Admiral almost spilled the beans in front of Brittany, combined with how quickly he told Dylan my mom's secret, makes me doubt only a few know what I desperately want to discover.

As I sit across from him, I ask, "Ever had your fingernails removed slowly, one by one? I know a guy."

The Admiral laughs. "Nice try." He takes a bite of his croissant and then says, "I apologize for telling Dylan the secret. I worried Wilma might have told Chad. And that's why he's been spending so much time in the back room during book club. You know it's rumored that Wilma and Chad have had a little, shall we say, alone time now and again."

This is new information. "She just told me only the two of you knew." I'm going to have to ask about her and Chad on Monday morning when I see her again. "How long had Chad been disappearing for long periods of time during book club?"

"Since he joined three or four months ago. At first, I thought it was because he was avoiding the more complex parts of our discussions. Or he had an overwhelming need to swab the deck back there." He stands and pours himself another cup of coffee even though the one in front of him is full. "Since we haven't had book club for several weeks, I was curious if Chad would even show up. He never seemed to have time to read our selections. For that matter, neither does Julie. At first, I assumed Wade and Chad were just there to gain Julie's affections."

Brittany had said the same. "Does Wade read the books?"

"Yes. He's been a good addition to the crew. Seems to get the finer points of the story. And the lad understands sea lanes. Very impressive for a landlubber."

I wish Wade would get busy with the finer points of *my* woodwork, but that's another problem I need to solve. "My sister wants me to move to San Francisco and open a restaurant there. If I did that, you'd have to tell me where the things are hidden, correct?"

"Yes." His erect shoulders slump. "It'd disappoint your mother, though. Greatly. She truly felt that you'd be happiest living here."

"I know." Now my shoulders droop too. I don't want to disappoint my mother. "It's why I'm staying."

A big grin lights the Admiral's wrinkly face. "That's excellent news." He stands and holds out a hand for a shake. "I'll wish you luck, then. I'm late to meet my men."

"Thank you." I return the shake and ignore the part about his men. He always says that. "How about a clue or two? I'm running out of savings."

"Can't do that. What I can do is offer some advice. There are a lot of old books in the back. Your mom always talked about putting them up for sale online to clear out some space. Said some were probably valuable to the right collector. Then she got sick and wasn't up for the task." He takes a pocket watch out of his sweater vest. "High tide soon. Have to ship out."

"Right. Can't miss your ship." Maybe selling the books online was actually a clue my mom left for me via the Admiral. "See you Monday?"

"Assuming I'm back in port by then."

"Okay. Have a good voyage, Admiral."

"Good luck, sailor." He salutes and heads for the door.

I'll take all the luck I can get.

Not ten seconds after the Admiral is gone, Brittany and Cooper return. She says, "How does he hold your fate in his hands?"

I smile deviously. "It'll be your fate too now. He gave me some good advice. If I go get my laptop, can you figure out how we can sell some of those old books in the back online?"

"Yeah." Brittany shrugs. "But unless we can get more than a buck or two for them, the shipping costs will be too much."

"My mom told the Admiral some of the books might be worth something to the right collector. We'll have to sift through the worthless ones to find the good ones. I want to get started right away."

"Sorry I asked," Brittany grumbles as she moves behind the counter. "We've had this scan gun I asked Gage to order for us for a while now, but your mom never wanted to hook it up. I'll rig this up to your laptop to speed things up."

"Perfect. I'll run home for my computer and be right back. Want me to take Cooper or leave him?"

"He can stay and keep me company." Brittany squats down and pets my dog. When Cooper lays his face in her lap, Brittany's face lights with one of her rare smiles. "He really grows on you, doesn't he?"

"Yep. Thanks for watching him. Be right back." I head for the door, and just as I reach to open it, in comes Dylan wearing his uniform. "I wasn't sure you work Saturdays too, Sheriff."

Dylan glances Brittany's way and then takes my arm and leads me outside. After the door swings shut behind us, he says, "I'm working every day until I solve Chad's murder. Do you have the golf ball?"

I grab the ball wrapped in tissue from my purse. "Cooper drooled on it before I took it from him and noticed the writing. Probably too late to lift a print."

Dylan frowns at the letters. "I'll write up a report so you can file an insurance claim. Any idea who'd want you gone?"

"My uncle, for one. Maybe Crystal. I had that run-in with her yesterday. Or Joe Kingsley about the matchy-matchy window-lettering thing."

"Okay. Let me see what we can do with this. In the meantime, be extra aware. And next time when you text, don't just say call me. Tell me what the trouble is. I would've dropped everything."

"I know, but you've got so much else going on, I didn't want to bother you."

"It bothers me to know you could be in danger!" He runs a hand down his face in frustration. When his temper cools, he says, "I need to ask a favor. Were you heading to lunch?"

"No, I was going home to get something. It can wait. What do you need?"

"I sent lab techs to your garden to take some samples. Yours was the last house Chad sprayed before he died."

I set my hands on my hips. "Don't you need my permission to do that?"

"That's why I'm here. To ask. I can still call them off. They're driving in from the city. But I'd rather you didn't tell anyone about it just yet."

"Fine. You can do your tests." I can't tell Dylan that Madge clued us in about her pesticide theory and the secret is already out. "Wade showed up this morning before I left for work. He might still be there, if that matters to you."

"Let's go check. You said you were heading that way anyway, right?"

"Yep." I start walking up the hill to my house. "Did anyone mention to you that Chad had spent a lot of time in the storeroom ever since he started coming to book club?"

"You've finally spoken with the Admiral." Dylan slows his long stride so I can keep up. "Yes. And I confirmed Chad's behavior with a few others too, to be sure."

I shake my head. "It makes no sense to come to book club each week when you haven't read the book. Unless he was just there because Julie was. I'm sure you know by now they'd been secretly dating. Or was he looking for an excuse to search the back room?"

"That's the million-dollar question." Dylan stops walking and faces me. "And it's why I need you to be careful, Sawyer. Your mother's letter said the things she hid were worth a lot of money. Probably enough for someone to have killed for."

My stomach takes a quick twist. "So you don't think Chad accidentally poisoned himself with pesticides? And yet you want to test my garden? That doesn't make any sense."

"How did you— Why do I bother trying to run an investigation by the book in this town? I have to eliminate all the possibilities." Dylan starts walking again. "I wish you'd stop playing junior detective and go live with Lance and Megan in the city until I make an arrest. Yet I know you won't."

He's right.

Picking up speed, I catch up with him. "So maybe money is an angle? Have you looked into everyone's financials?"

Dylan sends me a hard look that tells me I'm about to annoy him for real.

I lift my hands. "I'm just trying to help. Actually, if you looked into my financials, I'd probably go right to the top of your suspect list again. I'm probably the most broke. Except we both know I didn't know about the hidden things at the time of the murder." Maybe that's why Dylan paid for the groceries the other day. Maybe he's already looked into everyone's money situation. "Have you eliminated anyone yet?"

"What do you think, Nancy Drew?"

"Since you asked, I'll tell you. I don't think Madge or the Admiral could have done it because they were both by the door getting tied up with yarn and nowhere near Chad. After I cut everyone loose, Madge and the Admiral sat at another table, and I joined Julie, Chad, and Wade, who were already eating. So that leaves the mysterious customer and Crystal before Chad sat down to eat, or Julie or Wade could have poisoned Chad during the yarn confusion. But Wade was Chad's best friend. And Julie was dating Chad, so those two suspects don't make sense. At least not on the surface."

"Thank you for sharing." Dylan wraps his arm around my shoulder as we pass by Wade's truck in my driveway. "Want me to help you search the house tonight after your pal leaves?"

"That's it? No 'I agree,' or 'you're wrong because of this or that'? And he's not my pal. Not the way you mean it."

Dylan turns the knob on my front door and frowns at me because it's unlocked again.

I quickly say, "Wade probably didn't lock it because I don't have a key yet. I got new locks this morning."

Dylan mumbles, "Keep it up, and I'm going to lock you up at the station for safekeeping."

Ignoring him, I follow Dylan inside and then close the door behind us. A loud bang from the kitchen makes Dylan dash down the hall with me right on his heels.

Dylan pokes the swinging door open with his left hand as his right reaches for his gun. Wade is inside, crouching in front of the pantry and sweeping up the pieces of an old Pyrex bowl I keep on the very top shelf. Something yellow is sticking out of Wade's back pocket that looks vaguely familiar.

He looks up and cringes. "Hey, guys. Sorry about your bowl, Sawyer."

Dylan's gun hand relaxes, and he steps aside to let me go inside first. I ask, "What were you doing in the pantry?"

Wade throws the last of the pieces away. "I was looking for something old to mix a little touch-up paint in. I'll replace it."

"No. That's okay. I never use it anyway. You guys want the last of the blueberry crumble?" I head to the counter and find the dirty pan in the sink. "Oh, too late."

Wade smiles. "It was amazing, Sawyer." Then he turns to Dylan. "Are your people coming over to test the garden?"

Dylan nods. "Should be here in a few minutes. Any pot roast left from last night?"

"Time out! What do you know about my garden, Wade? And yes, help yourself, Dylan."

Wade jams his hands into his baggy jeans' front pockets. "When Dylan caught up with us at Skippy's last night, Crystal told him what she and Chad had been arguing about."

"Which was?"

Wade holds up both hands. "Just so you know, I didn't know exactly what Chad had been spraying on people's gardens. He only told me it was something he shouldn't be using, and that Crystal knew and wasn't happy about it. Crystal told us last night that when they were in Mexico last, she caught him buying it. And that she had threatened to tell Dylan if he didn't stop using it."

This makes no sense. "Chad told my mother he used environmentally safe all-natural sprays. Why would he use something he shouldn't?"

Dylan finds the pot roast and potatoes and dishes himself up a plate. "Because his father had been using it since the sixties. It got amazing results killing pests and made their gardening company the most popular in the area, but it's been banned in the US for many years."

I better keep Cooper out of the flower beds for sure now. "What is it?"

Dylan's face grows hard. "DDT."

I quickly google DDT on my phone and read all about the deadly pesticide that was banned in the US because it causes cancer.

Cancer? Did gardening kill my mother?

My knees grow weak, so I sit at the nook.

Chad and his father lied to my mother. Told her they were using environmentally safe sprays. Chad's father had been taking care of my mother's gardens since I was a kid. After he died, Chad took over. For the last thirty-five years, they'd been putting my mother and my family at risk. And how many others in the area?

My hands fist into tight balls, I'm so outraged. If Chad weren't already dead, I'd strangle him for exposing innocent people to something so lethal.

Through gritted teeth, I say, "Maybe someone else figured this out and decided to kill Chad with his own poison?"

Dylan nods. "Maybe."

CHAPTER 7

*W*hile Dylan and the lab guys are busy with my gardens, this is my chance to do a little golf ball sleuthing. I hop into my mom's old Honda and head out to the new golf course at the edge of town. Armed with my phone's photo, I pull up in front of the clubhouse and jump out.

Along with my uncle's new housing development south of town for the millennials who work in the city, he built a new clubhouse, restaurant, pool, tennis courts, and community center. Though this makes my uncle my first choice for the window-breaking crime, how often is the obvious person really the one whodunnit?

The pungent smell of chlorine smacks me in the face as I search for the pro shop. A big sign points me in the right direction.

The guy who runs the shop is a local guy I went to school with. "Hi, John."

He looks up from the golf magazine he's leaning on the counter reading. He pushes up his thick glasses and says, "Hey, Sawyer. How you been?" He swipes his longish black hair away from his eyes and stands up.

"Okay. But I have a question for you. Do many use this type of ball?" I pull up the picture of the ball's logo on my phone.

John smiles and points to a huge display of golf balls in cardboard boxes. "Everyone uses this brand. It's what we sell the most of around here. This one is the top-of-the-line model."

So, someone who plays a lot maybe. "Does my uncle use this brand?"

John's eyebrows scrunch as he considers. "No, actually, he buys special ones the pros use. He might use this type for the range."

Huh. "Does Joe Kingsley golf much?"

John shakes his head. "Maybe once a year? Why?"

I should have had that answer ready. My mind races for an explanation. "Some vandalism in town. No big deal."

"Oh. I see. You think Joe's kids did something?"

No, but that works.

"I don't want to point any fingers." I put my phone away. "Did you hear about Chad?"

"Yeah." John's eyes grow wide. "So weird, right? Wait. Does this have to do with Chad? Because he and Wade always bought new balls here before they played. And Chad had been teaching Julie how to play recently too."

Oh boy. Now we're getting somewhere. "How about Crystal? Does she play?"

"No. Not that I know of."

"Okay, thanks. I appreciate the information. Have a good day!" I plaster on a big smile.

"You too, Sawyer. Nice to see you again."

"You too." I head out to the parking lot, digesting what I've just learned. Wade and Julie both play golf. Joe does too occasionally. Joe is a major kiss butt to my uncle, so maybe my uncle put Joe up to it? Or, maybe my mystery customer plays golf too.

One thing's for sure. Better cameras at my store would be a good idea going forward.

After I get home, I park the Honda in the garage. Dylan and the lab guys are gone, so I grab my laptop, wave to Wade and then walk down the hill to my store.

When I arrive, Brittany is at the front counter, busy inputting inventory to sell online. I set my laptop beside her. Hopefully it'll go faster once Brittany hooks up her scanner. Cooper is happy to see me and runs across the store for a cuddle.

"Hey. Everything go okay?"

Brittany lifts her head. "Yeah. Except did you see the weird hole in the window?"

"I'll have to file an insurance claim." I join her at the counter. "Luckily, it's not too big."

Brittany nods. "I'm going to go in the back. It's easier than hauling the books out here."

"Okay." After Brittany is gone, I pull up the security files on the computer that's also our cash register. The files are all stored in the cloud, so I find the night Chad died and watch Brittany setting out the glasses by the front door.

Dylan was right: the quality is weak, and the images show up in sporadic bursts. The camera doesn't pick up the whole store. Absent is the little dining area near the back, and only the central part of the bookstore is seen.

Now that I know Chad had been spraying so many people's gardens in the area with a deadly poison, I'm even more curious about the mystery customer who was near Crystal and Chad during their argument. What if the man found out what Chad had been up to? Maybe the unknown customer had a similar reaction to mine when he found out, but took his rage to a higher level?

What I'd missed when Chad had come for book club that night was that he held an energy drink in a slender can. Then there's a big gap in the footage, and the open can is sitting on top of a low bookshelf while he argues with Crystal, and the mystery customer browses nearby. After another gap in the footage, the can is gone. And so are Crystal, Chad, and the customer.

Dylan told me to stop sleuthing, but now I have to know if he found that can and if that's how the poison was administered. Could the stranger have spiked his drink? If the unknown man had ever been in my mom's store before, he'd know most everyone takes advantage of the free coffee. What if Customer X brought something along hoping to poison Chad's drink?

I pick up my cell and tap Dylan's number. Buttering him up a bit before I go for the kill shot and ask about the can is my plan. When he answers, I say, "You were right. I'm taking your advice and getting new cameras. And I think I will take you up on your offer to help me tonight. I'll even feed you dinner first. I'm making chicken parm." Dylan used to beg me to make that for him. And he's actually had training in searching for things, so he could come in handy.

Dead air fills my ear for a good five seconds before he says, "Skip it. If I can answer your questions, I will, but no guarantees."

He's on to my plan.

"What gave me away?"

"You led with 'you were right.' I can't recall you *ever* saying that to me."

"Maybe that's because listening wasn't your strongest attribute when we were together? You probably missed it."

He chuckles. "That must be it. What do you want to know?"

"Did you ever find the energy drink can Chad carried in with him?"

Dylan is quiet for a moment. "We searched for it but came up empty."

Wow. "That's the equivalent of a smoking gun, right?"

"It's a piece of the puzzle."

A missing piece. "I don't get how anyone could have sneaked it out. You guys searched all of us and went through our things."

"All we know for sure is the can disappears in the footage, and so do all three people. Crystal or the customer could've carried it out with them. Or Chad could've carried it to the dining area with him. Anything could've happened in that large time gap in the recording."

"True. Have you asked people about the can?"

He sighs. "Of course, I have."

"You didn't ask me."

"Yes, I did. Late that same night, I had to wake you because you were the last one left to interview. You answered all my questions and then fell right back to sleep on the couch. *Now* who's the bad listener?"

I do tend to talk in my sleep. My sister used to ask me where my candy stash was while I was asleep. Evidently, the sleeping version of me always tells the truth, so I lost a lot of candy. And I never remembered the conversations afterward. "What other questions did you ask me?"

"You don't want to know. They might have been personal." I can hear by his voice that he's smiling.

He's just teasing me. I hope. "Do you have access to a facial recognition database you could run the customer through?"

A loud grunt fills my ear. "Do you want to know why I don't try to tell you how to cook?"

I know where this is going. "Okay, I get it. You're on it. I should let you get back to work."

"Thank you. Want me to bring a bottle of Chianti tonight? Or two?"

Chianti and Dylan are a combination that I used to find hard to resist. "Better stick with one. But this isn't a date. Just so we're clear."

"It can't be a date because I'm not allowed to date suspects."

"You can only have dinner with them?"

"It's a known interrogation technique. Lure them with good food, then ply them with lots of wine to lower inhibitions. Maybe flirt a little to rattle the subject. Then, while under my charming spell, she accidentally confesses, and I slap on the cuffs. Works every time."

That's so ridiculous, I can't help but laugh. "See you at six. If Wade is still there, it'll be fun to watch you try your charming interrogation technique on him."

"I'll bring my cuffs just in case either of you decides to confess. Or in case you'd like me to show you another charming way the cuffs can be used."

Probably best to ignore the fun-with-cuffs comment. "Bye, Sheriff." I'd forgotten how amiable Dylan can be when he puts his mind to it. No more than two glasses of wine for me tonight for sure. Got to keep those inhibitions just where they are.

As I disconnect the call, Brittany says, "You always say he's annoying. So why are you grinning like a loon? And having dinner with him?"

I quickly school my features. "He said something funny, that's why. And I plan to ply him with wine at dinner, so he'll tell me what he knows so far. What do you need?"

Brittany says to Cooper, "You'll have to tell me who plied what out of who tomorrow, buddy."

"Out of whom. Did you find something there?" I point to the book in her hand, hoping to change the subject.

"I did." Brittany's black-colored lips form a big smile. "This old Lee Child book just sold online for $105. We have five of the same editions, but ours are in better shape. And there's a whole lot more like this back there. Let's ask at least $120."

"I agree. Do it." This could be just what we need to keep the doors open until I can get the restaurant operational.

The front door swings open, and Madge hurries in. She must've spilled on her cat sweater and had to change it. The new one is a shade of green I associate with that emoji of someone about to lose their lunch. To each their own. "Hey, Madge."

"Hi there. Guess who Dylan has pulled into an interview? And she's bawling."

"No idea." I shut down my security footage and switch back to cash-register mode.

"Julie. And just before she arrived, Sam was grumbling that his eyes were about to fall out of his head for looking at so many banking records."

It's Saturday afternoon, not even forty-eight hours since Chad died. I can understand why Julie is still crying if she had feelings for him. "I didn't know you worked weekends."

"I don't usually, but Dylan needs all his deputies working on Chad's case, so I'm covering for Sam this weekend. Dylan and his men take turns taking the evening calls. We don't get many."

"Can you tell who they think killed Chad?"

"No. But..." Madge leans closer. "When I asked Sam if he thought we were all going to be working overtime next week too, he said it looked that way because more than a few people might have a motive. So naturally I asked if I was one of those people, and Sam shook his head. Thankfully. He said the murder weapon was adding a lot more complications."

The alleged DDT. "Who have you seen them call into the station?"

Madge holds up a hand to tick off fingers. "Yesterday, it was the Admiral and Wade. Which makes sense because they both ran to help Chad. And today, Crystal and Julie. Dylan made me take a break while they're interviewing Julie. Said he'd text me when I can come back. He's never done that before."

Dylan's probably on to Madge's gossipy ways. "What do you know about Julie?"

"Let's see." Madge leans against the counter and plops her chin into her hand. "She's a single mother who lives with her mom because Julie lost everything in her recent divorce. She's worked at the grocery store for a few months now but mentioned she'd been looking for a better job. Said she couldn't always afford to buy the books we discuss at book club, but enjoyed hearing about them anyway."

"Makes sense." Maybe that's why Julie wasn't prepared for the book discussions like the Admiral had said. "Crystal I knew from school, but what's been going on with her lately?"

"Dylan had to go to her house more than once for domestic disturbances when she was dating Chad. Oh, and I was behind Crystal in the grocery store a few weeks ago. She was in line at Julie's register. When Julie picked up a pregnancy test off the belt and swiped it, she says to Crystal she hadn't realized Crystal was dating anyone. And who's the lucky guy."

Uh-oh. So maybe Crystal asking Chad to do the right thing *had* been about a baby.

Madge continues, "So Crystal gets this weird grin on her face and says she still sees Chad and leaves. When I loaded my groceries on the belt, Julie looked like she'd seen a ghost. It was like Crystal had done that to upset her because it was obvious Chad was interested in Julie whenever we saw them together at book club. I shared all this with Dylan, just in case it'd matter."

I lean my elbows on the counter too. "So now we have two possibly scorned women, or Crystal just did that in the grocery store to be a jerk. She did some mean things to me in high school too over a guy." Dylan was that guy, but Madge didn't need to know that. She hadn't been around when we were in school. "Do you think we should skip book club next week? Out of respect for Chad?"

"Up to you." Madge shrugs as she digs out her phone and reads the screen. "Dylan says I can come back, so I have to go. Let me know what you decide to do about the meeting."

"I will. See you." Just when it looks like we can eliminate one of my four key suspects, something new comes to light. What if Julie and Crystal worked together out of revenge on cheating

Chad? Crystal distracts Chad while Julie makes him a plate of food complete with the poison Crystal knows Chad has. I read DDT is odorless and colorless, so it'd be easy enough to hide in food or a drink. Wade and Julie both helped themselves to food right before the yarn thing with Madge happened.

I hope Dylan's not on call tonight so he can drink enough wine to loosen his tongue. Mainly because I can't tell if he's worried about my safety because he's just being Dylan, or if he suspects someone might be looking for the things my mother has hidden. I intend to ask him that later.

I'M JUST PULLING the chicken parm from my oven when Wade appears in my kitchen, so I say, "Hi there. Staying for dinner tonight?"

Cooper sees Wade and slips under the nook's table. I've read online that goldendoodles are extra sensitive, and they have long memories. Time should help.

"Thanks, but not tonight." Wade walks to the sink and pours himself a glass of water. "Got a softball game."

"Good luck." I throw the garlic bread into the oven next.

"Hey. Do we have book club next week?" Wade reaches in his back pocket and grabs the yellow booklet I'd seen earlier. "I need to do some studying up if we do."

When he opens the book, I see it's a publication like I used in high school to get through the classics in literature. The pages state all the essential themes and subtext in books. Teachers called that cheating, but this is just book club, I guess.

I point to the pamphlet. "So, you don't read the books either? Just like Chad and Julie never did?"

"It was to impress Julie. At first." Wade's cheeks color as he holds up the booklet. "I started reading these or going online to research the books so Julie would think I'm smart like the others. Then I found out she'd started dating Chad, so it didn't matter anymore. Bro code and all. These books really help, though, especially the printed ones. They seem to dig a little deeper than a google search, so I just kept it up. I've actually read a few of the books. Although one a week can be too much."

I couldn't read one a week either. "Then why go to the meetings if you hadn't read the book?"

He shrugs. "It's free beer. And my friends were there too, so why not? Not a lot to do around here."

"Yeah. I guess. See you on Monday?" I'm hoping he takes the day off tomorrow so that I can have the house all to myself for a change.

"Bright and early." He lifts a hand and starts toward the swinging door, but then stops. "Do you think Gage could write my check a little early this month? I want to buy a new suit for Chad's funeral. Out of respect. You know?"

That sends a pang to my heart. "If it's okay with Gage, I'm fine with that."

"Great." Wade runs a hand through his shaggy blond hair. "Maybe I'll even get a haircut too, while I'm at it. His mom is always after me to wear it shorter."

I'd forgotten that Wade had lived with Chad's family senior year because his parents had died in a car accident. "I think that'd be a nice gesture."

"Thanks, Sawyer. I really appreciate it."

"You bet." After Wade leaves, I start on the salad. When the swinging door opens again, I look up and it's Dylan. Right on time. He's wearing jeans and a fitted dark green button-down shirt, with his gun holstered in a shoulder strap. He looks as handsome in civilian clothes as he does in his uniform.

He says, "Saw Wade on the porch. Glad he isn't joining us. For a change." He holds up his hands filled with Chianti. "Brought two. Just in case it's a long night." Cooper's at Dylan's feet, waiting for his new best friend to greet him.

My new mantra echoes in my head. Only two glasses. No matter what. "The opener is in that drawer over there." I point and then go back to chopping tomatoes. "Do you always come to a friendly dinner armed?"

"When there's a murderer on the loose, I do. Hi, Cooper." He sets the bottles down and then gives Cooper a generous rub. After he opens one of the bottles to breathe, he says, "Can I ask you a favor?"

"Maybe." I finish tossing the salad and set it on the kitchen table, all the while telling myself it's not weird to have dinner alone with Dylan. Family has always surrounded us since our breakup.

He sits and starts playing with the salt and pepper shakers again. "Since you've decided to upgrade your cameras, would you mind if I called in a favor from Ed and got them installed in time for you to have book club again next Thursday?"

"I wasn't sure I'd have book club next week." I pull the garlic bread from the oven and set it on the table too. "Still, getting the cameras in early would be great. Especially until we find whatever my mom hid. And to catch people hitting golf balls through my windows."

"Yeah." He nods. "That too. We didn't get any prints off the ball, so the sooner, the better. John told me you'd stopped by the clubhouse earlier."

I smile weakly. "Yep. So why are you so interested in having book club next week?"

Dylan rolls his eyes at my evasion. "So that I can observe people's behavior."

I pour our wine, grab the chicken, then sit across from him. "So, you don't think it's the mystery customer or Crystal but one of the book club members who killed Chad?"

"It could still be the mystery customer. Or Crystal." Dylan dishes up a plate and hands it to me. "If that customer comes in again, I'd like a better picture of his face. Don't confront him though. Call me as soon as you can after he leaves."

"Okay." I take a big bite of chicken parm as I absorb this. The warm cheesy red sauce sings in my mouth and almost distracts me. So I switch to the buttery, crisp garlic bread instead. And that's darn good too. I didn't eat lunch, and I'm starving. "Maybe the customer needs to return to the scene of the crime and all?"

"Something like that. This is amazing, Sawyer."

"Thanks." He's almost done with his first helping of chicken and spaghetti. He eats like someone is going to take his food away. Maybe that's from his military days in the field.

I stab some salad with my fork just to feel like I'm eating something green and healthy too. "What about motive? Who in book club has any?"

Dylan takes a long drink from his wineglass. He must not be on call tonight.

After he sets the glass down, he says, "If we assume that the secret of your hidden items is out, then everyone, except you, has a motive. If the secret isn't out, then we still have four with motives if we include the mystery customer."

I do the math and guess that Madge and the Admiral aren't included in scenario two. "I can see Crystal and Julie, but even Wade? He and Chad were best friends."

Dylan shrugs. "Motive doesn't make people guilty. It just opens the door to possibilities."

"Ah." We eat in comfortable silence for a few more minutes as I consider that statement. The wine Dylan brought is good and relaxes me a bit, but my mind is still swirling with questions. "How long before we get conclusive lab results on Chad's death?"

"Soon. Once we handed over the container of DDT from Chad's shed, things picked up considerably. Between you and me, though, DDT isn't what killed him. Chad's death happened too fast. He was poisoned with something else, but I don't want that to get out."

"Do you know what killed him yet?"

Dylan shakes his head. "We have to wait on labs for that. But because of the banned DDT, more agencies have gotten involved and are threatening to take over the case. The perils of being a small-town sheriff."

"And knowing you, that's lit a fire under you to solve the case before they get their red tape all figured out?"

"Exactly." He finishes his food and then takes his plate to the dishwasher. "And if we find the hidden items and let everyone know, that lowers the threat level to you as well."

My glass stops halfway to my lips. "You don't understand. We can't tell *anyone* if we find the things my mom hid."

"Why not?" He sits across from me again and pets Cooper, who's jumping on his leg for attention.

"Because then my uncle could claim my mother used funds from the trust to purchase them without his consent and demand I turn over the items. I can't think of any other way she'd have the money to buy whatever these things are. And if he can prove she violated the terms of the trust, I'd have no choice but to give him all the property, including this house, and go back to Chicago. The one thing my mother never wanted."

"Your mom made *that* clear to anyone who'd listen before she died." Dylan runs a hand down his face in frustration "Wait. You just found out about these hidden things. How were you planning to stay here before? You've told me in the past that the bookstore can't support you."

It's my turn to run the salt and pepper shakers around the table. Uncle Frank is in charge of the city that pays Dylan's salary, so I have to tread carefully. "I have a plan."

His eyes narrow. "What kind of a plan?"

I don't want to tell him the whole truth, no matter how much I trust him.

My mind races for an explanation. "Well, just today, Brittany and I sold almost $1800.00 in old books from the back room. We've created an online seller account, and we're working on our website. We're going to sell rare and limited-edition mysteries to supplement the storefront. And then maybe even branch out into other types of rare books."

"Because the Admiral suggested that today when you met with him. He told me the same thing the night Chad died when I questioned him about what he knew about the inventory in back. So, spill."

"Can I plead the fifth?"

"No." He takes my hand. "I can't protect you if I don't know everything."

"It doesn't have anything to do with Chad's death. I found a loophole in the trust, that's all. And Gage confirmed that what I plan to do will work and is perfectly legal. Unfortunately, my uncle could plug that hole if he catches wind of it before I can make it happen. It has nothing to do with the murder."

"At this point, we don't know what has to do with the murder and what doesn't. The golf ball is a good example of that." His hand tightens over mine. "Chad's behavior suggests he might have been looking for what your mother hid. Whoever killed Chad could simply have been taking revenge for using a banned substance or looking for the hidden items too. Desperation makes people do irrational things. And if I lose control of this case on Monday, we're both going to be in the dark. Let's go to the bookstore right now while it's closed and find what Chad was looking for to put a stop to all this."

I swallow back my rising panic. "If we find it, it'll be evidence, public record. My uncle will surely see, plug the hole I found in the trust, and it still might not prove who killed Chad."

Dylan tugs on my hand. "It might keep you out of danger,

though. Come on."

If we find whatever this thing is, my dreams of having a restaurant will evaporate, and my uncle will walk away with all the things that had been rightfully my mother's.

Hello, rock and a hard place.

I put Cooper in the laundry room with a rawhide bone, and then Dylan and I set off for the bookstore on foot. The summertime sun is starting its descent into the ocean, casting beautiful pink and purple hues onto the water. "Wow. That's something I'll miss when I have to go back to Chicago."

Dylan wraps an arm around my shoulder. "I know this is hard, but it makes the most sense to get you out of the loop. If there were any other way, I'd be all for it. I don't want you to go back to Chicago either. Still, I'd like you to stay safe even more."

"Yeah. Me too." As we walk, I try to be content watching the ocean waves crashing over the rocks just off the shoreline and hope for the best. But I've never been one to wait for fate to fix things. Growing up the way I have, I learned early on that I have to chart my own destiny.

Dylan steers me toward the rear of the store. "Let's not advertise we're here by going in the front."

The front of my store faces the middle of the town square with its park and specialty shops gathered around. It's always busy in the summer evenings filled with families and tourists licking ice-cream cones and eating from the food trucks that surround the park. Mom tried staying open later to get some of that business, but apparently, ice cream and burgers hold more appeal than mystery books after 6:00 p.m.

I follow behind Dylan, still trying to figure out a way to keep whatever we find secret, when he throws out an arm for me to stop.

He whispers, "Hide behind that dumpster and wait."

Before I can question him, I see what he sees. Someone is breaking into my store.

CHAPTER 8

*T*here hasn't been a burglary in Sunset Cove in twenty years, but it looks like that streak is about to be broken.

With my stomach suddenly tied up in knots, I take a quick peek around Dylan again before I hide behind the dumpster. A tall man with broad shoulders, dressed in black, is messing with the locks.

I'd recognize that full head of black hair with the dramatic touches of white at the temples anywhere. "It's my dad, Dylan. Put the gun down."

Dylan calls out, "Can I help you?"

My dad turns around, his eyes widening at the sight of Dylan's gun, and he raises his hands above his head.

And then he passes out.

Like a fainting goat, he's lying on his side with his arms and legs sticking straight out. He does this when he sees blood too. It's where I get my squeamish nature from.

We rush to his side, and I gently pat his cheek. "Dad? Can you hear me?" Dylan and I check for any injuries, but my father seems fine. My mom had always said my dad had the hardest head in the state. I used to think she meant he was stubborn, but apparently, his head really is hard. I can't even find a bump.

Dylan gently shakes my father's shoulder. "Come on, Max. Open your eyes."

I know what'll get his attention. I lean down and shout, "Max! You're on in two!"

My dad's shoulders jerk, and his stunning blue eyes fly open. "I'm coming. Be right there." He slowly sits up, and then a big grin lights his face. "Hey there, Jellybean."

"Hi, Dad." I point to Dylan, who's smirking, and say, "You ever repeat that nickname, and you're a dead man."

My dad turns and scowls at Dylan. "Well, if it isn't the galloping groom." Dad slowly starts to get up.

Dylan ignores both of us and slips his arms under my dad to help him. "Nice to see you again too, Max."

Once my dad is vertical, he slaps Dylan's hands away. "I'll thank you for keeping your hands to yourself, sir."

My dad has never forgiven Dylan for leaving me at the altar. Mostly because he couldn't get his share of the money back from the wedding planner.

I slip an arm through my dad's bent one and pull him toward the store. "I changed the locks this morning. What did you need?"

My father brushes the dust off his dark suit. It's the one he wears on stage. "Your mother was kind enough to let me keep my things in her attic. I've decided to pull some of my older tricks *out of my hat*. Get it?"

"Your top hat. Got it." Luckily, my father generally sticks to magic instead of dad jokes on stage.

I slip my key into the lock and then open the door. "I didn't even know this place had an attic."

"That's because you have to know where to look. Follow

me." My dad grabs the ladder by the back door and then heads toward the showroom as I stop the warning beep from the alarm before it goes off.

I start to follow my dad when Dylan's hand wraps around my arm to stop me. "Should I take off or stay, Jellybean?"

I raise a warning brow.

"Sorry." He holds up both hands. "I had to do it at least once. Wait until I tell the kids—hey! That hurts."

I drag Dylan by the ear toward the main showroom. "For your punishment, you can search the attic with my dad while I look down here." I release him and then head for the coffee that's probably cold by now, but we've got a microwave.

Rubbing his ear, Dylan whispers, "Your dad hates me."

I take a drink from my mug to test the almond roast. Warm enough. "Think of it as an opportunity."

"For what? More abuse?"

"No. To make up with him. Ask him to teach you a magic trick, and you'll be his best pal."

"I think I'd rather let him stay mad at me." Dylan glances over his shoulder. My dad is sliding a panel open in the drop ceiling, exposing a wooden pull-down staircase. "On second thought, that would make an excellent place to hide something for you." He heads my dad's way.

I can't blame Dylan for wanting to avoid my dad. He can be a bit much, telling exaggerated tales about his so-called exotic travels and spinning dramatic yarns about the famous people he has entertained over the years. Like the time he told us he'd just performed for the queen of England when we knew he'd been in Milwaukee. He must've forgotten that he'd asked my mom to wire him some money to pay his hotel bill. When my mom called him out on that fact, he'd said the lady in the front row had been the queen, or he'd eat his hat.

We love him anyway, flaws and all.

When my dad pulls out a wand and bellows, "Lumos!" light shines from the hole at the top of the stairs. I'll pretend I didn't see his other hand hit a light switch.

Dylan, halfway up the steps, looks down at me and says, "Harry Potter spells?"

"Yeah. He does it for the kids."

My dad calls out, "I have a rather good one for making sheriffs disappear too."

Dylan's jaw clenches as he climbs up behind my dad. Once Dylan's head is in the attic, he says, "Sawyer? I think you need to see this."

Curious, I start up the wooden steps and follow Dylan into the attic. It's huge. It must cover the bookstore and the empty space next door where the restaurant will be. There's a long aisle down the middle with boxes stacked to the ceiling on either side. But right in front of me, at the top of the stairs tucked away in a corner, there's a bed, TV, microwave, couch, bathroom, and a fridge. "What's going on up here?" I turn to my father, who has busied himself digging through boxes.

"Just a place to lay my head when I come to town. Your mother wouldn't allow me to stay at the house, remember? She offered me this instead."

When I open the fridge, there's bottles of ketchup and mustard, beer, and a few water bottles. "How often do you stay here?" The last I knew he was in town was for my mom's funeral six weeks ago. "And how did you get a queen-sized bed up here?"

My dad's brows hitch. "Magic, of course."

Dylan grunts as he digs through boxes. "More like through those doors right there." He points at two big doors at the rear. They must open up over the alley behind my store.

Dylan crosses the attic and turns the knob. He opens one side and peers outside before he slams the door closed again.

"These weren't even locked." He twists the dead bolt to secure them.

My father waves a hand. "Of course not. There's nothing anyone would want up here. It's just old books and some of my trunks."

I used to love playing with the things inside those old trunks when I was a kid on the road with my parents over summer breaks. The sparkly clothes my mom used to wear to get sawn in half, and the hats with secret pockets, and stuffed rabbits my dad would pull out of them. We couldn't have live bunnies because they had to be fed.

And what a great place for my mom to hide something for me! My heart rate jumps as I cross the dusty floor and open one of my dad's trunks. I rummage around inside, pushing the rings that aren't really solid but are made to look like it aside, and move the many packs of trick cards and silk scarves, but don't see anything of value.

Disappointment fills me as I sit back on my heels.

Dylan slips beside me and whispers, "See our footprints? The amount of dust covering everything suggests no one has disturbed things up here for a long time. The Admiral told me your mom placed the items just a few weeks before she died."

I glance over my shoulder. My dad is still mumbling to himself while looking for something in one of his trunks across the room. "The living area isn't covered in dust, though. Someone has been up here."

Dylan nods. "Do you think your mom would've told your dad about the things she hid? And maybe he's been here looking for them too?"

"No way." I shake my head. "I love my father, but if he got his hands on those things, they'd be hocked before lunch. My mom wouldn't have told him because she wanted me to have my restaurant one day."

"Voilà!" My father holds up an intricate box with little drawers. It's like a puzzle box but rigged for his tricks. "There you are, my little crowd pleaser. Now, if only I could find my throwing knives, I'll be back in business in no time."

Dylan's shoulder bumps mine. "Maybe you should ask your dad to stay with you for a few days. That way you won't be alone. And he could bring those knives."

"Right. If someone breaks in, my dad can pull out those fake knives, and then faint at their feet to give me a chance to get away. Good plan."

Dylan's shoulders shake with restrained laughter. "You said it. I didn't."

"You were thinking it." I stand and swipe the dust off my knees. "Besides, we need to search my house too. And tomorrow is the only day I'll have it to myself."

"Okay. But I need to confirm it's been him living up here and not someone else. He won't talk to me, so you're it."

"Fine." I brush the dust off my hands and stand by my father again.

He smiles at me before he wraps me up in a hard hug. "It's so good to see you, sweetheart. Can I ask a favor?"

Uh-oh. Here it comes. The part where he asks if I have any cash on me. "Good to see you too, Dad. Before you ask, though, I need to know something. Have you been staying here long?"

"No." He shakes his head. "Since the funeral, I've popped in a few times between gigs, but I've been on the road the last two weeks. Why?"

"Because you'll need a new key. And I'm changing the alarm code after new cameras are installed. Because of the murder here last Thursday."

"Murder?" My dad's face goes as white as his shirt as he drops on top of a trunk he's using as a coffee table. "Here? At the bookstore?"

"Don't faint on me again." I sit beside my dad and grab his hand. "Yes, in the stockroom downstairs. So you need to be honest with me, okay? It's important." I stand and grab a bottle of cold water from the fridge and hand it to my dad.

He takes a long drink, and his color comes back. "I've been here on and off for the past three months. Otherwise, I've been on the road doing state fairs." My dad points to Dylan, who has joined us. "Give him Carl's number if he doesn't believe me."

Dylan asks, "Who's Carl?"

"My dad's booking agent. I'll give you the number later." I look up, and Dylan is motioning toward the trunk with his eyes. He appears to be sending me a silent signal, so I glance down and see what he sees. There's a small note taped on the side of the trunk that says: Sawyer's Toys.

I can't recall saving any toys.

And the sloppy note was written by my mom. This is it. I can feel it. However, my faint father is sitting on the trunk, so I can't open it. And he's probably planning to spend the night. Maybe I can convince him to stay at the house if he's freaked out enough about the murder. Just as I open my mouth to invite Dad back to my home, Dylan says, "Max. Can you show me how that box works?"

My father's whole face lights up. "A good magician never reveals his secrets. However, I'm happy to show you the trick." He hops up and grabs the box. "Give me a twenty-dollar bill."

I smirk as Dylan digs in his wallet for a twenty. I should warn Dylan that he'll not get that back, but I'm more worried about what's inside the trunk.

My dad, with his back to me, says, "Great. Now open any drawer you like and place the twenty inside."

I quickly lift the trunk's lid, and there right on top is an envelope. With my name on it. Yes!

I grab the envelope, lift my shirt in the back, and put it in my waistband for safekeeping. I take a quick look at the other things in the trunk, but it's filled with boxes with hidden bottoms and more old costumes, so I quickly close the lid.

When I stand up, my dad is frowning and pretending to search for the twenty. "Maybe that's why I stashed the box away. It's broken."

I wag a thumb toward the stairs, and Dylan gives me a slight nod. He says to my dad, "You can get it back to me. Have a nice evening, Max."

I hand my key over because I have a spare at home. "Night, Dad. Come lock up behind us, please."

"Will do." My father has a smug grin on his face. "I'll be out of your hair before you open on Monday. I have a gig in Iowa."

I lay a quick kiss on his cheek. "Drive safe." Then I whisper, "There's about sixty bucks in the safe downstairs. I'm guessing you know the combination?"

"Max the Magnificent knows all. Love you, Sawyer."

"Love you too." I'm glad we sold those books online so I can go to the bank and get cash on Monday for the till. And grateful my father has kept his hand out of my safe up till now. He unabashedly asks for help but would never steal from me.

And hopefully, I'll solve my mom's mystery and won't even miss the sixty bucks my dad probably needs worse than I do.

My father follows me and Dylan downstairs and waves before he locks the door behind us.

Dylan says, "Technically, he just committed a crime. I could arrest him for stealing my twenty."

I give him a shoulder bump. "Maybe you should arrest yourself for being a sucker instead. How many years have you known my dad?"

Dylan laughs. "Too many. Still, I never heard the jellybean story."

"He only called me that because he hit his head. He stopped calling me that by the time I was ten."

"It's kind of cute. Did you find something?"

"Yep." I pull the envelope from my lower back and tear it open. Inside, there's a web address. My mom has written, *You might need this to stock your new restaurant. Sleight of hand and hidden panels are just illusion. I hope your new restaurant will be true magic.* I turn the paper over, and it's blank on the other side. "I don't get it. This looks like a wine website."

Dylan takes the note from me and examines it as we walk back to my house. "Maybe it's part of a series of clues?"

"Maybe. There's an old wine cellar in the basement at home. It's scary and filled with spiders, so I never go down there. Perhaps a brave, strong man like yourself would like to check it out when we get back?"

"Depends. Are we having dessert tonight?" He hands the note back.

"If you'll go down to the scary place, then I'm making dessert."

"Deal."

As soon as we arrive at my home, I free Cooper from the laundry room, and Dylan descends the stairs that lead to the icky basement wine cellar. I promised dessert, so I head to the kitchen to see what I have on hand. Tiramisu would have gone well with our dinner, but I don't have heavy cream or ladyfinger cookies. I only have the basics on hand: eggs, flour, sugar, and cocoa powder in the pantry, so brownies it is. I quickly whip up a batch from memory and then throw them into the oven. Cooper has grown bored watching me and sits in the corner chewing on his rawhide bone.

Just as I fire up my laptop in the nook, Dylan returns and sits across from me. He slides his phone my way. "I took pictures of the whole basement for you. It's mostly boxes filled with junk. And not a single bottle of wine."

After flipping through the pictures, I let out a sigh. Another dead end. "The Admiral was right. My mom didn't want to make finding whatever she hid easy."

Dylan points a finger toward my laptop. "The answer has to be on that website."

"Let's see what we've got." I study the landing page. It's a lot like the pages Brittany and I looked at earlier for rare books, but this one is all about wine. I flip the screen around so Dylan can see. "I don't get any of this. It makes no sense."

Dylan's brow creases as he studies the screen. "Maybe she was serious. Maybe she was simply pointing out a great place to buy wine for your restaurant. But then, why hide it in a trunk?"

As he's thinking out loud, I go check on the brownies. Not quite done, so I close the oven and then slide next to Dylan in the nook again. He's paging through screens of wine, but nothing stands out.

"Your mom didn't give you the website's home page address, so she must've given you a specific page for a reason." Dylan types in the original web address again, and it opens up with a page filled with expensive wine that I can't even pronounce.

He says, "I was just reading the other day how the assistant to a wealthy guy in New York embezzled hundreds of thousands of dollars by secretly selling his employer's rare wine. It was kept in a wine cellar in a house in upstate New York the employer only visited rarely. The thief sold seven bottles of wine to a collector for over $133,000."

"Really?" I lean closer to the screen and study it harder. "In the last restaurant where I worked, we had a few bottles kept under lock and key that were worth like $450 a bottle. I can't imagine anyone even paying that much."

"Most wouldn't." Dylan highlights the bottles of wine and cuts and pastes the web address in an email he sends to himself. "And our murderer probably wouldn't know that wine could be worth so much either. I've been thinking about how we could announce what your mother hid but keep the mayor out of it. What if we let it slip that your mom left you some valuable art?

That you'd found it right away and gave it to a broker to auction off?"

"My uncle will be all over me to claim the profits."

Dylan shakes his head. "I'll tell the mayor the truth. That while I can't discuss the details, we're using this false information to flush out the killer."

"So if whoever killed Chad was after what my mother hid, they'd think I found it first. And give up looking for it? Or, if it was the mystery customer or Crystal, it won't make any difference."

"Exactly. In the meantime, we'll keep looking. And we'll see how people react to the news. I think it might help keep you safe and keep your secret safe from your uncle too."

I hold up my hand for a high five. "I love it! Let's do it."

Dylan gently slaps my palm. "Do I smell brownies?"

Yikes! I forgot about them. "I hope you like them well done." I jump up and grab the pan from the oven. Got them just in time. "Want some vanilla ice cream on yours?"

"Absolutely." Dylan's phone rings, and he answers with, "Hi, Madge."

Dylan's brows scrunch as he listens. "Did you touch it?"

He listens for a few more minutes, then says. "I'll be right there." He disconnects the call and says, "Madge sat down to do some knitting and found an energy drink can at the bottom of her bag. Claims she didn't put it there."

"Chad's? She'd left her bag in the dining area. I overheard her say the yarn was such a mess, she couldn't use it to knit during the meeting like she usually does. I saw you search it."

"I did." He stands to leave. "If it is Chad's, someone put the can in there after I searched the bag. And it was conveniently in an area the camera doesn't cover. Maybe we'll get lucky and get a print. I'll call you tomorrow and let you know."

"Thanks." After he leaves, I slump into the nook. If someone put the can in the bag after Dylan searched it, that means the killer or his or her accomplice was still in the bookstore. So at least one of the book club members is guilty of murder.

A shiver runs up my spine at the thought of being locked in my store with a murderer next Thursday night.

CHAPTER 9

*I*t's Sunday afternoon, and Cooper and I have the house all to ourselves for a change. I'm exhausted because I couldn't fall back asleep last night after Renee texted to confirm she'd arrived home safely after her date. At 1:30 a.m. I guess I deserved that. I'm glad she checked in, though. One less thing for me to worry about.

I'd started the morning searching with gusto. Looking high, low, and in between produced zero. Nada. Bupkis.

I've just made myself a peanut butter and jelly sandwich with a handful of chips on the side, when the doorbell rings, sending Cooper into a barking frenzy.

It's Dylan at the front door with dark circles under his eyes that send a sympathetic pang to my heart. It looks like he's been up all night. "Hey. Have you had lunch?"

He shakes his head and follows me inside and back to the kitchen. After collapsing into the nook, he pulls Cooper into his lap and rubs the dog's ears. "Find anything?"

"Nope." I slide my sandwich in front of him and make myself another. "I've looked in the attic, torn apart my mom's study, searched the garage, all the closets, and looked under all the beds, but still nothing. I keep picking up knickknacks that I've seen around here forever and wondering if they're the valuable thing, but then I remembered the Admiral said the things are hidden."

Dylan nods as he tucks into his sandwich so fast, I hand him the second one I'd made for myself and start on another. Between bites, he says, "What if Wade, who's here a lot by himself, has found whatever your mom hid? Chad and he were friends. What if Chad told Wade your mom's secret?"

"Maybe. Although he doesn't seem the type to steal. He's such a laid-back surfer dude. I can't see him putting in that much effort. Into anything." However, Wade has been here a lot by himself. "Do you think I should tell him to take a few weeks off? Just until we figure this out?"

"I would. I'm still going with the theory that any one of the book club members could be the killer until I know for a fact they aren't."

"Okay." I set the bag of chips on the table and scoot into the nook across from Dylan. "I was just thinking about the can in Madge's bag. And how creepy is it that someone in book club either killed Chad or helped kill him?" A shudder runs up my spine again. "The thought of the next meeting freaks me out a little."

Dylan grabs a large handful of chips. "That's why I'm going to be hiding in the store watching the cameras at the next meeting. Any way to change it to Tuesday? Ed said he'd be at your store first thing tomorrow morning setting up the new cameras."

"I could ask Madge to ask the members. She's the one who sends all their emails. I haven't heard yet when Chad's service is going to be, though."

"There was a delay releasing his body to his family. They wanted to do more tissue and organ tests because of the DDT."

"I'll send an email to Madge this afternoon."

"Great. Any dessert left from last night?"

"Yep." I could use a brownie and some ice cream too, so I get busy. After the microwave beeps to alert that our brownies are warm, I add ice cream and join Dylan in the nook again.

After sampling a bite, I ask, "Was it Chad's can in Madge's bag for sure? And if so, any fingerprints?"

Dylan takes a bite, closes his eyes, and moans in sheer ecstasy. It's just a brownie, but I'm guessing Dylan is still starving even after eating two sandwiches. Bottomless pit, that he is.

His eyes pop open. "It was the right can but only Chad's and Madge's fingerprints showed up. She felt the can before she saw it. Didn't realize what she had until she lifted it."

My brownie takes a nose dive in my stomach. I was so hopeful for another print. The killer's fingerprint. Could it be Madge? "She is sort of obsessed with this crime. Maybe I was too quick to eliminate her from the suspect list. Yet, she couldn't have known Cooper was going to be there to steal her yarn and make such a huge distraction. And why tell you she found the can rather than just disposing of it if she is guilty?"

Dylan nods as he chews.

I continue with my theories, "The Admiral doesn't have any motive that I can see. Julie and Crystal working together is still on the top of my list. Any interesting things when you looked into bank accounts?"

"Lots. That, as you know, I can't discuss. What we do know as of this morning is that the can didn't have any trace of chemicals inside. Or it had been rinsed thoroughly, but then it'd be hard to maintain Chad's prints."

"So, it's fairly safe to say the can wasn't how Chad got poisoned." Relief fills me that it probably wasn't Madge after all, then. I like her.

"Yep." He pushes his empty dessert plate forward and sets Cooper on the kitchen floor. "Back to money issues. Why would you tell your dad to take the money from your safe when you obviously need it too?"

"You heard that, huh?" I take my time chewing as I compile an answer. Why does anyone help people who are lovable but major messes?

I finish off my brownie and push my plate away too. "Because I now know my mother was lazy when it came to returning books that didn't sell. Brittany said my mom could have returned many of those books for credit, but she held on to them. Probably hoping some would become valuable one day. And because the way the trust is set up, she could. So, I'm hopeful we'll have enough older books in the back and attic to hold me over until I can execute my trust loophole plan. And put my uncle in his place too."

Dylan's right brow hikes up. "Nice evasion."

I lift both hands in defense, but then let them fall. "I gave Max the money because he's my dad. I can always find a chef's job in San Francisco, if it comes down to that. My dad doesn't have any other options. He's an aging magician who can't keep up with the new crop of entertainers with all their glitz and glam. Old-school magic is all he knows."

"Fair enough." Dylan stands and puts our plates in the dishwasher, something he would've never done before he went into the military. He is a different person now, like my mom said in her letter.

He says, "So you've changed your mind? Thinking of sticking nearby if things don't work out? Not going back to the Midwest?"

"I came to that conclusion during my mostly sleepless night last night. I didn't realize how much I've missed my sister and the kids. Being nearby and seeing them whenever I want has been nice."

"Yeah. It's why I came home too. Lance, Megan, and the kids are all the family I have now."

That's not true. His dad is still alive, but I won't remind him of that now when he's too tired to argue with me.

Dylan's face lights up with one of his signature cute smiles, despite his obvious fatigue. "I'm glad you're going to stick close, Sawyer. Even if it ends up being San Francisco."

"Strangely, so am I. When I thought for a while yesterday that my uncle might win our battle, it became clear to me that I wanted to stay anyway."

"Good. Want me to help you search some more? I still feel like the kitchen might have something to do with this. Your mom always hired locals, and that she didn't this time is a red flag for me."

"You might not think that if you've ever watched Wade move at a snail's pace around here. My mom knew she had a deadline for once and needed to get things done."

Dylan's eyes scan the kitchen. "What if the kitchen is the clue? Hiding in plain sight. Maybe she wanted you to make a B&B out of this? It isn't your normal home kitchen. And there are a ton of bedrooms that aren't used upstairs. You'd be allowed to make improvements to the house, like add bathrooms, according to the trust, right?"

"Yeah, within reason. I have to get my uncle's permission for anything major." I stand next to Dylan and scan the kitchen with a new eye too. It is more a commercial kitchen than a residential one, based on my recommendations. I figured Mom would only get to remodel the kitchen once because of my tightfisted uncle, so why not go all out with the trust's money? Little did I know she was remodeling the kitchen for me. "You know what's interesting? I found all the paperwork for the remodel, except for a set of plans. Don't you think that's odd?"

He shrugs. "They got permits and had inspections, so the plans must exist. Maybe your mom had no use for a set of plans after the remodel was complete?"

"And yet she kept every scrap of paper otherwise? I don't know."

Dylan slowly nods. "I'll pull a copy of the plans tomorrow, and we'll have a look."

I open my mouth to warn against attracting my uncle's attention, but Dylan's quicker. He says, "I'll call in a few favors around the office. The mayor will never know."

"Thank you. I appreciate it, but please don't do anything to get yourself in trouble with my uncle. He can be a vindictive man."

"I'm aware. People keep voting for him because they're afraid not to. And no one wants the hassle of running against him."

"Maybe you should run against him. Everyone likes you."

"Maybe." He turns to leave. "Frank's term isn't up for a while, but I haven't ruled it out. I'm going to see him in the morning and start the process of telling everyone our fake news about your art find. It'll spread like wildfire as all gossip does around here."

"Perfect. I'll tell Brittany first thing too, in case anyone asks her. Now please go home before you pass out."

"Call me if you find something."

"I will. Get some sleep."

"Yes, ma'am." He sends me a snappy salute before he disappears through the swinging door and then calls out, "I'll lock up behind me."

After he's gone, Cooper and I head to the front door, and I turn the dead bolt too.

Dylan's right. We should assume anyone could be the killer until we know better. I should be more careful about Wade. I'll have to come up with a good excuse for him to hold up work here for a few weeks when I see him tomorrow.

Better safe than sorry. Though, with another delay I'll be lucky to have my woodwork fixed by Easter.

~

ON MONDAY MORNING, I'm clipping Cooper onto his leash to head to the store earlier than usual because I need to stop at the bank, when a knock sounds on my home's front door. Probably Wade. Ed, the locksmith/security guy in town, had left three sets of house keys on the kitchen counter Saturday morning, but Wade hadn't grabbed his set on his way out to his softball game. Thankfully. Now I won't have to ask for them back.

I open the door, and there's Wade with freshly cut blond hair. It's almost military short. He says, "Morning, Sawyer." He runs a hand through his new buzz cut. "Thanks for telling Gage it was okay to write me a check this morning."

Gage had emailed me at a little after eight and asked if I approved Wade's early paycheck. It was the least I could do before I tell him I won't need him around the house for a while. And luckily, Gage did my dirty work for me. He told Wade we'd found a pressing electrical problem that would make it hard for him to work with his power tools during a system upgrade.

I force a smile. "I see you've already put the money to good use. Nice haircut. I think Chad's mom will approve too."

"Hopefully." He shoves his hands into his front pockets. "This electrical box upgrade comes at a bad time, though. I cleared my schedule when your mom asked if I could do a long-term project for her. Gonna be hard with no paycheck for a few weeks, you know?"

I hadn't considered that Wade might have turned down other work for this project. And what did I care if the trust paid Wade while I figured everything out? "You make a good point. How about we call it a paid vacation? Take the next two weeks. Then if all goes well, you can start right where you left off?"

Wade grins, and he holds a fist out for a bump. "You're the best, Sawyer."

"Thanks." I return the bump. "Did you get Madge's email about book club being moved to tomorrow?"

He nods. "I'll be there. That actually works better. Chad's mom called me this morning and said they hope to have a small private service for him on Thursday. I'll just grab my tools from upstairs and load up my truck if that's okay? Shouldn't take more than a few minutes."

"Sure." I step aside and let Wade pass by. Just to be safe, Cooper and I wait for him to finish out on the front porch.

When Wade's done gathering his tools, he climbs into his truck and leaves with a wave. I lock up, and then Cooper and I hit the sidewalk and head toward the bank to get money for the till. A loud "gagooooga" horn sounds from behind and makes me smile.

I stop walking and wait as my dad rolls down the window of his red 1970s convertible two-door Cadillac. How that thing is still running is a miracle no one can explain. Of course, my dad says it's because of magic. "Hey, Dad."

"Morning, sweetheart." He points to Cooper. "Cute pooch. Megan called me last night with an idea. Can I give you a ride?"

"Okay." I withhold a sigh as I scoop Cooper up and then open the long heavy door. Megan is such a worry wart. I suspect this idea will have to do with me moving in with her. "I'm going to the bank."

"The bank it is." My dad puts the Magic Mobile—what my sister and I have always called it—into gear, and we head off. Dad pats Cooper as he says, "Megan is worried about you staying in Mom's house all alone. Especially with that …*thing* that happened in the back room. She told me you could be in danger. Something you neglected to mention to me the other night." He reaches under the seat and comes up with a long knife. "You should take this. For protection."

I laugh. "This is one of your collapsible knives. How will this protect me?"

"It's all about illusion. You don't like blood any more than I do. This way, you won't have to see any, and you can still chase a bad guy away."

My father and his logic. It's not worth arguing about, so I tuck the blade into my purse. "Thanks."

"Megan wishes you'd let the corrupt blowhard mayor win and then move into a house she said she wants to buy and fix up in the city."

"Since when is Megan buying another house? I just saw her on Friday, and she didn't mention that."

Dad shrugs. "She thinks between you and me, we could have it ready for resale in a year or so. We'd be doing her a big favor, and she'd be willing to cut us in on the profits along with giving us free room and board while we renovate. What do you think?"

I think my very kind sister is trying to be sure both my father and I have a roof over our heads. She and my dad don't think I can beat my uncle because my mom never could. That just makes me more determined to try.

"You should take her up on the deal, Dad. I have other plans." We arrive at the bank, so I open my car door and step out. "My restaurant will open very soon. You can take that to the…" I hold out my hand toward the bank.

My dad chuckles. "I told Megan you'd never go for it. I'll wait for you."

"That's okay." I shut the massive door. "I know you're in a hurry to get to Iowa."

Frown lines crease my dad's forehead. "I tried to get out of my gig after I talked to your sister, but I can't. So, I did something to ensure your safety."

Oh boy. This should be interesting. "What have you done?"

"You'll see. If you reject my offering, it'll break my heart. Love you, Sawyer. See you in a few weeks!" He waves as he takes off toward the highway.

"Love you too." He's like my sister. They never wait for an "I love you back" before they both move on with whatever they're so focused upon.

But break his heart? Way to lay the guilt on thick.

I glance down at my cute white-chinned dog who I swear is smiling while wagging his tail at me. "You think this is funny? You just better hope he hasn't asked some of his weird circus pals to stay with us. Like Fred the fire-eating sultan, or Samantha the snake charmer." The thought of reptiles in my house makes me shiver.

Cooper's tail droops, and he blinks at me.

"See? Not so funny when snakes are involved, right? Let's go get some cash."

After we're done in the bank, Cooper and I head toward the bookstore to beat Wilma before she shows up with the coffee I so desperately need this morning. I've already got a stress headache. And I need to talk to her about the Admiral's allegations about her and Chad.

Cooper and I arrive in the back alley just as my mother's best pal loads up her rolling cart with coffee and croissants. "Good morning, Wilma."

She glances up and smiles. "Morning, Sawyer. How are you?"

"Good." I unlock the door and deal with the beeping alarm. "I have a question for you, though. It's delicate."

Wilma laughs. "I've known you since you were born, Sawyer. You can ask me anything."

I follow behind as Wilma rolls her cart to the dining area. "It's not about me delicate. It's about you delicate."

Wilma glances over her shoulder, and her brows disappear under her bangs. "Well, now. This should be fun. What would you like to know?" She starts her routine of swapping out carafes and setting out the fresh, flaky, buttery croissants.

"It's something the Admiral said on Saturday." I unhook Cooper, and he runs straight for his favorite love seat by the front window to soak in the sun. "That there are rumors. About you and Chad? That maybe you've been …intimate?"

"Me and Chad?" Wilma's whole body shakes with laughter. "I wish! I haven't seen a hard body like that since my twenties."

My cheeks must be flaming red. This is so awkward. "The Admiral said he worried that you might have told Chad about the hidden things? Like pillow talk?"

"Sawyer." Wilma closes the gap between us and hugs me. "The Admiral is a nice man. A genius, really. He knows lots of things about a lot of things, but we both know he's one book short of a boxed set. You can't trust everything he says."

I lean back and stare into Wilma's eyes. She didn't deny it, and I need to see the truth for myself. Too much rides on her answer. "So, you never told Chad Mom's secret?"

"No. Nor have I ever been with Chad in a biblical sense. I've kept your mom's secret strictly between the Admiral and myself because I loved your mom. And I want what's best for you too, sweetheart."

The sincerity beaming back at me sends a fresh wave of relief through me. "Thank you, Wilma. I just had to be sure."

"I understand." She runs a hand up and down my arm before she releases me. "Do I need to talk to Dylan about this too?"

"Couldn't hurt. I'm sure the Admiral told Dylan the same thing, but now I don't know if I can trust that the Admiral kept the secret."

"You can trust him, honey, because he loved your mom too. They'd been quietly seeing each other since you left for college."

Say what?

My mouth opens, but nothing comes out but a squeak.

Wilma tucks her finger under my chin and closes my mouth for me. "You would've found out eventually. This town is way too small for that big a secret."

My *mind* is way too small for that big a secret. Everyone must know but me. "But… He's so. Old. My mom was still young. In her fifties. Like you! And the Admiral *is* sort of …nuts!"

Wilma chuckles as she packs up her things. "We can't choose who we fall in love with. And people in this town thought your mom was a little nuts too. Right?"

"Well, yeah. I guess that's true." I still can't wrap my head around this. "You said on Saturday that my mom was no saint when it came to men. I assumed she dated a lot but wasn't ever serious."

"That was true for a time." Wilma starts pushing her cart with the empties toward the back. "She dated a few different guys along with the Admiral. In the end, she finally realized he was the one for her. They were exclusive for the last five years or so." She stops pushing, and says, "I promise, the Admiral has your best interests at heart. See you tomorrow?"

"Yes." I'm rooted in place, nodding like a bobblehead doll as Wilma slips out the back door.

I need to call my sister. She'll never believe this.

I reach for my phone but stop when tapping on the front door interrupts me. It's Gage, dressed as sharp as always in his Italian suit and loafers. The man could model for *GQ*.

I cross the showroom and unlock the front door. "Good morning. Thanks for taking care of Wade for me earlier."

"Yep." He smiles, and that dimple on one side shows up as usual. "I need to talk to you about something. Your dad stopped by to see me this morning."

My stomach drops to my toes at the mention of my father. "What about?"

"Protection." Gage's grin fades, and he blinks nervously at me. "Your dad asked if I'd stay at the house with you. Until the murderer is caught."

So, this was my dad's clever plan.

I close my eyes and picture Samantha and her snakes. It could be worse. "I'm fine, Gage. Thanks for offering."

He clears his throat. "Your dad said he would've asked Dylan, but he thinks the guy is unreliable. His words, not mine. And if I didn't agree to do it, he'd tie me up in court for months asking for his common-law marriage rights to your mother's estate. I don't have time for that nonsense."

"You'd rather fall for his blackmail?"

He lifts his palms. "I'm the only lawyer in town. And I only have two hands, Sawyer. It could put a freeze on the trust and slow down the opening of your restaurant."

Can't have that. I'm on thin ice financially as it is.

My mind races for a way out of this mess while battling the guilt of breaking my dad's heart.

Before I find a solution, Gage says, "Knowing your past and all, I cleared it with Dylan. He said he thought it'd be a great idea if I slept on your couch until he finds the murderer."

"He did?" I'm offended by that. Dylan has been flirting with me nonstop since I've been back. "Then fine. I'll be home a little after six. And you don't have to sleep on the couch just because Dylan says so."

Gage's lips tilt into a nervous smile. "Where exactly will I be sleeping?"

"In the guest room. I'll even cook for you during your stay as a thank-you."

"Great!" He quickly dims his smile. "I mean, thanks. I haven't had a home-cooked meal in a long time. I'll pick up the groceries if you text me a list."

"Will do. See you later."

Gage waves and then turns and walks away as I lock up again. I lay my forehead against the cool glass and close my eyes.

Moving here was supposed to uncomplicate my life. Not make it worse.

Hopefully, Dylan will find the murderer soon, and my life will get back to normal. I have to tell myself that three more times before finding the strength to open my eyes again. When I do, Cooper is at my feet, furry face between his paws and eyebrows arched in a "May I please help you" kind of way. It melts my heart.

I drop to the floor, and Cooper crawls into my lap. A cuddle from my adorable, soft dog is just what I need right now.

After I've had my fill of doggy love, I slide my hands on either side of Cooper's teddy bear face and say, "We can do this, right, Coop? You and me?"

"I'm here to help too!" says a male voice behind me that makes me jump.

I whip my chin over my shoulder. Ed, who's round, bald, and in his sixties, is standing behind me with his hands full of equipment. "The back door was unlocked. Ready to get wired up? Or in this case, wireless?"

Wilma must've forgotten to lock it behind her.

Ed has no idea how badly I want to catch the murderer and get my life back. "Yep. Let's get started." And I'll have Ed make the back door lock automatically from now on too.

Ed grins. "We'll do your house after we finish here. Dylan said to keep your house cameras on the down low, though. You'll be able to sleep like a baby at night when I'm finished."

"Thanks." I think. Dylan never mentioned keeping my home cameras a secret, but I hope Ed is right. I haven't had a good night's sleep since last Thursday. Maybe having Gage around at night will be a good thing after all so I can relax a little. Old Victorian houses make strange creepy noises at night. And I'll avoid breaking my father's heart.

I'll just ignore that dimple and how darn handsome Gage is.

CHAPTER 10

*E*d is busy installing my new cameras at the bookstore, while I'm trying to help a customer who's looking for a book for her mystery-loving mother. I lead the woman to the bestseller table in the front when Brittany appears by my side.

My black-clad employee says, "I know just what your mom likes, Claudia. Follow me."

Huh. I'm impressed. Not only is Brittany only fifteen minutes late this morning, but she's been paying attention to what the customers want. Maybe I've underestimated her.

I go back to sipping coffee and looking up older books that have sold well online when Madge barrels through the front door. Does she ever walk normally?

Today her red sweater has little white blobs of something all over it, like she tossed whipped cream at it, but maybe they're supposed to be stars? "Hey, Madge."

"Hi, Sawyer." Madge joins me at the front counter and then glances over her shoulder to be sure no one can hear us. "Have you heard the latest?"

"About you finding the energy drink can?"

"No. That came up a big zero. It's about Crystal. She's missing. No one knows where she's been for two days now."

Brittany and the woman customer join us by the register to pay for the book Brittany recommended, so I tilt my head toward the dining area, and Madge follows along. I whisper, "Who reported her missing?"

"No one." Madge pours herself a cup of mocha roast and grabs a croissant. "One of the deputies has been trying to contact her for some follow-up questions. I heard him call the office where she works, and they said she called in sick today. Dylan went to her apartment this morning, but no one answered. And her car wasn't in the parking lot. Oh, and get this. I got a glimpse of the murder board in Dylan's office."

"He left it uncovered?" I find this hard to believe.

"Not exactly." Madge waggles her brows as she takes a long drink from her china cup. "I was dropping off some paperwork in Dylan's office while he was out looking for Crystal and couldn't resist just a little peek. The four key suspects are who we thought they were, but they all had something written by their names. I'll tell you if you promise not to tattle on me to Dylan."

Okay, this is so not fair. I really should tell Dylan that he can't trust Madge, but then, my best source of information will dry up. If curiosity killed the cat, I'm probably about to get run over by a bus. "I promise."

Madge pulls out a chair in the dining area and sits, so I settle in across from her. She says in a low voice, "The mystery customer has two names by it. They used facial recognition software, so I'm guessing that it came up with two choices. Or maybe someone thought they recognized the guy? I'm not sure, but I heard them say the video wasn't as sharp as they'd like."

"What are the names?" I pull out my phone and tap the notes app to open it.

Madge pulls out a sheet of paper from her pants pocket. "John Walker and Michael Jones."

"Have you googled them?" I ask as I type the names in my phone.

"Yes. Multiple names came up, so we need to do some more research. I can't do it at the station because someone might notice."

"I'll get on that."

"Sounds good." Madge swipes the crumbs from her fingers. "Crystal disappearing might be because she's involved, but she, Julie, and Wade each had a dollar sign by their names too."

"I assume that means they have money motives?"

Madge nods as she sips her coffee. "Chad has a dollar sign by his name too."

So maybe they owed Chad money? Or vice versa?

Wade had asked me for his check early, but that was to buy a new suit. Julie works in the grocery store and stated she was looking for a new job. They could both need money. "Where does Crystal work?"

Madge sets her cup down in the saucer. "She works in the IT department in town hall."

Brittany slips beside me along with Cooper and says, "Crystal is the big-chested redhead who was fighting with Chad, right?"

Madge nods. "There's an old saying about redheads having fiery tempers, and Crystal fits the mold to a tee. She and Julie are at the top of my list."

"Maybe." Brittany smacks her gum. "I saw Wade making some big moves on Julie at the softball game on Saturday night, though. Maybe he killed Chad so he could have Julie all to himself."

"Scorned women." Madge shakes her head as she rises from her chair. "They are not to be messed with. I have to get back. My break is up. Let me know if you find anything interesting about our mystery customer. And have fun spending the night with Gage tonight." Madge winks before she heads for the front door.

"Wait. What?" Brittany's face whips toward me. "I thought you and the sheriff were having pajama parties."

"Nope. My father asked Gage to sleep at my house until the murderer is caught. As friends. Like Dylan and I are."

Brittany's lips slowly form into one of her signature smirks. "You've got the two hottest old guys in town drooling over you. Get some game, girl!"

To fifteen-year-old Brittany, men in their thirties probably did seem ancient. It's making me feel old at thirty-two. "Speaking of old, did you know my mom and the Admiral were …?" I can't bring myself even to say it.

"Kicking boots? Yeah. Everyone knew. Never could figure that one out. But I heard something weird from Claudia just now. She said she heard that you found some rare paintings here that are worth a fortune. How do I not know this?" Brittany crosses her arms and looks hurt.

I hate to lie to her, but only Dylan and I can know the truth if our plan is going to work. Can't afford even an innocent slip of the tongue. "We don't know exactly how much people are willing to pay for the paintings yet. Now, how about you get back to work uploading books online so we can keep the doors open another day?"

"Fine." Brittany's forehead scrunches. "After you get the money, are you closing the bookstore?"

"I don't know." I can't give her false hope. My uncle could figure out what I'm up to and shut me down. "All I know for sure is that our best bet for staying open right now is selling our old inventory online. And there's a whole attic we can go through when we're done in the back."

Brittany looks up. "There's an attic up there too? Great."

"It is great. More opportunities for book finds we can sell on our new amazing web page that you designed. Thanks for all the hard work."

Brittany's lips begin to tilt, but then she quickly shuts her grin down. "It was nothing. I'll be in the back if you need me. Come on, Cooper."

"Thank you." I hope I don't have to shut down my mom's bookstore. Because if I don't find whatever my mom hid, it might come down to that sooner than later.

Brittany stops and sits across from me again. "What *is* the deal with you and Dylan?"

I start to brush Brittany's question aside, but she looks sincere. Like she actually cares and wants to know. "We dated for seven years starting in high school. And were even going to get married, but he decided not to show up for that."

Brittany cringes. "Ouch."

"Yeah." I drain my coffee cup. "He left for the military the next day. Then I decided I didn't want to be an engineer, so I went back to chef's school while I licked my wounds. The next time I saw Dylan was at my sister's wedding when she married his brother."

Brittany nods. "Your mom said your sister's wedding was the only time she'd ever seen you cry. Was it because you still loved him? And it hurt to see him again?"

"Yes." I'm surprised my mother would have mentioned that to Brittany, but it's true. I used to pride myself on being tough. Now I've come to realize it's not weak to cry when I hurt. It actually helps. "And because I knew I'd have to keep seeing him and reopening the wound. It felt overwhelming that day, but it's fine now."

"That *would* be tough." Brittany stands and pushes in her chair. "He wants you back. Can you ever forgive him for ditching you like that?"

"I've forgiven him. He was going through a tough time after his mom died. However, taking him back? I don't know about that. I'm not sure my heart could stand to be abandoned twice."

Brittany nods in understanding. "It's hard when the person you love most keeps letting you down. Or dies."

Is Brittany talking about my mom? "Who lets you down?"

"Doesn't matter if I don't let it." She shrugs. "Your mom always said I reminded her of you. I've been trying to figure out why that is. I'm no food nerd, and we don't like any of the same books or television shows. Maybe it's because I'm tough like you. I don't cry either." Brittany turns and walks away.

I call out, "A lack of tears doesn't mean what's hurt you is any less painful. Been there, done that, got the T-shirt. Anything I can help with?"

Brittany shakes her head and disappears into the back.

If she's anything like I was at that age, she won't tell me what's wrong until she trusts me. I won't give up asking, though, so maybe I'll annoy her enough to get to the bottom of her troubles soon.

Brushing away my sadness thoughts of Dylan brought back, I get busy on my phone googling the two names written beside the mystery customer on Dylan's board. I start with John Walker and find a ton of listings under that name. Luckily, I saw the customer and have since seen the security video. Although the picture wasn't as clear as it could be on the recording, between the two, I think I can eliminate men who don't match.

The results pop up, and I'm a little gobsmacked. Who knew there were so many men named John Walker just in California? Hundreds of thousands in the US. So, while the guy could live anywhere, I'm going to narrow the search to the San Francisco area first and hope I get lucky.

I'm scrolling through pictures and eliminating men when Dylan walks in. I quickly lay my phone facedown on the countertop. "Well, if it isn't the man who thinks it's a good idea for Gage to spend his nights with me. The news has traveled fast.

The gossips will have him and me engaged by tomorrow afternoon for sure."

"Hey. It was your father's idea." Dylan lifts his hands palms out and says, "Besides, would you have let me stay with you?"

"No." I cross my arms.

"I rest my case." He leans against the glass and whispers, "I don't like it either. Gage is attracted to you. Until you're ready to give me a second chance, though, this is the best option to keep you safe."

I whisper too, so Brittany won't hear in the back, "If you were me, would you give you a second chance?"

"Probably not." His jaw twitches. "I'm willing to wait as long as it takes for you to see I've changed. Because we both still have feelings for each other."

Oh, I have a lot of feelings for Dylan, not all of them so nice. Not all bad either. "Fine. Truce. What did you need?"

He leans even closer. So close, the warmth of his breath against my lips sends a tingle up my spine. "I came in to apologize for the way I handled Gage. I shouldn't have acted like it was my place to give permission for him to stay with you. Other than the fact that I *am* your concerned brother-in-law."

"If you'd said that up front, it would have gone a long way toward improving this conversation."

The twinkle in his eyes tells me I probably just fell right into whatever trap he'd laid for me. He says, "Yeah, but then I wouldn't have been able to see you tilt your chin and get all snotty. Because you were upset that I gave in so easily to Gage's request to stay with you."

He can be so annoyingly right sometimes. "Glad I could be your morning entertainment." I lay a hand on his chest and give an ineffective shove. Mostly because having him so close makes me remember those good feelings for him. "Please go away and catch a murderer so I can have my life back."

He leans away. "Are we good?"

Reluctantly, I say, "Yes."

"Good enough for me to chaperone your dinner tonight with Gage?"

"Nope." I shake my head. "Not that good."

He smiles. "Okay. What was Madge doing in here earlier?"

"She finds me entertaining too. And she likes croissants."

"Uh-huh." His eyes narrow. "If you find something of interest, I'll be in my office."

"I have no idea what you're talking about. Have a good day."

Dylan raises a brow but doesn't respond before he turns and heads out the door.

He's totally on to Madge. And me.

After helping two more customers and drinking two more cups of coffee, I finally dive back into my search for the mystery customer. I've been through all the John Walkers who have pictures online. A couple sort of looked like the mystery customer, but none rang a bell. Now I'm about ninety percent through the Michael Jones listings, so I start where I left off.

Swiping pictures of younger guys and some much older away, it sort of feels like those dating apps where you slide your judgmental finger left or right over potential dating profiles.

When a dark-haired man with forehead creases and a particular tilt of his head appears on my screen, I pause. This guy is close.

He lives in San Francisco and works for an advertising and marketing firm. He's won a few awards for his outstanding work, so he seems like an upstanding guy. I click further and find his company's web page. They specialize in representing "green" organizations from manufacturing to food preparation to produce.

I click on the "Our Team" button and find glossy headshots

of Michael Jones. Is it him? I'm not sure, so I move through the rest of the names that came up in the google search. When I run out of names, I go back to the marketing guy and study his face some more. Then I pull up the old camera footage and compare.

It could be him, but I don't know. At least not with enough certainty to tell Dylan and expose Madge's peeking-at-the-murder-board antics. Besides, not all the John Walkers and Michael Joneses had pictures online, so it could still be one of them. Maybe Madge and I should leave the facial recognition up to those smarter-than-us computer programs.

Ed appears before me with a triumphant grin. "Ready to test the new security system?"

"Absolutely." I shut down my phone search and give him my full attention.

After some brief instructions, I can declare the new system amazing. It displays multiple views at the same time or individual camera shots. As I switch back and forth, I find Brittany sitting on the floor in the back with Cooper in her lap, emptying a box of books and scanning them. The back room, attic, dining room, main sales floor, and even the front and rear of the store are completely covered by cameras now. And with the touch of a button, I can zoom back and see all the views at once.

"Ed, this is great. Thank you."

"Welcome." He glances over his shoulder as he packs up his gear. He says in a low voice, "I'll start at your house in the morning. Say, nine?"

I appreciate his efforts to keep the cameras at my home a secret, although I'm still not sure why that is. "That would be great. See you then."

"Betcha." Ed hitches up his tool belt. "Oh, I almost forgot. The sheriff said to clear it with you about allowing him access to the cameras from his phone too. Just until the person who killed Chad is caught?"

"Sure." I agree but then hesitate. "He meant here at the shop, right? Not at my house too?"

"I assume he meant both." Ed shrugs. "You can get back to me on that tomorrow. See ya." He disappears through the back door that now locks automatically behind him.

Okay, that's it. Dylan has something up his sleeve. He failed to mention the cameras at my house were secret, and now he wants access to them? I call out, "Hey, Brittany? Can you watch the store for a few? I need to run an errand."

"Sure." Brittany appears with a sandwich in her hand and Cooper at her heels. "Can I request a sandwich upgrade? I'm getting tired of turkey and PB&Js."

"Sell more books online, and we'll see. Be back in a few."

Brittany nods as she chews, which I'll take as a yes to selling more books and watching the store.

It's nice and warm outside as I cross the park to town hall. Tourists stroll with babies in carriers on their chests and their hands filled with packages. It restores my faith that some people still like to shop in stores rather than online. However, not so much for books anymore, it seems.

Maybe I'll knock a few holes in the wall between my bookstore and new restaurant so people can browse books while they wait to be seated? I could make the restaurant and menu book themed too. Might be cute. I'll have to think some more about that. If and when I actually open my restaurant.

A waft of ocean breeze brings salty air along with the aroma of spicy lamb from the gyro truck. The growl of my stomach, also tired of my budget lunches, leads me to the cart, and I order two. I point to the churro sticks, and the kid operating the register adds two of those too. Dessert for Dylan depends on how much he spills.

Armed with a bag of goodness, I climb the steps of town hall, yank the heavy glass door open, and almost run into a screeching little boy. Julie is in hot pursuit.

"Grab him, Sawyer. Please!"

Grab a child?

Instead, I beat the grinning toddler to the door and shut it. Then I block his way. "Sorry, little man."

The dark-haired kid, laughing and trying to get me to move by pawing on my slacks, is playing a game Julie has had enough of.

Julie growls, "Stop it, Cody! Now!"

Cody, who looks between two and three, looks up and blinks as if suddenly realizing he's the only one playing catch me if you can. And he's probably going to be in trouble for it.

Julie swoops the kid up, slams him on her hip, and then turns her pretty face toward mine. "Sorry, Sawyer. He's been like this all day."

I shrug. "No harm done. Is Cody your son?"

She nods. "It's my day off. Cody had to come along with me to talk to Dylan. Again. It's getting old. I don't know how many more times I can tell the same story over and over. They should interrogate Crystal. She's the one who ran away, probably because she's guilty!"

This is interesting. "You and Crystal aren't pals?"

"Hardly." Julie grunts. "She tried to trick Chad into taking her back by telling him she was pregnant with his kid. Chad swore it couldn't be his. And I believed him. You remember how Crystal was in school, right?"

"I do." I don't know what else to say, so I add, "I'm sorry about Chad, Julie. This must be so hard on you."

"It has been." Tears bubble up in the corners of Julie's eyes as she waves a hand. "I'm sorry. I shouldn't have said that. I don't like Crystal, but that doesn't make her a murderer. I haven't been sleeping, and I'm overtired. I'll see you tomorrow night at book club."

"Yeah. See you. Bye, Cody." So she's planning to come? Less

than a week after Chad's death? Everyone grieves in their own way, I guess.

The little boy smiles and waves as Julie carries him down the front steps.

Julie *seems* honestly upset about Chad. Maybe Brittany is right and Julie comes to book club to get a break from her kid. Being a single mom can't be easy. And Julie was also an aspiring actress who moved to Hollywood right after high school and married the first director she met.

More to think about as I head to Dylan's office and open the door. I'm hit with a buzz of activity. Ringing phones, fingers flying across keyboards, and deputies rushing to do whatever task is at hand.

Madge lifts her chin as she speaks into a headphone, so I make my way to her desk. When she's done with her call, she whispers, "Any luck with the Johns and Michaels?"

I lean closer and say, "I think one of the Michael Joneses could be the guy, but not for certain." I lower my voice even more. "Can you do me a favor? I need to see something Joe Kingsley and my uncle have handwritten. For my golf ball problem I'm sure you know about by now. Could you get that for me?"

"Easily. I know the woman who types the town council's notes." Madge's eyes scan the office before she says, "Something big is up around here. I'm not sure what. It might take me a few minutes before I can slip out to get that for you."

A buzz runs through my veins. "Maybe they caught the killer?"

"Maybe. I assume you're also here to see Dylan, since you have lunch in your hands. You can wait in his office. He'll be right back." Her phone rings again, so she points to the biggest office in the corner.

"Thanks." I've never seen Dylan's office before and head

toward it filled with curiosity. Will it be neat and clean, or a mess like my mother's study?

When I walk through the door, I'm met with efficiency. Not neat or clean, but tidy stacks of brown files on a desk that holds no personal pictures. Just a lone soda in a to-go cup and a legal pad alongside the piles.

He has a credenza behind his desk with some awards on top, and a bookshelf full of what looks like procedural manuals. Against the opposite wall is an easel with a heavy cloth draped over it. Probably the infamous murder board Madge peeked at.

After I sit in one of the chairs in front of his desk, I spot two sets of rolled-up plans on the floor leaning against the credenza. Probably my kitchen remodel, so I stand and retrieve a set. Then I see the plans have Dylan's last name on them and an address. Maybe a set of house plans?

When I turn around to spread the plans out, I nearly bump into a khaki-clad chest. "Oh, hi, Dylan. I brought you lunch."

"And made yourself at home." He plucks the plans from my hands. "These aren't yours. Those are." He puts the plans back and then picks up the other set. Then he snaps, "Is this what you wanted? I'm in the middle of something important."

"No, actually." I hurry and sit in a guest chair again. I haven't seen Dylan this short-tempered in a long time. "Are you building a house?"

"I don't have time to chat, Sawyer." Dylan flops his big body in his chair and rubs a hand down his face. "What can I do for you?"

"You need to eat. You're hangry." I take out the gyros and set one in front of him. "And while we eat, you can tell me what the big plan is at my house you're not letting me in on."

Dylan's sandwich stops halfway to his mouth. "Plan?"

"Ed told me about your request to monitor my cameras. And the secret ones at my house too?" I take a big bite of my spicy delight and wait for his answer. By the look on his face, grumpy Dylan just got busted.

"Oh. That." He sighs before he sets his gyro down. "I was hoping I wouldn't need to go there. It was a back-pocket kind of thing. In case all else failed."

"Mmmm?" I nod while still chewing and listening. This ought to be good.

"I want to establish, with the art rumor, that the hidden items at the store have been found. And then, as soon as Ed gets the cameras installed inside and outside your house, I plan to ask—politely—if I can set up a trap to catch the killer. Without you in it, of course."

I swallow and then reach out and take a sip of the soda sitting on his desk. "Cameras *inside* my house too? With you able to access them from your phone? No wonder you had me run Wade off. And where was I going to be during all this?"

Dylan winces. "Megan and Lance's? Or I was going to offer to swap houses with you if it came to it. This is totally a plan C, or it was until about ten minutes ago." He stuffs a big bite of gyro into his mouth.

"What happened ten minutes ago?"

He holds up a finger while he swallows. "I was asked to gather all our evidence and turn the case over to the San Francisco office. You can still say no to the house cameras." He sets his sandwich down and sips his drink.

I'm running through the pros and cons of his plan as I finish off my sandwich, but then something else pops into my head. "This is why you so eagerly agreed to my dad's plan to have Gage sleep on my couch, isn't it? You were going to have me shipped off anyway, therefore not needing Gage's protection for more than a night or two?"

He shrugs. "It's still a night or two too long."

Men.

I lift my chin. "I don't understand how a guy who wants to

win my trust again thinks it's a good plan to sneak around behind my back."

"Because you've been sneaking around behind mine meddling with Madge even after I asked you to stop." He sets his palms on his desk, leans forward, and gets in my face. "I'm worried you're going to get yourself killed. And I'm willing to risk your *wrath* to keep you safe!" He huffs out a breath before he leans back and picks up the rest of his sandwich.

Wrath is a little harsh. I brought him a sandwich along with my wrath.

I slowly fold my empty gyro wrapper while Dylan inhales the rest of his sandwich. He's not wrong. I have been meddling even though he asked me to stop. "So, if I agree to this plan, are we going to set the bait at book club tomorrow night?"

He nods as he crumples up his wrapper and throws it in the trash. "Assuming Ed gets all the cameras working at your house." Then he leans back in his chair with his arms crossed, apparently still upset with me.

"Fine. Let's do it. And for the sake of full disclosure, would you like to know which Michael Jones I think was the customer in my store? It was in the way he holds himself as much as his face. I could still be wrong."

Dylan's eyes cut to his murder board and then back to mine before he digs the heels of his hands into his face in sheer frustration. Finally, he mumbles, "Actually, I wouldn't. At least until I've handed everything over. Then we'll discuss it."

"Because you're not supposed to be investigating anymore? However, if you're simply protecting your sister-in-law because you're worried that she's in danger and happen to catch a killer, then it's okay. Right?"

"Yeah." He lifts his hands away from his face. "Anything else you've stumbled across oh so innocently?"

I shake my head. "That's as far as I've gotten. I'm sorry they took your case away. That must be as frustrating as my innocent meddling," I say with just a touch of sarcasm.

He reluctantly smiles. "Not quite, but close. Thank you for lunch. I *was* hangry. I didn't mean to snap at you."

I can't say I didn't mean to meddle, because I did. I'm the curious sort.

"No problem. I'll do whatever needs to be done to catch Chad's killer." I stand and grab the kitchen plans and the churros. If he's going to be snippy, I'll bring dessert back for Brittany instead. "So, are we good?"

"Yeah." He taps his tented fingers against his lips like he's thinking. "In the spirit of full disclosure, I'm worried we're getting close, and the killer knows it. That's why I made sure Madge and therefore everyone else knows Gage is going to be on your couch tonight. I'm sorry if that causes you any embarrassment."

"Thank you, but you don't have to worry." I set my things down and reach into my purse. Then I whip out my dad's knife. "Because I have this!"

Dylan frowns. "If you use that, things will be bloody, and you'll be faint. Hand it over." He waggles his fingers.

"If you insist." I jab the retractable blade into Dylan's palm.

His eyes grow big before he lets out a laugh. "Nice trick. Your dad would be proud." He tosses the knife back to me. "Go away, please. I have files to hand over."

"'Kay." I gather my things again but stop in the doorway. "Are you being overly cautious because of that 'we still have feelings for each other' thing, or do you honestly think I'm in danger?"

He slowly shakes his head. "I just know I'd never forgive myself if anything happened to you. And as much as I hate it, part of me is glad Gage is sleeping on your couch. Mostly because I know he has a concealed carry license. He's armed with some real firepower to keep you safe."

The walls around my heart crumble a bit at that. "Thank you

for worrying about me, Dylan." I set the bag with the churros on his desk. "For your kindness, I'll share my dessert to show my gratitude."

Dylan peeks inside the bag and grins. "You don't even like these."

I shrug. "But you do."

I turn to leave, and Dylan mumbles, "You're killing me, Sawyer."

"And you're saving me from being killed, so we're even. See ya."

He calls out as I leave, "That makes no sense."

I can't help my grin, knowing he's sitting there grumpily chomping on churros and trying to figure out what I meant. That the churros are a simple thanks for watching out for me. Not a romantic gesture.

I wave to Madge and then reach for the door. When it opens before I reach the handle, I nearly run into Crystal.

She's got a black eye and is being escorted inside by one of the deputies.

$\mathcal{I}$'m rooted in my spot, standing just inside the door to the police station as Crystal is escorted past me. Her bruised face is varying shades of green and yellow, suggesting the injury isn't a fresh one. I smile in greeting, but Crystal quickly looks away to avoid eye contact.

Under her breath, she grumbles, "Can we hurry and get this over with, please? I have things to take care of."

Dylan meets them at his office door, and then shuts it behind them.

Madge pops up from her desk, grabs my arm, and pulls me out into the hallway. "While you were in with Dylan, I heard they tracked Crystal's credit card. She's been in San Diego. I wonder if she went back to Mexico for more DDT? Maybe she plans to off someone else!"

I almost slip and tell Madge, Chad didn't die because of the DDT, but I catch myself. "I think Crystal's dad lives in San Diego. She used to come back really tan after spending summers with him when we were kids."

"Oh." Madge's expression falls so fast, it's comical. "Did you see her face? She told one of the deputies she fell. A crock of phooey if you ask me. She probably got into a fight with her coconspirator about something. Like who to kill next!"

I'm trying to be like Dylan and keep an open mind until we find the killer. "Well, no matter what happened, she just got totally busted for playing hooky from work in a pretty dramatic way."

"True." Madge chuckles. "Speaking of which, I'd better get back to work. I'll let you know if they arrest Crystal. And I'll get those handwriting samples." Madge waves and then turns to leave.

"Thanks." I start for the main front door and see that my uncle is power walking toward me down the shiny marbled hallway.

He looks mad. As usual. And he's seen me, so I have no choice but to stop and talk to him. "Hi, Uncle Frank."

"Sawyer." He tilts his head toward the double doors. "Let's talk outside."

My hands start to sweat. Is my restaurant secret out?

When we hit the grass across the street, my uncle stops. "I talked to Dylan. About the art story." He crosses his big arms. "While I know it's a story you two have made up, I need to make something clear. If you *should* find something of great value among your mother's things, it will belong to the trust."

I cross my arms too. "Do you have a reason to think I would find anything of great value?"

"Maybe." He clears his throat. "There was something my father spoke about my mother owning that was never found after she died. So it's possible."

"What kind of thing?"

"A signed first edition Mark Twain book with author's notes inside. Before he became famous." My uncle waves a hand. "Your mother might have found it and sold it years ago, but apparently, your great-great-grandmother and he had some sort of romantic relationship. She was a flaky poet or some such."

"And she kept it because she was in love with him?"

My uncle nods. "My father said the book had been handed down to the youngest woman in the family rather than the oldest male. His grandmother thought it was unfair that the elder male heir always got everything back then. My father saw the book once, but never again after my mom died."

Huh. That's pretty amazing. Why hadn't my mom mentioned that? I need to call my sister and see if she knows anything about the book. Or the affair. "Well, I haven't seen it either. And I really need to get back to the store."

"Yes, because it's probably chock-full of customers," he says with sugary sarcasm.

"No, because it seems I have a Mark Twain book to find!" I don't wait for a reply and head across the park to my store. I'm checking for traffic before I cross the street, when a thought hits me.

Mark Twain's most famous character was Tom Sawyer. Could that be where I got my name from? Because I'm the youngest too, as was my mother, and hers too. Is the book what my mom hid for me? It'd have to be worth thousands, especially if it's an early limited edition. I've learned a lot about rare books in the last few days, and how authors often used to do special editions with limited print runs back in the day. Often with mistakes in them. Those are the ones collectors pay for.

It's starting to feel like the Admiral suggesting we sell the older inventory was all part of my mom's plan. Along with giving me Cooper, leaving me the bookstore, and planting men in my life everywhere I turn.

Could there be a Mark Twain book among all those books in the dusty attic? Or did my mom sell the book and name me Sawyer instead? If she kept it, would she keep it at the store? Or at home?

Enthusiasm for the hunt makes me pick up the pace as I jog to my store and open the front door. Brittany is taking pictures of books to upload to our online store. I grab a cup of coffee and then join my employee. While I give Cooper a belly rub, I say, "When you get a chance, can you look up how much a first edition Mark Twain book would be worth? Signed. With author notes. Throw in a spelling error while you're at it." If the book was given as a gift, it might have had flaws. Twain wouldn't want a book with errors circulating.

Brittany nods, and her fingers fly across the keyboard. "Looks like anywhere from $500 all the way to $65,000 depending on the condition." She looks up and blinks. "Do we have one of those I don't know about?"

"Not sure. My mom might have had one. If you come across it, though, don't say a word to anyone, please."

The corner of Brittany's mouth curves up. "Especially not Mayor Mean, right?"

"Yes. Him the most." I grab my laptop from under the counter and look up Mark Twain. There's a lot of information about his life. About his time on ships sailing the Mississippi River, when he worked at a newspaper, until he sold his now-famous books. And sure enough, he'd lived in San Francisco in 1864 and had artistic pals, like my poet great-great-grand-mother, apparently.

I'm still deep into the Mark Twain rabbit hole when Madge walks in. I close the lid of my laptop to give her my full atten-tion. Hopefully, she's here with some good news and the hand-writing samples for my golf ball problem. "Hey there."

"Hey back." She sits next to me on the couch I'd moved to when I got tired of standing at the counter. "Here are the samples you wanted."

"Thanks." I take out my phone, and we both examine the writing on the ball.

I shake my head. "Neither of these are even close."

"Yeah. Maybe the person disguised their handwriting?"

"Could be." I'm disappointed but won't quit until I've seen Wade's, Judy's, and Crystal's handwriting too.

"Sorry about that, Sawyer." Madge pats my leg. "I have other news, though. They didn't arrest Crystal. And some arrogant guys wearing suits came and took over boxes of evidence. We found them an empty office down the hall. I don't know why they didn't trust Dylan to take care of this. Compared to the last sheriff, he's been amazing at his job. Now he's basically taking orders from the new guys until this murder is solved."

Not entirely. Dylan has a trick or two up his sleeve that I can't share with Madge. "Did anyone say why they wanted to follow up with Crystal so badly?"

Madge stands to leave. "Nope. Crystal deciding to go to San Diego in the middle of a murder investigation doesn't sit right with me, though. And where did that black eye really come from?"

"I agree." I stand and walk her to the door. "Dylan knows we've been working behind his back. I didn't tell him about you seeing the murder board. I let him think I looked when I was in his office. I don't want you to lose your job."

Madge grabs the door handle and pulls. "He had a talk with me, and I confessed about the murder board. He said all is forgiven if I keep him up-to-date on what the men in suits are doing." She grins. "My nosy nature has helped solve a crime or two around here over the years, so Dylan gives me freer rein than he should. Thank you for caring about my job, though. You're a real peach, Sawyer."

"So are you, Madge. See you tomorrow." I wave her off and then head to the dining area for more coffee.

A few moments later, in walks Dylan. "Do you have a second to talk about which Michael Jones you think was in your store?"

"Sure. Let me show you." We sit on the couch where I'd left my laptop. "I was researching Mark Twain when Madge dropped by." I quickly close out the screen and find the Michael Jones page I'd bookmarked earlier.

Dylan stretches out his long legs. "Why Mark Twain?"

After I tell Dylan about the book, he nods. "That sounds like it could be one of the things we're looking for. Have you tackled all the books upstairs yet?"

"Nope. We're still working our way through the ones in the back room for now." I hand over my laptop. "This is the Michael I think was here. The other name was close, but something didn't sit right with him."

Dylan studies the screen. "That's the Michael I chose as the closest match too. His office says he's on vacation. A relative had a medical emergency. They expect him back next Monday. If he checks in, we might hear from him. The suits are following up now. The other name we found had a singing gig in the city on the night of the murder, so he's all alibied up."

"Was this Michael Jones gone last week too? During the murder?"

"Yep." Dylan blows out a long breath. "Have you thought any more about our plan? Would you be willing to go stay with Lance and Megan?"

I stand again and start the process of closing up. I hadn't realized how long I'd been researching Mark Twain. "I don't want to have to drive that far every day to come to work."

"Then would you reconsider and swap houses with me?"

The cameras on the screen at the front desk show Brittany is still hard at work in the back. I don't want her to hear our discussion. "Maybe it'd be better if Cooper and I stayed put. If someone thinks there's something hidden in my house, they'll be watching it, won't they? Why not break in while I'm here all day rather than when we're home?"

"Because if they're desperate enough and think you've found what your mom has hidden, they might want to make you talk. I wonder how many people know about the book your uncle mentioned? He seemed mad enough about it to stew out loud."

"I have no idea, but you're probably right. He'd want his share of the money if Mom sold the book. Don't you think between the cameras and Gage in my guest room, I'd be safe? It's not like you don't live only a few blocks from me."

"Gage was your father's idea. Now that we know about this Twain book, the best solution would be to let me sleep on your couch. It's my job to protect people around here, not Gage's."

I run all the possibilities through my mind. As much as I don't want Dylan on my couch, I'm not a fan of getting hurt either. "What if Cooper and I stayed here? Upstairs, in my dad's little apartment? We're going to tell everyone tomorrow at book club that we found the art, right? So they'd know nothing was still hidden here."

"Not if they thought the Twain book was still hidden. What better place than a bookstore to hide it? Maybe that's why your mom kept so many books. To make the Twain hard to find?"

Could be. "Okay. Fine. You can sleep on the couch. My dad will just have to get over it. I still owe Gage dinner tonight, though. You can come over after Gage goes home."

Dylan grins. "Or you could invite me for dinner too."

"Gage already bought the groceries. There won't be enough for you and your bottomless-pit stomach. Besides, I draw the line at providing more than one meal in a day. Could give you the wrong impression about us."

He sighs as he stands up. "You've made it perfectly clear where we stand. Can I walk you home? As a concerned brother-in-law?"

"Okay." Brittany and Cooper join us precisely at closing time, so I grab my kitchen plans, set the alarm, and then lock up behind us.

Brittany says good night to us and heads the opposite way.

Dylan is quiet as he walks, and I jog behind Cooper up the hill to my house. "Care to share what has you so deep in thought?"

"Between the mayor and his twice-daily updates along with the new red tape the suits have to adhere to, it's giving me a headache. And it looks bad to my staff that I've been taken off the case." He holds a palm out to take Cooper's leash, so I hand it over. As usual, my dog falls right in line.

"I think out of everyone in town, your staff understands the most that we don't have the same resources that they have in San Francisco. This is a complicated murder case including a banned substance that has been transported over state lines. No one will think less of you."

Dylan nods but remains silent.

I want to cheer him up, and he loves trivia, so I say, "I learned something interesting today about why Samuel Clemens picked Mark Twain for his pen name."

Dylan glances my way. "Because Mark Twain is what they used to call out on the boats on the Mississippi to indicate they had twelve feet of water?"

"Right." He never was fun to play trivia with. He's tough to beat. And I hate to lose. "I was being easy on you, though, seeing how you've had a bad day. How about this—who's sold more books, Agatha Christie or J. K. Rowling?"

Dylan thinks for a moment before he says, "My first thought was J. K. because those Harry Potter books sold like wildfire, but then Agatha Christie's books have been around a lot longer. Agatha Christie."

Really? I thought I'd get him on that one for sure. I just read that statistic in my trade pubs. Yesterday. "You're right. It's estimated that Christie has sold four billion to Rowling's five hundred million. How about this one? Who is the most annoying person to play trivia with?"

Dylan laughs "You. Because you're a sore loser."

"Nope. You. Because you're so smug when you're right."

Dylan is still grinning as we walk up my front steps and I unlock the door. He says, "There's no one else I love more to beat at trivia than you. May I look around before I leave you to your date?"

I'm ignoring the date part. "Yes, please. However, technically, you didn't beat me because I knew the answers to all the questions too." I send him my own version of a smug smile and then drop the plans in the hallway before I unhook Cooper's leash. My prancing dog knows it's his dinnertime, so we head down the hall to the kitchen to feed him.

I open the pantry and grab his bag of food from the floor. When I stand up, my gut tells me something is wrong, so I study the pantry closer. My spices are mixed up. Call me a little OCD, but I always alphabetize them. And three are out of order. I quickly fix them and chalk it up to my recent distractions before I see some of my cans, which I also alphabetize, are wrong too. Maybe having Dylan on my couch will be a good thing after all. I haven't slept much since the murder.

Shaking my head, I close the pantry and pour out Cooper's food. While he digs in with the same enthusiasm as Dylan eats, I grab Coop's other bowl and fill it with water at the kitchen sink. As I wait for the bowl to fill, I notice the plant that sits in the windowsill is backward. I always place the decorative daisy on the clay vase toward me because daisies remind me of my mom.

A big hand lands on my shoulder, and I jump a foot into the air as I lunge for the knife block. I'm not going down without a fight.

"Hey. What's wrong?" Dylan's voice in my ear calms my racing heart.

"Oh. It's just you." I let go of the knife I was about to pull from the wood and turn around. "Some of my things are out of place. I don't know if it's because I'm overtired and I've been careless, or if someone has been in here." I quickly show him the cans and spices I rearranged.

Dylan's forehead scrunches with concern. "Nothing's ever out of place in one of your kitchens." He heads for the back door and examines it. Then he jogs to the front and does the same. After he's tested all the downstairs windows, he says, "No signs of forced entry. Does anyone else have a key?"

"No. Ed left me three sets just as I asked him to. I have all three."

Dylan rubs a set of knuckles against his five-o'clock shadow as he considers. "Let's look around some more. Don't touch anything that's out of order this time, please."

Dylan reaches into the back pocket of his uniform pants and produces a pair of latex gloves. "Let's start with your precious pots and pans always neatly nestled so properly."

"Hey. Chaos in the kitchen spills over into the food prepared there. Neatness brings order and peace with a side of Zen."

"Okay, Gandhi. Whatever you say." Dylan opens the cabinet next to the stove. "My food tastes just fine no matter how my pans are stacked."

"Says the guy who can burn water." All my pots and pans are stacked nice and neat. Just as I left them. "These all look perfect."

Dylan shakes his head, and then we repeat this process with all the cabinets until we've checked the whole kitchen. Everything else looks fine.

Drawing in a deep breath, I say, "Maybe it's just sleeplessness and stress. Thanks for looking around for me, or I'd be freaking out right now."

Dylan is chewing his lower lip and nodding at the same time. "I'll be back with some gear about eight."

"What kind of gear?" I'm picturing all sorts of tactical gear like he used in the army.

"Cameras mostly. And my pj's, of course." He forces a smile. "Does this gig come with breakfast?"

A knock sounds on the front door. "We'll see. Gage is here.

Be nice and I might be persuaded to make you an omelet in the morning." I poke Dylan's big shoulders to get him moving down the hallway.

"Deal." He pulls up short in front of the mirror in the entrance, gently moves me in front of him, and lays his chin on my shoulder. Into our reflection, he says, "I have a trivia question for you before I go. How big does the human eye get when it looks at something pleasing?" Dylan smiles his biggest smile. The one that makes his eyes twinkle with blue mischief.

Luckily, I know this answer. "The pupil dilates as much as forty-five percent."

He squints. "Yours appear to be at thirty-five percent. Looks like I still have a chance."

"Very funny." I lightly jab my elbow into his rock-hard gut. "Go away, please."

Dylan is still chuckling at his clever self as he opens the door.

Gage, his arms filled with groceries, blinks for a second and then says, "Dylan. Nice to see you. Didn't realize you were joining us for dinner."

"I'm not. But we've had a change in plans, so you're off-duty after dinner. I'll be back later. Enjoy your meal." He turns back to me and winks before he saunters down the steps, but then stops. "By the way, I've checked the handwriting on the golf ball too. It doesn't match with any of the suspects. So stop already."

"You could've told me that earlier when I was in your office."

He grins. "I forgot. Bringing me lunch and being nice to me threw me off my game. And reminded me how much I miss you." He jogs down the rest of the steps and heads for his house.

I sigh inwardly. It could be a long few days living under the same roof as persistent Dylan.

Gage forces a smile, showing off that cute dimple. "Tenacious, isn't he? I hope you don't mind that I took the liberty to pair some wine with our meal tonight? And brought a lovely vintage of rawhide for Cooper."

I laugh. "Not at all. Thank you. Come in." Wow. He even remembered Cooper. I need to dim the smile that's stretching across my face, though. Gotta keep those priorities straight if I'm going to get my restaurant up and running before my uncle finds out. Men have no part of my master plan. This year. Maybe next year, I'll give dating a go again.

I step aside to let Gage in. He bends down and pets Cooper and then gives him a rawhide that my dog races away with as though I'm going to take it away. Actually, I'm thrilled, because it'll probably keep his nosy little furry body busy the whole time I cook and out from under my feet. As per usual. "Thanks again, Gage."

"Couldn't pick up groceries and forget Coop. Right?" His sumptuous cologne tickles my nose and puts my hormones on notice. Or maybe it's the dimple and that eye-catching face of his.

"Cooper wouldn't let you forget it if you forgot him. He thinks everyone comes to see him, not me. Come on back to the kitchen." I need to ignore my traitorous body. He's just an attractive guy here to have dinner. That's all.

I glance at my eyes in the mirror as we pass.

My pupils look the same size as when I looked at Dylan.

Not good. Not good at all!

CHAPTER 12

While my dog happily chews on his rawhide in the corner of the kitchen, I unpack the groceries Gage brought for us. I didn't want to ask him to pick up expensive steaks or lobster when he's paying, but he's a foodie, so I chose a menu that's delicious without breaking the bank. "Wow. This all looks fabulous, Gage. Thank you."

"I'm excited to see what we end up with." He pops two bottles of white into the wine fridge and then takes a seat at the large island to watch.

I ask, "Want an Aperol Spritz while the wine cools?"

"What's in it?"

"It's slightly bitter with a touch of orange and a light tang of herbs. The prosecco gives it sparkle. And it's pretty and red."

"Sold."

I make mine half as strong as the recipe in my head calls for as I pour the liquor over ice, stir, and add a few splashes of soda water before I top them off with orange slices. "Cheers. Thanks for coming."

Gage taps his glass against mine and then takes a drink. His eyebrows spike before he sets his glass down. "This is my new favorite drink."

"Mine too." I get busy cleaning the mussels and then drop them in a bowl of water to soak for twenty minutes before I steam them.

Gage takes another sip. "What are all the things I brought going to end up being tonight?"

"To start, we have a kale salad with apples and currants topped with a warm pancetta vinaigrette. Then for our main, we have steamed mussels in white wine broth, with a hunk of that crusty baguette on the side to soak up the luscious broth. For dessert, I got up this morning and made a Nutella semifreddo that we'll top with crushed hazelnuts and whipped cream."

Gage's brows form a V. "What's a semifreddo again?"

"Basically, a frozen mousse made with sugar, eggs, and whipped cream. I cheat by adding more Nutella than the recipe calls for, because you can never go wrong with a little extra Nutella, right?"

Gage lifts his glass. "Cheers to that." After a long drink, he asks, "Does this mysterious change in plans Dylan referred to earlier have to do with the rumor I heard today about you finding some rare, expensive art at your store?"

I raise my eyes to meet Gage's as I cut the pancetta. "Did my mom ever mention hiding something for me?" I don't know if I can tell Gage the truth or not. Dylan and I are the only ones who are supposed to know about our plans to catch the thief.

"No. I do know your mom and the Admiral had something up their sleeves before your mom passed."

Quickly changing the subject, I say, "Speaking of that, my uncle mentioned a Twain book today." I dice apples for the salad while recounting my uncle's story. "If I did find that book, would the trust own it as my uncle said?"

Gage steals a slice of apple off my board and pops it into his mouth. "So we're skipping the art question?"

I stop mincing shallots for the wine sauce and lay my knife down as I take another long drink. My mind races for what I can say. Finally, I give up and go with the truth. "Dylan said not to talk about it. With the ongoing investigation at my store and all."

"Hmmm." Gage smiles. "Interesting how the art just came up today when you were supposed to have found the paintings right after your mom died. And how you never mentioned it to me. But back to your question. It depends."

I'm so flustered by circumventing the truth that I've forgotten what my original question was. "Depends?" I toss the pancetta for our salad dressing into a hot pan and then get busy washing the kale.

"We could argue that your grandfather never put the book into the trust for a reason. Your uncle said his father saw the book, so it seems to me your grandfather wanted to respect your great-great-grandmother's wishes for passing down the book to the youngest female."

"I like that." I throw shallots into my pan and then wipe my hands on my towel. "What about if I found something else of value? Is my uncle correct that it wouldn't belong to me personally?"

"Maybe. It'd all depend on what it was. Any other rare books, besides the Twain, because they discussed it before your grandfather died, would belong to the bookstore and therefore the trust. Now, assuming it was something like that art you apparently found, that would depend on a lot of factors. Is this why you offered to cook dinner for me tonight? To pick my brain?"

"No! Not at all. Sorry. Let's change the subject. What brought you to Sunset Cove?" I remove the pan from the heat and whisk in some olive oil, dark mustard, and red wine vinegar.

"My aunt. You know her. Betty Franklin? My mom's sister. We used to visit her often."

I pour the dressing over the salad and then slide a bowl in front of Gage. "Yes, I was sent to the principal a time or two in high school. Your aunt is tough but fair." I cover my kale, apples, and currants with the rest of the dressing and slide my bowl next to Gage's.

"She said to say hi. She just got back from a long river cruise in Europe."

"That must be why I haven't run into her yet." I quickly smash the garlic and mince it up to add with the wine to steam the mussels. After I pop on the lid, I sit beside Gage. "So you fell in love with our little town on your visits here?"

He waits for me to take the first bite of my salad and then picks up his fork. I love a man with manners.

Gage says, "Who can resist the cliffs, the ocean, and the tight-knit community here?" He takes a bite, and his eyebrows hop up again. "This is fantastic too. And it's just a salad."

"Thanks." There are pros and cons to growing up in a place where everyone knows your business. It's refreshing to hear his differing point of view. "Did you try city living first?"

"Yes. LA. Hated it. Like you, I had a job with ridiculous hours. Constantly tried to convince myself it'd all pay off in the end."

I nod as I swallow. "I figure if I have to work that hard, then why not for myself? I've got the experience under my belt now, and the scars to prove it, so I'm ready." I lift my sleeve and show Gage what years of splattering oil and hot pans carelessly trotted down the line in a tight, busy downtown kitchen leave on a working chef's skin.

He takes my arm and winces. "Geez. I guess the next time I

get a paper cut, I'll have to suck it up." He gently runs his fingers over my scars.

It makes my spine tingle.

"Papercuts hurt too." Before he sees my goose bumps, I pull my arm away and grab our wine from the fridge. He's picked a Chardonnay that will pair perfectly with our mussels. "Nice choice."

"Confession? I had to ask which one would go best with mussels at the liquor store."

His honesty warms my heart. Most guys would lie to make themselves seem an expert. "Tell me you've actually ever stopped and asked for directions when lost, and I'll be a goner." I smile as I grab two glasses and pour.

The cute half smile on Gage's face when I hand him his glass makes me realize what I just said. "Wait. Sorry. That was a joke. I didn't mean ..."

He holds up a hand. "I get it—no problem. Let's toast to your sticking around. And maybe after your restaurant is open, I'll get lost and ask for some directions."

I'm an idiot, but power through my embarrassment. "To sticking around." I tap my glass against his and sample the wine. Rich buttery goodness slides down my throat. Perfect.

To cover up my awkwardness, I check on the mussels. Then I throw the bread into the oven to warm it and grab big bowls.

"Oh. I meant to tell you something." Gage cuts through the thick silence hanging in the air. "People on the town council have been stopping me on the street asking for hints for who the new mysterious celebrity restaurant owner is."

I glance over my shoulder. "Celebrity?"

"They added that part. Not me. You know how people are around here. It's like a game of telephone that starts with a small fact and then ends an urban legend."

"True. I can only imagine how disappointed they'll be when they find out it's just little ole me."

Gage picks up his wine. "They'll get over it once they've tasted your food."

"Hopefully." I dish out our mussels with broth and set the bowls down. Then I add an empty bowl for the shells. I grab the bread that's smelling yeasty and warm and sit again. "Because council members are asking, does that mean my chances of getting approved are good? Or are people afraid a rich celebrity restaurant might bring in too big a crowd a smaller restaurant can't handle? Please. Dig in."

Gage nods and then dips his spoon into the broth. "Serve them this, and they'll do anything you ask. Wow." Gage picks up the little fork and frowns at a mussel. Like he's not sure of the polite way to eat them.

I grab a mussel shell with my fingers, use the little fork to dig out the meat, then I toss the empty shell in the bowl in front of us.

Gage follows my lead and then tosses his empty shell into the bowl along with mine. "It means they're interested and not unhappy about the restaurant, so far. The vote won't happen until next month at their meeting. In the meantime, I think we can move forward with the construction plans if you want to risk it. They could still say no."

"I'll think about it. Now, enough business. Tell me all about you. Any sibs?"

Gage shakes his head. "My father left right after I was born. He was a trust fund baby and decided he'd like to pursue his love of mountain climbing and bird-watching rather than be with us. My mother waited for him to get bored and come home, but he never did, so my parents divorced. My mom still lives in LA with her second husband, who is a temperamental screenwriter. He required utter silence in our house at all times. They never had kids because they'd make too much noise, as I did."

"Who could ask a child to live like a monk in a monastery? Or your mom, for that matter."

He shrugs. "My mom spends a lot of time in her garden. When school was out, she and I would take trips up the coast to visit Aunt Betty."

I'd always chalked up his quiet nature to basic politeness. Something I find attractive in people. "I wonder why we never ran into each other?"

"Oh, we did." Gage finishes off his wine and then pours us both another glass. "You just never noticed. Probably because you assumed I was just another tourist. The locals here do that. They look at you but don't really see you."

Gage is right. When you live in a town full of tourists, you don't pay them much attention. They're all temporary people who you'll most likely never see again. "I apologize for treating you like a tourist, Gage."

He smiles. "You were always nice to me when I came into Renee's parents' shop for ice cream. I was painfully shy back then. I'd sit in the corner and eat my treat, watching all the cool kids who hung out there. They weren't very nice to you."

"No. They weren't." Memories of that time of my life aren't pleasant. "Renee was my only real friend back then, besides Dylan. Her mom was nice enough to give me a job, but I hated it. It was embarrassing serving ice cream to the mean rich kids."

"I didn't fit in either at school. It wasn't until college that I finally grew into my gangly body and came out of my shell. And I got Lasik and dumped my glasses." He takes another long drink. "It used to pain me to see how those kids treated you back then."

"Now I'm embarrassed that you felt sorry for me."

"I didn't feel sorry for you as much as I understood how not belonging felt. But you never let them see you sweat. You held your chin high and gave it right back to them. I admired that about you."

I wave a hand because I hate talking about that part of my life. "One does what one has to do to survive in a small town. So back to you. Did your dad ever come back?"

"No. Never. He wrote and occasionally called. Eight years ago, he died and left me his trust fund, thereby allowing me to move here and practice the kind of law I enjoy."

That explains the fancy suits and slick sports car Gage drives. "And make all the noise you'd like to make?"

"Exactly." He lifts his glass in a mock toast. "I've never told anyone in town about my trust fund. I only told you because I want you to know I'm not after the millions in yours. I have plenty of my own."

"And you of all people know I don't really have access to those millions in my account." I take a drink too. "I've wondered why you've never asked out Julie? She's the prettiest girl in town."

"She's not my type. And because I've had a crush on you since I was fourteen, Sawyer."

That totally catches me off guard. What am I supposed to say to that? "I still can't believe I didn't notice you back then." He's so darn good-looking, how could I have been so blind?

I stare deeper into his greenish-turquoise eyes, searching for something familiar. It's hard not to get lost in his entrancing gaze. There *is* something about Gage's eyes. "Wait a minute. I *do* remember you. Tall, skinny, black glasses, and two scoops of rocky road in a cup with caramel, nuts, and whipped cream. No cherry. Right? You came in often. So much, I remember asking you if you lived in the area. You just shook your head and walked away."

Gage slowly nods. "Told you. Painfully shy. And I still hate cherries."

"Well, you'd think I'd hate ice cream after working there for so many years, but unfortunately, that's not true. It's still my guilty pleasure. And speaking of frozen dessert, are you ready to bust into it?"

"Absolutely." Gage stands and clears our dishes to the sink.

I slip off the stool to grab the semifreddo. When I close the freezer door, I wake my snoozing dog. Cooper grumbles a bit and then goes right back to his nap. "Excuse me, your highness, but I believe it's time for you to do some business outside." I open the kitchen door and wait. Cooper slowly stands and stretches like a cat before he heads outside. Just past the doorway, he freezes, yelps, and runs back inside and behind my legs.

My heart starts pounding. "Is someone in the backyard, buddy?" I toss the dessert onto the counter and stick my head out the door. "Gage, there is!" Someone dressed all in black with a white football team logo on the back and hood pulled over his or her head is running away.

Gage jumps in front of me and closes and locks the door. Then he grabs his cell. "I'll call Dylan."

"Tell Dylan he's running toward my neighbor Bill's house. At least I think it's a man. It's hard to tell."

Gage nods as he reports to Dylan and then hangs up. "Dylan says to sit tight. Is the front door locked?"

"Yes. I locked it behind you." I peer out the kitchen window —all clear. Yet, Cooper can wait to go out until Dylan gets here. I place the dessert back in the freezer and then join Gage at the kitchen island.

Gage lays his hand over mine. "So much for a nice dinner, huh? You okay?"

"Fine." I nod, but it's hard to settle. "Things just got real. Dylan was never sure I was in danger, he was being cautious, but I think now we can establish I am. No one would have any reason to be lurking in my backyard other than for no good."

"I agree. Here." Gage slides my wine in front of me. "Dylan will be here soon."

"Thanks." A loud bang makes me jump.

"Sawyer? Open up." Dylan's voice sounds at the back door.

Relief fills me as I hop up and let Dylan in. He drops a duffel at his feet before Cooper runs and jumps into Dylan's arms. I don't call my dog Chicken Coop sometimes for nothing.

Cradling my dog in one arm, Dylan locks the door behind him. "All clear outside. Any idea about height and build?"

I answer, "Looked like a guy, but who knows? The person had on baggy black sweats. And the jacket had a pirate logo on the back, for the football team. Could be a tall woman, though."

Gage shakes his head. "I didn't see anyone."

Dylan sets Cooper on the floor and then runs a hand down my arm. "In the morning, you and I need to go see the Admiral. Ask him to turn over what's in his safety deposit box. Your mom's scavenger hunt isn't worth your life."

I turn to Gage. "You sure you don't know what the Admiral left for me in his will?"

"No. My instructions were to hand the envelope from his box to your mother's heirs after the Admiral dies."

I turn back to Dylan. "Okay. You're right. Let's hope he'll go against my mother's wishes and tell us where the hidden items are."

CHAPTER 13

$\mathcal{E}$d showed up bright and early to my house and is busy installing the new cameras. He promises to finish this afternoon. So book club should still be on for tonight.

I slide a ham-and-cheese omelet in front of Dylan and then sit opposite him in my nook. I'm on my third cup of coffee, and it's only eight thirty. "Did you get any sleep last night?" I ask Dylan.

He shakes his head between bites.

"Yeah. Me neither." I play around with my veggie omelet, but I'm not hungry. "I say we go search Wade's, Crystal's, and Julie's apartments. There has to be something they forgot while planning the crime. There's no such thing as a perfect one, right?" After last night's dark-clad visitor, I'm officially spooked.

Dylan slips a bit of ham to Cooper, who's under his feet in the nook. "Search warrants don't work that way. We have to have a reason to look."

"The *reason* is that one of them either killed or help kill Chad!"

Dylan sets his fork down. "Things have to be done in the proper order, and the suits are checking off all the boxes.

151

Painfully slow. So, let's talk about book club tonight. We need to tell everyone about the art you supposedly found and about the cameras Ed installed so people think the bookstore is a dead end. And then tell everyone about the Twain book that must be hidden at your house."

"Okay, but can I have first dibs on your taser gun when we catch whoever did this? Chad made a mistake using the DDT, but he didn't deserve to die like that."

"No, he didn't. I'm just as eager as you are to see justice served on his behalf. Please let me do the serving, though. And it's too soon to write off the mystery customer."

"Yeah, yeah." I'm grumpy from being up all night. "What kind of evidence are we going to get from book club?"

"Don't know, but I'd like to see their demeanor when they're not talking to a cop. For now, let's go visit the Admiral so we can find whatever your mom hid."

"Fine." I take a few more bites and then clear the dishes while Dylan puts Cooper into a harness I haven't seen before. "What's that?"

Dylan snaps on the leash. "It'll make him behave when you walk him."

I like this idea. "Great. Let's go check it out."

After I tell Ed to let me know when he's almost done so I can come home and lock up after him, we head down the steps and toward the cliffs to the Admiral's house. And my little doodle boy is walking as well for me as he usually does for Dylan. "Thanks for this."

"Welcome." Dylan gives me a shoulder bump. "How was the date last night?"

"*Dinner* was enjoyable. Gage is a nice guy."

Dylan grins. "Yeah, but I win because I got to spend the night."

Brother. "On the couch with your gun. That hardly constitutes a win."

"Bet Gage would disagree." His big shoulder bumps mine again.

"I'm changing the subject. What was the Admiral's reaction when you called him this morning and said we need to go against mom's plans?"

Dylan lets out a long breath. "He doesn't take breaking the promise he made to your mom lightly, but after I explained things and told him what happened last night, he agreed to go to the bank with us. He knows your mother would never have knowingly put your life in danger."

"No. She couldn't have planned for any of this."

We walk along in silence for a few moments until Dylan says, "Getting excited to find what your mom left for you?"

"I might've been, except now I don't even know if I can legally keep anything I find today." I glance at Cooper who is happily trotting ahead of us with his tongue hanging out. I'm super thankful to my mom for my pooch, though. He sometimes reminds me of her with his sweet goofiness, and it makes my heart lighter.

Dylan nods. "You'll figure it all out."

"Hopefully." We avoid the busy town square and head toward the sounds of the ocean pounding the cliffs. The steady rhythm of the waves, the cries of the seagull, and the tang of salty air bring back memories of Dylan and me walking this same path each morning to high school. No one dared to mess with me if he was around. He was protective of me back then too.

I give *him* a shoulder bump for a change. "The big-city cops made a mistake taking you off the case. Still, we'll get 'em anyway. Right?"

"Absolutely. Because our team has a wild card the suits don't have." He slips an arm companionably around my shoulder. "You and the book club members."

I blink at him as I process, and then a lightbulb sparks in my head. "Oh, because we've already established our inclination to snoop? And could get ourselves into trouble. So now that you're off the case, you've taken it upon yourself to keep us all safe while we continue to spy? That's what you'll tell the suits?"

"Yep." Dylan grins as we approach the Admiral's house. "Let's find out what your mom hid for you and worry about the rest later." He holds out a hand for me to do the honors.

The Admiral has a brass knocker shaped like an anchor on his front door. I lift it and then let it fall. We wait for a few minutes, and then I repeat the process all over again. "Maybe he can't hear it. Is there a doorbell?"

Dylan and I look around and finally find a doorbell. He pokes it, and the song *Anchors Aweigh* rings from inside the house.

We wait some more until I ask, "You told him we were coming here, right? Not the bank?"

"Yeah." Dylan tries the doorknob, and it turns freely, so he pulls his gun from the holster on his belt. "You and Cooper should stay out here."

"Nope. We're sticking with the guy with the gun."

He sends me a sideways look before he calls out, "Admiral? You home?" Dylan pushes the big wooden door with his shoulder, and it makes a noise like rusty hinges scraping a chalkboard. It sends shivers up my spine.

Dylan whispers, "Stay behind me."

Once inside, Dylan doesn't have to ask me twice to stay behind. The dark place smells like dusty library books and burnt grease. It's spooky.

I lay a hand on his shoulder blade and stick close as we creep inside with Chicken Coop bringing up the rear.

There are brass ships' bells on the wood-paneled walls, yellowed framed maps, ships in bottles on coffee tables along with lamps with nautical scenes. His home takes vintage nautical decorating schemes to whole new levels. As if a sailor and a hoarder combined forces and then gave up and just parked a shipwreck here instead. Not to mention the boxes and junk stacked everywhere that create eerie shadows.

The dust motes dancing in the rays of sunlight from the barely cracked-open curtains add to the ambiance, as if we're entering a dark scene in a movie where everybody dies.

A low moan sounds.

I'm ready to bolt, but too frightened to leave Dylan's protective bubble. "What was that?"

He holds up a hand, shushing me. I don't like to be shushed as a rule, but in this case, I'll make an exception.

With the leash on my wrist and both hands on Dylan's back, my fists grabbing what little material I can gather on his tight uniform shirt, I match Dylan's steps as we slowly make our way toward the direction of the noise. It sounds out again, and it's definitely human. Someone's hurt.

Dylan picks up the pace, so I have no choice but to do the same, but then he stops suddenly. I smash against his back, and Cooper crumples against my legs. Dylan doesn't flinch at the impact, and instead says, "Admiral? What happened?"

Against my squeamish nature, I peek around Dylan to see for myself. The Admiral is on the dining room floor holding his head. Thankfully, there's no blood.

Cooper doesn't hesitate. He runs to the Admiral's side to comfort him.

The Admiral pets Cooper and then faces us. "I was drinking my coffee at the table when someone snuck up behind me. A gloved hand slipped over my mouth, and then a note appeared on the table in front of me. I read the note but couldn't answer the question. Next thing I know, something smashes me on the side of the head, and I fell to the floor."

Dylan scans the rooms and then says to me, "Call for help. I'll have a look around."

"'Kay." I pull out my cell and dial. When Madge answers, I

say, "We need an ambulance at the Admiral's house. He's had a home intruder and has a nasty bump on his head."

Madge agrees to send help, so I hang up and jog to the nearby kitchen, keeping an eye on the Admiral. I step inside what I can only imagine a ship's galley would look like. A kitchen on a wooden pirate ship, not a fancy cruise liner, though.

Grabbing a towel hanging on a rack, I fill it with ice from the freezer and then hurry back to the dining room.

I squat beside the Admiral, who is still prone on the wooden floor with Cooper snuggled against his side. "Hold this over the bump. Help is on the way."

Dylan joins us again and holsters his gun. "Do you recall anything else?"

When the Admiral tries to sit up, Dylan lays a hand on the old man's shoulder. "Stay down, please. You said there was a note?"

"It's right over …" The Admiral blinks and looks around. "It should be on the table right there. It was written on lined yellow paper."

"There's no note up here." Dylan presses, "What did the note say?"

The Admiral's forehead scrunches as if he's having trouble thinking. "It said to write down where the things are hidden for Sawyer, and nobody dies."

My stomach clenches. Now we know for sure someone is after what my mom hid. "Did you do it?"

"I couldn't." He shakes his head. "Your mom sat right over there, wrote the note, then handed me the sealed envelope that I placed in my safety deposit box. It's what I told the intruder too."

This makes me wonder, "Why did she type out the note she left for me, but write the one she gave you in longhand?"

The Admiral closes his eyes. "The one she left for you was

written just a few days before she died. She dictated, and I typed that note out on her computer because she'd become too weak to write. She wanted to be sure you could understand what she was trying to tell you, Sawyer."

That makes sense. And he called me by my real name for a change. Guess he does know what it is.

Dylan asks, "Can you give us a description of the person who hit you?"

"I only caught a glimpse after I fell to the floor. Black sweats that had a sports team logo on the back." He opens his eyes. "A football team. Very familiar, but I can't place it."

Could it be the same person who was in my backyard? "A pirate?"

"Yes! That's right, Sailor. A pirate with a dagger between his teeth."

Guess we're back to Sailor.

Dylan presses on, "Shoes? General build?"

"White tennis shoes, I think. I'm not sure." His eyes flutter like he's going to pass out.

Dylan squeezes the Admiral's shoulder. "It's okay. We can talk later. Where's the key to the safety deposit box?"

A bony finger points to a rolltop desk in the corner. "In one of the drawers on the top row. Never can remember which one."

"I'll look for it." Dylan grabs gloves from his back pocket and slips them on. The rolltop is lifted, exposing rows of little drawers for Dylan to search.

Amid the banging of drawers opening and closing, the rescue team arrives, followed by the suits who took over Chad's case. Cooper and I step out of the way as the paramedics help the Admiral. One of the suits points at me and says, "Take the dog and wait outside please, miss."

I want to tell the guy that the reason the Admiral is hurt is because of my mom's note and that I feel obligated to stay and help, but the hardness in his glare warns me not to argue.

Cooper and I go outside and sit on a bench on the front porch, watching people go in and out and waiting for Dylan to fill us in.

Finally, the Admiral passes us on a gurney. He gives me a thumbs-up on his way to the ambulance. A few moments later, after all the officers are gone, Dylan locks the front door and then sits beside me. "They're going to run some tests on the Admiral to be safe, but they think he'll be fine."

The tension in my shoulders finally leaves. "I'm glad to hear it. My mom would've just been sick to know she caused anyone to be hurt. Especially the Admiral."

"Hopefully, he'll feel well enough to meet us at the bank tomorrow morning. Never found the key, though. The intruder might've taken it." Dylan stands and rests his hands on his utility belt. "Luckily, it takes a bank employee's key along with the Admiral's to open the box. Can I walk you to the store? I don't want you to be alone until we catch whoever has done this."

"Okay." I stand and say to Cooper, "I guess you don't count. You're no guard dog, but you're always good for a cuddle."

Dylan reaches down and pats Cooper. His response is to roll on his back for a tummy rub. "He let you know someone was in your backyard last night, so that's something."

"True." We start walking toward my store as I run the events of the morning through my head. "I thought it was so weird that whoever broke in handed the Admiral a note until it dawned on me why. Because the Admiral probably knows whoever the intruder is, right? And might recognize a voice?"

"That'd be my guess." Dylan pulls a pair of sunglasses from his top pocket and slips them on. The morning fog is burning away, exposing what threatens to be a beautiful day.

"Can the bank let the Admiral into his safety deposit box without a key?"

"About that." Dylan's jaw tics. "The suits are going to file the paperwork for a search warrant. It'll most likely get approved this afternoon or first thing in the morning. I'm sorry, Sawyer. It can't be helped."

"I understand." If they publicly expose what's in the box, my uncle will surely hear about it. On the other hand, I don't want anyone else to be hurt. Especially me. If I have to turn whatever we find over to the trust, so be it. I'm not here for the money anyway. And if I can keep the bookstore going with online sales, then maybe my restaurant plans will still work.

Dylan says, "Maybe we'll catch a break before it comes to that. You still up for book club tonight?"

"Yes. I want this over with as soon as possible. And if it'll help us catch the killer, I'm all in. As long as you and your gun are there, that is."

DYLAN AND BRITTANY are feverishly looking through book boxes in the back, and I'm at the front counter watching the store and studying the plans for my kitchen remodel. I'd grabbed them from home when I'd locked up after Ed finished with the camera install. Dylan thought the kitchen might have something to do with our mystery, but I don't see anything unusual. Just a bunch of dimensions and lines that look just like the kitchen turned out. The appliance specs seem in order too. There might have been an opportunity to pad the bill there, but the appliances all match what's in the kitchen now to a tee.

Sighing, I roll up the plans and stuff them back into the tube —another dead end.

Where could my mom have hidden something in the house where I haven't looked? Maybe I'll look in the garage again. And my mom's car.

The front door opens, and Madge jogs inside. Today's bright blue sweater has an animal that looks like a beaver on her chest, but it's probably supposed to be a cat.

Out of breath, Madge lays a hand on the front counter for support. "Terrible what happened to the Admiral. But it looks like he's going to be fine. He even wants to come to book club tonight if they release him soon enough."

"Then he must be feeling much better." That's a relief to hear.

"Yeah. Here's the really big news, though. The suits are searching Wade's house right now. I overheard one of them say Wade was the only one who voluntarily agreed to a search. Julie and Crystal refused. What do you think that says about their guilt?"

"Nothing good." This news sends a jolt of adrenaline straight to my gut. "They've all had time to get rid of any incriminating evidence by now, though. Did the women say why they refused?"

Madge leans closer. "Crystal told them her dad the lawyer advised against it. Seems that was what she was doing in San Diego. Getting legal advice. She passed the same advice on to Julie and Wade as well. The three of them were huddled up in Skippy's last night. And get this. Wade was wearing a black team jacket that fits the Admiral's intruder's description, according to Skippy. I called him myself. When I told the suits, they jumped on it."

"Most everyone around here has the same fan gear. Dylan does too. It doesn't make him guilty." Or any of them for that matter.

A memory of seeing Crystal in a similar jacket niggles my brain. She's a jogger, and I've seen her running at the high school track. And the school is near the Admiral's house. Maybe his home was a quick stop on her morning jog.

Crystal is a big-boned woman. Tall, large chested, and could have been the one I saw running away from my house. Her red hair would be hard to miss, but not if it were tucked under a hood. Julie is small and slightly built. No way it was her. Wade is on the thin side, but it could've been him too. Or maybe the mystery customer.

Madge crosses her yarn-covered arms. "Well, if they're not guilty, why not let the authorities have a look inside their homes and cars? I might have a chat with Julie tonight at book club. Tell her how bad it's making her look. I like her."

That'll fit right into Dylan's plan too. Besides watching their reactions when I tell them about the found paintings and the Twain book, Dylan hopes to see if anyone still wanders to the storage room anyway. We decided not to tell everyone about the new cameras here at the store. "Even though she's not a member of the book club, do you think Crystal would come tonight too if you invited her?"

She's the one who interests me the most right now, and it's her facial expressions I'd like Dylan to study.

"Why? She's not a reader, as far as I know." Madge's forehead crumples in confusion.

Good question. Why would Crystal join us tonight? I don't want to share my jogging theory just yet. I could be wrong about Crystal, and she already hates me. She used to make my life so miserable as a kid. I don't need to falsely accuse her of anything and then have to endure her harassment. This town is too small. There's nowhere to hide.

I scramble for a coherent reason other than I think she's guilty because she's mean.

A scene from a book I've been reading before bed—because Brittany shamed me into it after I revealed I hadn't read a murder mystery in years—flashes in my mind. "You guys like to solve murders, right? So what if we go all Agatha Christie and reenact the crime scene tonight? Everyone will do exactly what they did the night Chad died. You can tell Crystal we'll need her help to do that. And I'll ask Brittany to stay for a few extra minutes too. Maybe by going through what we know, we can figure out how Chad got poisoned."

"That sounds amazing!" Madge's eyes go round as saucers. "I'm on it. See you later." Madge heads for the door, squeeing with pleasure.

I probably should have cleared that with Dylan first, but I'm sure he'll be okay with it. And what I'm going to do before book club is see if I can take a look at the high school's camera footage. Maybe I can find images of Crystal running the track to see if she might be the one who was in my backyard and who hit the Admiral over the head. Dylan can't ask for the footage without involving the San Francisco police and their rules, but I can.

I don't know where I've left my cell, so I pick up the store's landline and call Gage. Maybe his aunt Betty could help me see the school's recordings. These days, all schools have cameras everywhere. Hopefully, they have one that covers the track. Who knows? We might get lucky, and Crystal will be wearing the same outfit. I'd love to help lock whoever did this away so we can all rest easy at night again.

As Gage's phone rings in my ear, the front door opens again, and my heart nearly stops. Michael Jones, the mystery customer, is walking straight toward me. It's him for sure. His head tilts in that particular way that made him stand out to me in the first place.

And he looks mad enough to hurt me.

CHAPTER 14

*A*s a scowling Michael Jones, aka the mystery customer, storms toward me at the bookstore, my heart pounds so hard, it's difficult to draw a deep breath. Gage's voice mail echoes in my ear, so I hang up the store's phone—in case I need to dial 9-1-1. Dylan is in the back. If I knew where my cell was, I could've texted him. Shouting out might let the guy get away.

There's a pair of scissors on a shelf below the phone, so I wrap my hand around them. "Hi. Can I help you?" my voice barely squeaks out. Dylan said to act normally.

This is as normal as I can get with a potential murderer two feet in front of me.

He places both hands on the counter and says, "I'm looking for someone."

"Who?" My hand is sweating on the scissors, but I grip them even tighter.

"The sheriff. I got a message that he was looking for me. Someone told me he's here. Is he?"

Relief whooshes through me. Michael hasn't come to kill me. Not at the moment, anyway. "Yes. He's in the back. I'll go get him."

Doing a sideways shuffle around the counter and trying to keep my pace in check, I head for the storage room. As soon as I cross the threshold, I run. "Dylan!"

Dylan looks up from the boxes of books he and Brittany are rifling through. "What's wrong?"

"He's here." I cock my thumb over my shoulder. "Mystery customer. Michael. Said he got a message. He wants to talk to you. He seems agitated."

"He must've finally checked in with his work. Thanks." Dylan takes off at a jog, and Brittany, Cooper, and I follow behind. I'm braver now that a man with a gun is leading the way.

Dylan stops and holds up a hand. "Wait back here. I need you to call Madge and tell her what's going on."

"I can't find my phone."

Brittany whips hers out. "On it."

Dylan nods and then heads through the door to the showroom.

I plaster my ear to the door to listen while Brittany talks to Madge. Michael is telling Dylan he's pressed for time and to please tell him what this is about.

Brittany presses her ear on the door too. She whispers, "Madge said two men are on their way."

We both strain to listen but can't quite make out what they're saying. They must've moved closer to the front door—something about Michael's mother and an operation.

Cooper flops on my feet and is making chewing noises. I haven't given him a rawhide, so I crouch to take whatever he's stolen from the wastebaskets again. "Cooper! No!" It's my phone he's chewing on. It must've fallen to the floor, fair game as far as my dog is concerned.

I hit the app to connect to my cameras so we can see and hear what's going on out front. Dylan is taking notes when the two suits come through the front door and take Michael away to be questioned.

Brittany, Cooper, and I hurry to the front to join Dylan. "So? What do you think?"

Dylan slaps his notebook closed. "He says he just stopped in for a book on the way to his mother's house down south for her to read while recovering from her surgery scheduled for last Friday. He knew who her favorite author is, but then wasn't sure she hadn't already read it, so he left without buying the book. Said he was running into the city today to take care of something at the office, and then he had to get right back to his mom."

Sounds reasonable enough. "So now what?"

Dylan tucks his pad into his top pocket. "They'll run him and check out his story. Then we'll see. What research I've already done on him doesn't show any connection to Chad. Or gardens and DDT."

Brittany asks, "Did he hear what Chad and Crystal were arguing about?"

Dylan nods. "It jibes with what Crystal told me. I have to go to my office for a few minutes. I'll be back as soon as I can." Dylan's eyes zero in on mine. "Keep your phones on you at all times, please."

I lift mine so he sees I've found it. "Will do. See you later." That reminds me. I need to call Gage again to see if his Aunt Betty can look through her school surveillance files. Maybe we'll get lucky and find that Crystal went for a jog today. Better yet, I'll send Gage a text and explain what I'm hoping to do.

After I slip my phone into my pocket, Brittany blows out a long breath and says, "And then there were three."

"It's looking that way. When Dylan gets back, I'm going to run to the grocery store for book club." And hopefully, Gage and Betty will get back to me by then. "Any requests for snacks tonight?"

Before Brittany answers, the door opens again. It's Renee. Even better, she's brought ice cream from her shop.

She smiles at Cooper, who has run to greet her. "Hey there, Cooper. We haven't actually met yet." She gives Coop a rub all over.

I ask, "Heard from either of your weekend dates?"

Renee smiles. "Both of them. I'm surprised you'd even feel the need to ask."

True. Renee explains to guys she doesn't want commitment, and it has the opposite effect. They take it as a challenge and sometimes get a little clingy. Why this works is a mystery to me.

When Renee's had enough doggie love, she hands over a bag with two mint chocolate chip sundaes inside. Then she leans her elbows on the counter and lays her chin in her hand. "What's new, ladies?"

Brittany's face lights up. "Ice cream for lunch? So much better than turkey sandwiches! Thanks, Renee." Brittany and I both dig in.

"Welcome. Where are we in Chad's investigation? Who are the remaining suspects?"

Brittany and I practically inhale the minty chocolate and whipped cream. I finally say, "As far as we can tell, Wade, Julie, and Crystal are the three suspects left. Or a combination of them."

Renee frowns. "Crystal is the obvious choice. She has a wicked temper, but Julie has been acting distant. We're friends, but I didn't know she'd been dating Chad until you told me the other day in my shop, Sawyer. If I had, it'd make me wonder why she and Wade have been running together all of a sudden. That girl doesn't like to sweat, but I saw them almost every morning before I left for my convention last week."

This makes my antennae tingle. "At the high school?"

Renee shakes her head. "The trails in the woods. North of town. I don't like the track. It's boring. I mostly saw them in or around Wade's truck, but I did see them actually running a few times. If you can call what Julie was doing running. It was more like a fast walk."

Brittany licks the last of the chocolate syrup from her plastic spoon. "Did Chad run?"

Renee says, "Not that I knew of. Wade just started in the last few months."

I finish off my treat too. "Apparently, Chad didn't stick with women long. Maybe Wade was setting the groundwork for when Chad got bored?"

"Maybe. You want to come bunk with me for a few days, Sawyer? Until this blows over?"

Brittany says, "She has Gage to protect her."

I haven't said anything to anyone about Dylan guarding me instead, and I think I'll keep it that way.

"Gage, huh?" Renee's full lips tip into a mischievous grin. "Do tell."

Brittany adds ever so helpfully, "She made him dinner last night."

"The way to a man's heart. Or ice cream works too." Renee leans closer, making her long dangly earrings ting. "Anything happen after dinner?"

"No." I hold up a hand. "Stop. We're just friends. My dad asked him to stay with me." That's all true. I'll leave out the part about who actually stayed.

Renee pushes off the counter. "I have to go. Want to come over later? I brought back some amazing wine from my weekend adventures."

"Can't. We have book club tonight. Soon, though."

"Yep." She reaches her long arms over the counter and hugs me. "Be careful. Think some more about staying with me, please."

"Okay." I squeeze my pal. "I'm glad you're back in one piece." If you listen to the news, it's filled with dating dangers.

"Glad to be back in one piece, but you worry too much, Sawyer. Bye, Brittany."

"See you." Brittany lifts a hand and sighs as she watches Renee saunter out the door with her usual attitude. "She's so cool. How are you two even friends?" Brittany's lips tilt at the corners as she teases me.

"No idea. Now get back to work, please." Maybe Brittany and I are becoming friends too. She never used to tease me. She hardly talked to me.

"Fine. Nachos. And sliders. Maybe some chili cheese fries."

"For tonight?" That's gross teenager food. I did ask her, though, so maybe I'll keep the goodwill going and comply. "You got it." Although it might be fondue rather than processed cheese on chips.

As I input my grocery list into my phone, the door opens again, and it's Gage's Aunt Betty. "Hi, Principal Franklin. How are you?" She's dressed in yoga pants and a matching jacket, and has her mat tucked under an arm. I see now the family resemblance. Principal Franklin is blonde and attractive like Gage.

"I'm great, but you can call me Betty now, Sawyer."

I open my mouth to try, but it just won't come out. She'll always be my former principal. "I'll work on it."

"I get that a lot." Smiling, she joins me at the front counter. "Gage forwarded your text to me. What are you looking for?" She sets her mat on the floor and pulls a cell phone from her jacket pocket. "I can access the cameras from my phone."

Just like mine. Probably because Ed installed a similar system. "Can this stay just between the two of us? Unless we find something important, of course."

Principal Franklin tilts her head. "If I can. Gage told me about your backyard intruder last night. Which camera are you interested in?"

"The track. This morning. Anyone run there?"

"We usually have a few." Gage's aunt taps her phone and scrolls through the cameras. "Who are you looking for?"

"Crystal. Or anyone wearing black sweats."

The principal's eyebrows arch. "Doing detective work behind Dylan's back?"

She could always see right through people. Probably from all her years dealing with kids in trouble. "Yes, but he's on to me."

"Mmmm. Well, the school is public property, so I don't see any harm in me looking."

Nervous anticipation makes my fingertips tingle as the principal scrolls. Finally, she shakes her head. "No sign of Crystal today. Just your neighbor Bill wearing red and white."

Darn it. Maybe Crystal didn't have time to run if she made a stop at the Admiral's house. "Would it be too much trouble to look back the last few weeks? See if we can spot black running gear?"

"Since there's always incredible coffee here, I could take a few minutes and look." She makes her way to the dining area and pours herself a cup. Then she grabs a croissant and sits. "I was so sorry to hear about your mom, Sawyer. I haven't had a chance to tell you that."

"Thank you." I pour myself another cup of coffee and sit across from her. "I guess you've been away for most of the summer?"

"Yes. Glad to be back home, though." The principal's finger stops scrolling, and she meets my gaze. "Gage mentioned what an incredible chef you are, Sawyer. Are you interested in doing some catering? We're having a party in a few weeks. A fundraiser thing for my mother's artsy pals. Lots of hoity-toity types from the city."

"I'd love to. Text me when and where." Maybe if people like the food, I can pick up a few more private dinner parties in the city to help me get by for now.

"Great. You'll be saving my life." She scrolls some more. "I keep seeing Crystal—she jogs by a few times a week—but not the black sweats." The principal's coffee cup stops halfway to her lips. "Wait. I think we found what you're looking for. This was back in May." She turns the phone my way.

There's Crystal jogging the track, wearing a Raider's jacket, black sweatpants, and wearing white tennis shoes. The gait seems familiar, but that might be from when I'd seen her around town. Was she the one I saw running away from my house? It's hard to tell. It'd been dark.

"Can you send that to Dylan, please?"

A deep voice says, "Send what to me?"

I was concentrating so hard on the video, I didn't realize he'd come back. "It's Crystal, wearing exactly what the Admiral described his intruder wearing. I knew I'd seen her wearing that before."

"It's not an uncommon look around here." Dylan takes the phone from Principal Franklin and watches the video for a moment. "This should be enough to get us a search warrant. Or, maybe once we show her the video, she'll voluntarily agree to let us search her house. Can I email this to the station?"

Betty nods. "Sure. Whatever you need."

"Good work, ladies."

Principal Franklin lifts her hands. "That was all Sawyer, not me. Glad I could help. Good luck, Dylan. Nice to see you, Sawyer." She grabs her yoga mat, takes her phone back, and heads toward the front door.

"Thanks again …Betty." It still feels wrong to call her that.

I turn to Dylan, "Any news on the Admiral? Can we all go to the bank this afternoon? Before the search warrant comes through?"

"He won't get out of the hospital until a doc signs him out. Might be too late today by the time he gets back here. The search warrant might come through any minute, though. I told the bank we'd like to be there too."

"Will the police keep the letter?"

"If it has valuable information, yes. They'd bag it as evidence."

Shoot. I wanted to be the first to read the letter. "When you got back, I was going to the grocery store to get stuff for tonight, because after this morning, I don't want to leave Brittany here by herself, but I want to be at the bank when they open the letter too."

He hooks his thumbs in his utility belt. "Why don't you lock up and send Brittany home? Leave a note here in the window that book club is still on at six. Then you can stick with me in case they get permission to open the Admiral's safety deposit box."

I hate to miss a sale by closing early—I could really use the money—but that makes the most sense.

DYLAN IS TAPPING texts out on his phone while I toss ingredients into the shopping cart at the grocery store. He hasn't left my side since we left the bookstore and he's been on his phone the whole time, so I ask him, "Did Crystal agree to the search?"

He looks up and blinks at me as if his eyes have been staring at his tiny screen so long, my full-sized face is too much for his pupils to take in. "Yes. They're searching her house right now. Wade's house and car came up with nothing significant."

"Nothing significant? So, something?"

He nods as his thumbs go back to work on his phone. "We already knew he had a Raiders jacket too. So nothing new there."

Both Wade and Crystal have the same jacket. And who doesn't have a pair of black sweats? Not a lot to go on, but enough to make Crystal realize she'd get searched with or without her permission. So mission accomplished there.

After all the ingredients are in my cart, I head for the front checkout. And guess who's on duty? Julie. She must've been on a break when Dylan and I arrived. This could be an opportunity, but not with Dylan by my side. He's too much of a truth teller to go along with what I'm thinking, so I say to him, "Why don't you wait for me by the front door? I have to grab one more thing, and then I'll be ready."

He looks up from his phone again. "I'll go with you."

Brother. "I don't want you to go with me. I have to buy something …personal."

"Oh." His eyes shift from me to his phone in a flash. "Got it. See you up front." He scurries off like there's a fire by the front door to put out. He was never one to delve into all the personal things women have to do that men don't. And I don't feel at all bad about using that fact in this case.

I take my chance for freedom and hightail it to Julie's line. There's a person in front of me, so I grab the rubber stick to separate our orders and start unloading. Dylan is making a point of *not* looking my way, so I'm good to go.

When it's my turn, I say, "Hey, Julie. How's it going?"

Her eyes shift toward Dylan and then back to me. "As well as to be expected. Under the circumstances and all."

Here's my chance. "Yeah, I hear Wade and Crystal both had their houses and cars searched today."

Julie's head turns so fast, I fear for whiplash. "She's the one who told us not to let the cops inside. Her father said it was a civil rights thing."

I nod as I keep loading groceries onto the belt. "Something about their jackets being the same as the person who attacked the Admiral or some such, so Crystal gave in to the search before she was ordered to. Kind of makes *you* look a little guilty now, though, being the only holdout, huh?"

Julie stops scanning. "I guess it does. But I don't have anything to hide. I was just following advice."

"Oh, I know. Maybe Crystal had always intended to let them search her place? To make you look bad and shift the blame to you?"

Julie's face turns from perfect porcelain to beet red. "That scheming mean girl strikes again. I wish she'd find a hole and bury herself in it up to her neck!"

Well, this is working better than I could've hoped. "I'd call Dylan over and beg him to search your place if I was you. Can't let Crystal win, right?"

"Yeah." Julie's chewing her thumbnail in thought. "Why not?" She calls out, "Hey, Dylan?" She curls her fingers in a come-hither motion.

Dylan glances up from his phone and then walks closer, but stops a few feet away. Probably to avoid seeing something embarrassing. "Yes?"

Julie throws her shoulders back. "What do I have to do to let you search my house and car? I'm ready."

Dylan glances my way fighting a little grin. "I'll call the officers in charge, and they'll be right here. Thank you for helping with Chad's case."

Julie jerks a shoulder. "I want the killer found as much as anyone."

Bam. Two for two today.

Hopefully the searches don't turn out to find "nothing significant" like Wade's did. Now that the mystery customer is out of the picture, I think the women worked together to kill Chad.

CHAPTER 15

*W*hile still waiting to hear about the search warrant for the Admiral's safe deposit box, Dylan and I unload the groceries at my house. I sent Cooper home with Brittany for the afternoon in case we get the call from the bank. It's the longest I've been away from my adorable little dog, and I miss him. Who knew I'd ever be able to fall in love again so quickly? It hasn't worked with any of the men I've met since Dylan, but at least I know that part of my heart still works.

Just as I've put the last of the veggies in the fridge, Dylan's phone rings. Is it about the search warrant at the bank?

His blue eyes cut to mine as he listens to the caller. Then he shakes his head and leaves the kitchen to finish up his conversation. A part of me is disappointed and another part happy that maybe we can still get to the note before the search warrant comes through. Maybe the Admiral will be well enough to meet us right when the bank opens in the morning.

I'm folding the cloth grocery bags when Dylan joins me again. "Michael Jones's story about his mother's operation checked out. He was just passing through town on his way south. They're searching Julie's house and car now. Her mother gave them access."

"Oh, that's right. I forgot that she lives with her mother."

Dylan nods as he slips into the nook with a frown. "What's this Madge tells me about you guys reenacting the crime tonight?"

Madge's big mouth works both ways. "You don't think that's a good idea?" I pour two cups of coffee, doctor up his, and then slide in across from him.

"No." He takes a long drink from his cup and then sets it down. "If the murderer feels cornered, who knows what he or she will do. This isn't the movies, Sawyer."

His phone dings with a text, so he picks it up and reads the screen. "They got the search warrant for the Admiral's box. Let's go."

By the time I chug half my coffee Dylan is already at the front door. "Wait up. I have to find my purse." I look around the kitchen, but it's not there. I finally spot it on the little table by the front door with my keys, so I scoop them both up.

Dylan breathes down my neck as I turn the key and then slip it back into my purse. "All set."

"About time." He takes my arm and practically carries me down the steps along with him. "We need to hurry. They won't wait for us. Actually, the cops don't know we're going to be there. Let me do the talking, please."

I'm jogging to keep up with his long strides. "Why wouldn't I have a right to be there? It's my letter!"

"Because you were at the scene of the crime too, Sawyer. I know you didn't do it, but they don't. I'm hoping we get lucky and they'll need an interpreter for your mother's handwriting."

That makes sense. The Admiral said my mom sat down and wrote the note out and then handed him a sealed envelope. The cops have handwriting experts, but it'd be faster if I read it to them. "This all seems a little unfair. Just saying."

"Agreed." Dylan is still half carrying me by his side. "If the killer is who I think it is, we need this information now, not after the lab works on it in a day or two. The murderer is going to act again. I can feel it."

That makes my heart pump faster, not only from the running. "Whoever it is will give up once I find the hidden things, right?"

"That was what I'd hoped at first, but things have come to light that have changed my theory."

"What thing—?"

Dylan holds up a hand to cut me off. "I can't discuss it."

"Seriously? Then don't say stuff like that. It just makes my imagination run wild."

He sighs. "It's a money thing." We're in the bank parking lot, so Dylan picks up speed. "The killer might get desperate enough to take the hidden items from you by force. After killing once, it's easy to do it again."

My stomach hurts all of a sudden. "Maybe I don't want to know what's in that letter."

"Too late." We bolt up the steps and slide to a stop in front of the bank manager, Mr. Sanchez.

Dylan asks, "Are they still here?"

"Yep. Follow me." Mr. Sanchez leads the way to the vault filled with men in suits and little locked boxes lining the walls.

One of the cops turns and holds up a hand. "Sheriff. You don't need to be here."

"Realize that." Dylan smiles and holds up both hands like he's just the small-town cop they think he is. "You've never tried to read Zoe's handwriting. Thought you might need some help." Dylan moves me in front of him like I'm our invitation to the party. "This is Sawyer Davis. The person the note is intended for."

"Hang on," the tall man in the black suit says to the gray-clad man with his gloved hands inside the box. "You want her to verify?"

Mr. Gray Suit nods. "Couldn't hurt." He holds up a white #10 envelope. "Do you recognize this handwriting? If so, what do you think this says?"

I smile. This guy wouldn't be the first to think my mom learned to write from a Martian. "It is my mother's handwriting, and that's my name on the front."

Gray Suit frowns. "A nickname?"

"No. Sawyer. Tilt your head a little to the right, and the envelope to the left. It's all in the angle."

Dylan quietly chuckles as the cop in the gray suit contorts his body and the envelope to try to see what I'm seeing.

Finally, Gray Suit says, "Maaaybe?"

Mr. Dark Suit asks, "Is it the only envelope in the box?"

When Gray Suit nods, Mr. Black Suit says, "Okay. We'll bag it. Thanks for your help, Ms. Davis."

"Wait." Dylan jumps in. "The Admiral was hurt over the contents of that letter. I still have a whole town full of folks to protect while you take the time to analyze that. Why don't we let Sawyer read it? You can verify after. It could save another life."

Gray Suit and Dark Suit go to the back of the vault for a consult. While they make a phone call, Dylan whispers, "Do you have a recording app on your phone?"

I shake my head. "Why would I have one of those? Don't you have one?"

"Can't use mine. Download one. Now."

"Fine." I scan the app store and start downloading the first one I see with decent ratings. It costs me four bucks but hopefully will reap much more than that.

I'm begging the little circle that indicates how much time is left for the download to move faster as the suits continue their debate with whoever they have on the phone with them. Gray Suit says something about the worst handwriting ever and that the Admiral confirmed the note was intended for me.

Finally, the download circle is complete, so I poke the "get" icon, and the app opens up. I start reading the directions, impressed with all the features I just got for so little money, when Dylan whispers, "Just hit Record now and put it in your front shirt pocket."

I whisper back, "Only guys carry phones there. Besides, this blouse is too flimsy. They'll see it weigh down the pocket."

Dylan takes my phone and tucks it into my top pocket. Then he frowns and takes it back out. "You're right." He grabs Mr. Sanchez, who is still standing behind us, and slips it into his top shirt pocket. "Stay right behind Sawyer, please."

Mr. Sanchez smiles and winks at me, apparently amused by the whole situation. He probably doesn't think the suits should've taken over Dylan's case either. Why else would he have agreed to call Dylan when the others got here to search?

After much debate, the men return, and Mr. Gray Suit opens the letter with his gloved hands. Then he holds it up. "Do you need for me to tilt it or something?"

"No." I lean my head to the right and try not to think about my mom sitting in the Admiral's house writing it. I want to cry, but there's no time for that. "It says, *Dear Sawyer, if you're reading this, then you've decided not to stay in Sunset Cove. While this saddens me, I understand. I'm sure you tried your hardest to make things work. Your father and I didn't make it easy on you girls, because being an individual in this town isn't an easy thing to accomplish. Please don't ever forget to embrace what makes you special.*"

I have to stop and blink back my tears. As hard as I always tried to fit in here, part of me needed to go away and see what it'd be like to live in anonymity. It wasn't as great as I thought it'd be.

After clearing my throat, I keep reading. *"In case this falls into hands that are not Sawyer's, particularly my brother's, I'll leave clues that I know only Sawyer will understand. The first item can be found inside the chest that used to hold your imagination and dreams, remember? One that reading often will eventually reveal."*

I glance at Dylan, who's frowning as he tries to decipher the clue but I need to read the next one and worry about the details later.

I lean closer and read, *"The second item I've left for you is easily found in your own advice to me about a chef's kitchen. That I should always keep at my fingertips ingredients filled with spice and life that, when combined, will fill the soul with love."* I scan the words to the bottom of the note. "The rest is about how my sister and mom want me to be happy and that I should use the things she left to remember her by fondly."

Gray Suit asks, "Do you know where the items are hidden?"

I glance at Dylan and then back at the two cops. There are so many things running through my mind, but nothing is making any sense. "Not off the top of my head. I'm sure it'll come to me. I just have to think like my mom for a few minutes. Then I'll figure it out."

Gray Suit folds the paper and slips it and the envelope into a baggie. "We'll take this to the station. Meanwhile, no one here mentions that Sawyer read this. For her safety. Understood?" After everyone nods, he turns to me. "We'll be in touch, Ms. Davis."

"Thank you." My mind is still racing to put the pieces together.

While Gray and Black Suits pack up their things, Mr. Sanchez slips my phone back into my purse. Dylan thanks everyone and then leads me out the front door.

He says, "The trunk in the attic, right? That was the first part of the clue? You used to play with what was inside when you were a kid. Where you found the envelope your mom left with that website."

I nod. "Yeah. But my mom knows I don't read much." I keep rolling the words "reading will reveal" around in my mind as we walk back to my house. "Wait! Brittany had told me that my mom wanted me to start up book club as soon as I felt up to it. It was important to her. And what do we serve at book club?"

A slow smile lights Dylan's face as he takes my arm and steers me toward the bookshop. "Wine. Illegally, but we'll ignore that for now. Have you ever gone through all the cases of wine in the back?"

I shake my head and start to jog. "It's all marked the same on the outside. An inexpensive California wine I assumed my mom found on sale." Oh boy. Could I have been sitting on top of the prize the whole time?

We skid to a stop in front of my store, and I unlock the doors. After I hit the alarm, I lock up behind us, and we run for the back. Way in the corner, stacked in two piles, are cases of what I thought was cheap wine. "You take that stack, and I'll do this one."

I've already opened the top case, so I move it aside and open the next sealed case. Inside is the same brand as was in the first case, so I move that one and go on to the next. "Any luck?"

Dylan shakes his head and keeps looking through his stack too.

"Would my mom risk us accidentally drinking the wine? That'd be an expensive mistake."

"That was my thought too. Maybe this was too obvious."

Dylan is on his last case when he says, "Here we go. A note that says, *If you need more wine, look for a trunk with your name on it in the attic, Sawyer.*"

"So, it's back to the note that leads us nowhere. I'll grab the ladder. Maybe I missed something." I swipe the dust from my slacks and head for the ladder, but Dylan has beaten me to it.

I follow behind him in silence, concerned that my mom's cryptic messages might be too convoluted even for me to figure out.

Dylan pushes the ceiling panel aside, yanks the wooden ladder down, and heads upstairs. I follow behind, recalling the words my mom wrote about the wine website. Something about tricks being an illusion and how she hoped my restaurant would be true magic.

Dylan lifts the lid on the trunk where we found the note. "It's got to be something in here."

I kneel beside him and sort through the old costumes and broken tricks inside. Dylan picks up a box and says, "Is this one of those puzzle boxes? Like your dad used to steal my twenty?"

I nod and keep looking. "Many a sucker besides you fell for that one."

"Don't rub it in. Your mom said her clues were ones that only you'd understand. What did you and your mom know that your uncle didn't about these things?"

I shrug. "How the tricks work, I suppose." I grab the box Dylan has in his hand. "There's a little pin in this one— maybe that's it! One of these puzzle boxes might be what we're looking for." I hit the button, revealing an empty drawer, so I toss the trick aside and grab the largest in the trunk.

The box is complicated and needs the exact sequence to make the hidden drawer open. "This one is the hardest to open. I hope I can remember how."

It's been a long time, but I spent many hours bored out of my skull in the summers playing with these old tricks, so I close my eyes and let my fingers take over. Without directing my hands, I allow them to move in the pattern buried deep somewhere inside my head like a pianist playing a song etched on her heart.

After my fingers do their dance, a pop sounds and a drawer slides out. I'm almost afraid to open my eyes, but I force one open and then the next. Dylan has a huge grin on his face.

"You did it, Sawyer."

I glance down and can't help the grin stretching my lips either. There's a key with a tag along with an envelope that says, "Taa Daa!" on the outside. The extent of my mother's lines in my father's magic show.

Dylan picks up the key while I read the note inside. He says, "This is from that new storage place up north. The environmentally controlled one, which would make sense for storing wine."

I fold the note and stuff it into my pocket. "Yep. The wine is safe inside. She says she left me an explanation of how she came to own it in the storage unit." I glance up at Dylan and nod my approval. "Man, that was smart of my mom. My uncle would've never found this."

"Most everyone underestimated your mom. Never understood that just because she forged her own paths in life, they weren't necessarily the wrong ones." He stands and then holds out a hand to help me up.

My hand is dwarfed by his big strong one as I accept his help. "Maybe I was one of those people too. Always feeling like I had to make excuses for her and my father's oddities, rather than accepting them. Running away to college the first chance I got to find a 'normal' life and a 'real' job."

Dylan nods. "And now your mom is giving you the opportunity to give up all that normalcy you went to years of college for. She's helping you do what will make you happy by owning your restaurant."

I can't help but love my mom even more for that. "Well, let's wait and see how she pulled off all this expensive wine later now that we know it's safe. Maybe being an eccentric hippie was an excellent cover all these years for her side gig as an international jewel thief."

Dylan laughs. "Right." Then his feet stop midstep as he follows me down the ladder. "On second thought, maybe I don't want to know how she got that wine."

"Me either."

At the bottom of the steps, he says, "Would you please consider staying with Renee tonight? Let me stake out your house alone? I'll ask Gage to pick you up after book club and stay overnight with you guys."

"Okay. If you think it's best." I'm not sure now if I'm safer with Dylan in a house we're setting up to be robbed, or with Renee and Gage at this point. All I know for sure is that we need to figure out who killed for the things my mother hid. Maybe by sticking to our story tonight at book club, we'll finally find out.

AFTER I'VE SET out all the food at the store that I made for book club, I turn to Dylan. "Okay, my story is I found the art here in the store shortly before I reopened it, and now a broker has it?"

He nods. "And that you think there might be a valuable Twain book hidden somewhere in your house, but you've never found it. You can add things about how your uncle wants the book too, if you think it'll help."

"Okay." I'm rubbing my hands together to shake off the nerves. "Have you heard any more about Julie's and Crystal's searches from this afternoon?"

"No. I think showing up at the bank earlier made the officer in charge clamp down on the chatter. I've been cut out of the loop entirely now."

"Sorry about that." I glance at my phone. "It's time. You should go hide."

"Hey." Dylan grasps my arms. "Try to act normal so everyone else will too. No one will know I'm watching and listening in the back except you and Brittany. I'm here if you guys need me."

"I'll make sure everyone knows I'm spending the night with Renee tonight too. So if I don't see you before I leave, be careful.

Okay?" I've given Dylan a set of keys to lock up the store after everyone is gone.

"Will do." He squeezes my arms. "You be careful too. Maybe by morning, we'll have our culprit. And all this will be over."

"Let's hope. My nerves can't take much more of this."

I wait until Dylan disappears into the back before I unlock the front door. Brittany and Cooper are the first to arrive, and my dog is acting like he hasn't seen me in a month, jumping on me with excitement. "Hey, buddy. Good to see you too." I glance at Brittany. "Change of plans tonight. No reenactment. You don't have to stay."

"Then I'm out. I'll put the glasses out before I go. And maybe I'll grab some food?"

"Sure." I take a minute and cuddle with my sweet boy while Brittany sets out the glassware like she always does. "Take some for your mom too."

"Thanks." Brittany dips bread into the fondue and takes a bite. "Good. Still, nachos would've been better. Wonder why Madge didn't tell everyone the enactment was off?"

"I don't know. Maybe she got busy? We can ask, because here she comes now."

Madge comes hurtling through the front door. "Sorry I'm almost late, but you won't believe what happened this after-noon. Oh, is that fondue, Brittany?"

Brittany pops another piece of cheesy bread into her mouth and gulps it down. "If you say so. What happened?"

Madge lays a hand over her ample chest while she catches her breath. She's changed sweaters from the one she had on earlier. I think her orange sweater has a black bat on the front, but maybe it's a seal?

Our out-of-breath dispatcher says, "They found a container of DDT at Crystal's house, and Julie's clothes from the night of the murder have traces of DDT on the sleeve. I wouldn't be surprised if they're getting the paperwork ready to arrest both women."

This makes Brittany stop midchew. She slowly lowers her wooden skewer and says, "Then maybe we better watch our food and drink tonight, because here comes one of the murderers now."

CHAPTER 16

*B*rittany, Madge, Cooper, and I are cemented in our spots in the dining area as Crystal walks toward us. Her expression is hard, her black eye fading a bit and her clenched fists a pretty good indicator that she's spitting mad. However, now that I know the DDT didn't kill Chad, I don't know if the found evidence will really matter.

Madge clears her throat. "Thank you for joining us, Crystal."

Crystal crosses her arms. "I figured I couldn't afford *not* to join you and your gossip club, especially because you and your little group of want-to-be sleuths seem to have an inside track with the sheriff. One could even argue *undue influence.*" Crystal's eyes cut to mine.

I hold both hands up as if she's pointing a gun at me. "I'm only the host. I don't join in around here." Cooper quietly whines as if in agreement with me. Besides, this was also a test to see if someone didn't show up. Probably because they're guilty.

"Whatever." Crystal shakes her head and turns to Madge. "Let's get started. I don't have all night."

"We're still waiting on a few." Madge gestures toward the food. "Help yourself to some refreshments."

"Yeah. No thanks." Crystal tosses her red hair over her shoulder and then finds the nearest couch to flop onto. "I don't have a death wish."

Brittany whispers, "I'm out. Want me to take Cooper?"

"Renee and I are having a sleepover at her house tonight, and she wanted me to bring Cooper along. But thanks," I say loud enough for Crystal to hear.

"Okay. Good night. And good luck." Brittany heads for the door just as the Admiral enters.

"Hello, Sailor. How are you this fine evening?" says the Admiral, who's not afraid to dish himself some food.

"Good. How's the head?"

"Never been better." He moves next to me and whispers, "Did the clues make sense?"

"One did. I'm still working on the other."

He taps his forehead. "Just have to let the subconscious do all the work. Think about something else. It'll come." He joins the others on the couches as he eats his food.

Easy for him to say. The second clue has me baffled.

After Wade and Julie join us, I lock the door to prevent tourists from wandering in, and Cooper and I sit in the dining area to observe while Madge calls the group to order. I need coffee, but Brittany has me spooked about drinking anything.

Madge begins the discussion of the chapters they were all supposed to have read, and Crystal interrupts. "Wait a minute. I came here to clear my name. So, let's do this."

The Admiral says, "Well then, why don't we lay out the facts of the crime. Sailor, do you have a whiteboard I can borrow?"

I shake my head. "We don't have one of those. How about some paper?"

"That'll have to do." He turns back to the group. "Who'd like to defend themselves first? We'll ask questions, then you can tell us why it couldn't have been you who committed the crime."

The Admiral clearly didn't get the message that Dylan didn't want this to happen, but it looks like it's happening anyway. I grab a pad of lined paper and set it in front of the Admiral along with a pen.

Crystal says, "I'll go first because I know many of you think I killed Chad, but I didn't."

Madge raises her hand first. "Then what were you two arguing about before our meeting? And why go to San Diego in the middle of a murder investigation? What *really* happened to your face?"

Boy, way to pack all she could into that question. I move to the edge of my seat because I want to hear Crystal's explanation of all these things too.

Crystal rolls her eyes. "Chad and I were discussing his use of DDT on people's gardens. When we were dating, he took me to Mexico, and I caught him sneaking it back home. I told him if he didn't quit, I was going to tell Dylan. I lost a grandfather in Vietnam to chemical poisoning." She turns to Wade. "And you knew about it too, because Chad told me when he asked you to repay him for all the money you've borrowed the last few years, you told him he had to wait, or you'd go to Dylan about the DDT as well."

Holy moly. This is new information. I wish I had a big bowl of popcorn, because I think things are just getting started.

Wade shakes his blond head. "I knew he was using something he shouldn't. I never knew it was DDT until a few days ago."

Crystal's right brow pops. "Chad also told me that you were finally going to pay him back soon because you'd found a pot of gold or some such. What was that all about?"

Wade yawns and stretches out his long legs. "The job over at

Zoe's. I'm on a retainer, and it'll take months." Wade points to me. "Right, Sawyer?"

"Yep." Cooper isn't comfortable with all the raised voices and wants in my lap. Usually, that'd be a no, but I think I could use the cuddle, so I pick him up.

Wade says, "So, why'd you go to San Diego with your black eye? To get rid of evidence?"

"No. I tripped when I was out jogging in the woods. My face hit a tree. And I had already planned my San Diego trip to visit my father before Chad was killed. My dad's been sick."

Madge says, "Then how do you explain the DDT they found under your kitchen sink?"

Crystal throws her hands up in exasperation. "Chad and I lived together for a long time. He must've put it there. Do you think I would've left it for the cops to find if I'd killed Chad? And just because I have a Raiders jacket just like most of you in this room doesn't make me the killer. It's all circumstantial evidence."

I guess Crystal is right. It is all circumstantial evidence, but when does enough circumstantial evidence become too much to be a coincidence?

Crystal leans back and crosses her arms with a huff. "What I don't understand, Madge, is why you guys didn't think it was strange when Chad, Wade, and Julie all just randomly showed up for book club. Didn't you think it was odd that all three would join at once?"

Madge frowns. "Well, now that you mention it, maybe it was a little off." She turns to Julie. "Why did you all join at once?"

This perks me up too. That's a great question. Why would all three randomly join?

Julie, who has been silently wringing her hands all evening, says, "I'm with my kid twenty-four seven when I'm not at work. I needed some mental stimulation, so I mentioned one night at Skippy's I was going to join, and Chad said he'd like to as well.

Wade just tagged along for the beer, I suppose, but he's taken a real interest in it now."

"Seriously? Chad and books?" Crystal narrows her eyes. "Well then, answer me this, Julie. If you and Chad were dating, then why did I see you and Wade huddled up in his truck by the running paths so many mornings recently? What have you two been plotting? Chad's murder, maybe?"

"No, of course not." Julie shakes her head. "We were talking. About my divorce and what I'm going to do long-term. Life stuff friends talk about."

Crystal says, "You owed Chad money too. He and I got into a big fight about it. I didn't understand why he was so eager to loan you money the minute you stepped back into town after your divorce."

Julie's mouth opens and closes like a fish stranded on the shore when Madge says, "And why would the sleeve on the shirt you wore last Thursday evening test positive for DDT?"

Julie blurts, "How would I know? Chad probably touched my arm that night. He must've had it on his hands from spraying earlier in the day. How do we know he didn't poison himself?"

Madge says, "Because DDT is a slow-acting poison. Although his energy drink showed no traces of chemicals when tested, someone put the can in my knitting bag after Dylan searched it to throw suspicion on me."

Julie says, "Maybe you killed Chad, Crystal, because you're pregnant with his kid and he dumped you. Told you he never loved you. Wanted nothing to do with you ever again."

Oooh. That was harsh, but a valid accusation. Crystal and revenge were synonymous in high school.

Crystal laughs. "I'm not pregnant. I was just messing with you in the store the other day because I think you, Wade, and Chad were up to something. Suddenly, you three had become best buds, always huddling up at Skippy's and whispering. Then you all three join the book club. And then Chad is found dead in the back. Nowhere near the bathroom, from what I've heard. There are rumors that he was looking for something."

Julie shrugs. "We're friends, Crystal. Something you wouldn't know much about."

"Funny." Crystal leans closer to Julie. "I think you and Wade killed Chad to get a bigger piece of whatever golden pie you thought you'd found because you're both in dire financial straits."

"How would you know anything about mine and Wade's finances?"

"Because Chad told me how much money you both owed him. Are you guys planning to pay his estate back? His mom could probably use it to run the business now that Chad's gone."

Wade threads his fingers behind his head. "How do you know we hadn't already paid him back? You and Chad haven't been together for months."

Crystal shoots back, "Because I asked Chad's mom last Friday after I heard he was dead. We still talk. She confirmed you hadn't paid him back, because he would've told her. She thought the three of you were up to something too."

Wade finally sits up. "She's like a mother to me. You had no right to upset her like that with your fantasy and lies."

"Oh, wait!" Madge's face whips toward me. "Sawyer, do you think Chad could've known about that art you found in the back before you reopened? Or the Mark Twain book your uncle is always going on about that he thinks is still hidden in your house?"

Thank you, Madge, for doing my one job here tonight. "I don't know. My mom never mentioned the paintings before she died. I just stumbled across them." I'd cross my fingers behind my back, but they might notice. Besides, technically, my mother never mentioned the art. Because it doesn't exist.

The Admiral adds, "I was dating Zoe, and I had never heard her speak of those paintings in the back either. Anyone else?"

His eyes scan the group of people all shaking their heads. "Crystal, do you have any facts on which to base an accusation of collusion between Chad, Julie, and Wade?"

"No." Crystal huffs out a breath. "Except I dated Chad for a long time and knew him well. I always knew when he was keeping something from me. We fought about his sneakiness often. He was definitely hiding something from me when we broke up."

Probably that he wanted to be with Julie, but I'll keep that thought to myself.

Crystal points to Wade. "You've had a crush on Julie since high school. I bet it chapped your butt that Chad stole her right out from under you, because Chad beat you at everything, didn't he, Wade? You pretend to be a laid-back dude, but those fights the two of you got into at the bar were always because Chad beat you at something again. Weren't they, Wade?"

He shrugs. "Chad and I were like brothers. We fought, but we were always friends. You're just making up stuff because you killed Chad, Crystal. We all know you did it!"

Julie and Madge are both nodding, so Crystal says, "Tell us why we shouldn't think you killed Chad, Julie. You and Wade are clearly a team now. And you had DDT on your sleeve. Your looks aren't going to get you out of this one like they always have before."

Wade says, "And your bullying tactics aren't going to save you this time either, Crystal."

Crystal's face is turning so red, I'm worried she might blow out a blood vessel when she yells, "When could I have poisoned Chad? I talked to him for like five minutes, and then I left!"

"I have a theory about that, Crystal." The Admiral, who's been watching the accusations fly, his eyes shifting left and right as if watching a tennis match, says, "It seems to me that you and Julie could have been working together. Perhaps Chad the Cheater, as he's known around here, scorned you both? Maybe it was your job, Crystal, to distract Chad while Julie plated up and poisoned his food? It seems pretending to be enemies and both having circumstantial evidence against you would be a fine way to muddle the case."

Crystal and Julie both send the Admiral scathing looks before Crystal says, "That's just stupid. Everyone knows Julie and I can't stand each other." She turns her glare toward the others. "You call yourselves a mystery book club, but you're nothing but a bunch of hacks sitting around reading books because you have nothing else to do with your sad little lives!"

My phone dings with a text. It's from Dylan telling me to cut things off. Now!

I put Cooper on the floor and stand. "Okay, guys. Maybe that's enough for—"

Loud banging interrupts me and silences the group.

I turn around, and my uncle, Mr. Black Suit, and Mr. Gray Suit from the bank are standing outside the front door. This can't be good. My uncle must've found out about the note my mom left in the Admiral's box via his daily mayoral briefings.

Cooper prances to the door ahead of me, probably eager to get away from all the screaming and carrying on. "Cooper, sit."

His little rump hits the floor, and he waits for me to join him at the door. "Good boy." Dylan worked with my pup on that last night, so I'm glad he listens to me too.

With a twist of the key, I unlock the door and in barrels my uncle. "Your mother can't get around what's legally mine with some silly riddles. What has she left you?"

The whole store has become as quiet as a tomb. Everyone is waiting for my reply.

The problem is I don't like to out-and-out lie. I don't mind a little innuendo that can be misconstrued now and then, or even some omission of the truth to protect people sometimes, but straight-up lying has never worked out so well for me. The facts always come out. And then I just look like a liar. "Dylan and I figured out the first clue and found a key to a storage unit. We didn't have time to investigate what's inside. I haven't figured out the second clue yet."

My uncle waggles his fingers. "Hand over the key."

I shake my head. "My mother left the key for *me*. I will let you know if what I find is something relevant to you."

"I think these gentlemen would agree that what is in that storage unit might be relevant to this case." My uncle's grin is a smug one.

"The storage place is closed right now, so we'll go check it out tomorrow. I'm pretty sure the other thing of value she left is still in the house somewhere, but I'll have to think on the clue some more to figure it out."

"That Twain book is as much mine as it is yours, Sawyer. Or whatever else she left in the house."

"I'm spending the night with Renee tonight, so we'll deal with this tomorrow. Whatever Mom left has been hidden all this time. I'm sure whatever it is isn't going anywhere." Everyone in the store now knows I won't be home tonight. Please don't let my uncle ruin our catch-a-thief plans and insist we go to the house and look. "Now, if you'll excuse us, we're in the middle of book club."

"Hold up, Ms. Davis." Mr. Gray Suit moves around the mayor to stand in front of me. "We have some business with one of your members."

Black Suit joins his partner, and they confront Crystal. "Ma'am, will you hold out your hands, please? You're under arrest for the murder of Chad Fellows." Black suit slaps on the cuffs.

A collective gasp sounds. Not that most people didn't think Crystal did it, but to see her arrested slams the reality home.

We all watch in shocked silence as Crystal gets Mirandized. Or whatever it's called when they read you your rights.

When they're done, Crystal says, "My father will have me out within the hour. You've got nothing on me!"

Mr. Black Suit says, "We'll talk about that when we get to the station. Let's go."

Crystal sends one last sneer at Wade and Julie before she reluctantly lets the cops haul her out of her chair and to the front door.

As everyone begins talking at once about justice being served, I'm not so sure. Because if Crystal acted alone, who put the can in Madge's knitting bag after Crystal left?

CHAPTER 17

I'm staring at the ceiling of Renee's tiny guest room in her adorable little cottage by the ocean. The first rays of sunlight are creeping through the mostly closed curtains, and I can't sleep. I haven't heard from Dylan, so I don't know what's going on at my house, but I don't want to call or text. In the movies, it's always the phone making noise giving away people's location when they're hiding from bad guys. So I throw my covers back and get up. Cooper lifts his head from his blanket on the floor and wags his tail, always ready to start his day. I wish I had even a fraction of his enthusiasm for mornings.

I tiptoe down Renee's creaky stairs and let Cooper out the back door. Yawning, I start the coffee and then rummage through Renee's fridge. She's not big on cooking. The best I can find for breakfast is leftover pizza from last night's late-night delivery. It'll have to do.

I don't want to wake Gage, who's sleeping on the couch in the living room, so when the coffee is made, I take my mug and the pizza outside to the back deck and set them on the table. The scream of seagulls scavenging for their breakfast and the cool, salty breeze from the ocean remind me why living in

Sunset Cove long-term could be a good thing. It sure beats the stifling summer Chicago heat.

Cooper flops at my feet. "What do you think, Coop? Cold pizza? Or should I go inside and heat it?"

"I like mine cold." Renee, dressed in a silk oriental robe and with her coffee mug in hand, joins me and snatches a slice from the box. "How'd you sleep?"

Renee is one of those people who can fall asleep in an instant and always wakes up looking perfect. It's annoying. "Hardly at all. You?"

"Like a baby. Probably because of all the wine we drank last night." Renee takes a huge bite and then swallows. "Yet, even I'd have trouble sleeping if I had two handsome men pursuing me, a murderer after my stuff, and an uncle ready to foil my restaurant plans at the slightest misstep. Much easier to casually date guys from the city and run an ice-cream shop."

I whisper just in case Gage is up inside, "Casual dating isn't fun anymore." I take a long drink from my mug. "I wouldn't mind selling ice cream all day long again, though. It's a happy job."

"It is." Renee leans closer. "Perhaps your dating discontent is because of Dylan? Have old feelings resurfaced? Or are you thinking about a relationship with the hunky town lawyer who was looking at you last night like you were the last scoop of ice cream on a hot summer day?"

"Who knows?" I wave a hand and take another long drink. "Let's talk about your dating life. It's much more interesting than mine."

"Don't change the subject again. And to ensure you answer this time …" Renee grabs my mug. "No more coffee until you spill your guts."

"Taking away an addict's coffee is just mean."

Renee, who's about a foot taller than me, raises the mug over her head. "Answer my question, or this gets poured out."

"Fine." I cross my arms and lower my voice again. "Part of me thinks Dylan has changed and maybe we should give it another go. Another part tells me I should go on a few dates with Gage. See if there's anything there."

"Gage is a nice guy." Renee replaces my mug on the table. "And Dylan I only pretend to hate on your behalf. You can't go wrong either way, but there's one big problem."

"What?" I take a sip from my mug, bracing for what I'm pretty sure I know Renee is going to say about my lingering feelings for Dylan.

My pal leans closer and whispers, "One of them you still love." She grabs another slice of pizza.

That's the rub. "Loving someone and being *in love* can be two different things."

"Or the same thing." Renee's lips slowly grow into a huge smile. "'Bout time you admitted it. Sort of. Maybe dating Mr. Hunky on the couch *would* be a good idea. It might make a certain sheriff realize he needs to step up his game."

"If I decide to go on a date, it won't be to play games with Dylan. I'll talk with Dylan first. He'll know exactly where I stand."

Renee nods. "Assuming you figure that out. Right now, I'd say you're sitting smack dab in the middle of the fence. But there are worse problems in life. Like running out of hot fudge at my shop."

That makes me smile. "I know choosing between two attractive men isn't a problem in most people's minds, but I don't want to hurt anyone's feelings. Especially mine again."

"Admit it. You're afraid Dylan will move on if you date Gage. That it matters to you speaks volumes, my friend."

Renee's right. She knows me way too well. I'm not ready to make this decision. "Let's not forget that I have to see Dylan every national holiday if I want to spend them with my family. There's a lot at stake here."

"I know." Renee leans over and wraps me up in a hug. "Listen to your heart. Then do what it tells you. No pain, no gain as they say. And I'll take whichever one you don't choose."

"You would've already had one of them by now if you'd wanted either one, you man-eater." I lightly swat the back of Renee's head before I release her. "Must be a curse to be so good-looking and perfect. Brittany asked how we were even friends because you're so much cooler than I am."

Renee smiles. "Feed her free ice cream for dinner as I do, and you'll quickly surpass me in the coolness department."

"Do you do that often? Feed her ice cream for dinner?"

"Yeah. Or I share my 'leftover' pizza with her." Renee shrugs. "I feel sorry for the kid. I offered to let her stay with me, but she refused. Don't say anything, especially to Dylan, but her mom took off with a guy a month ago. Brittany has no idea where she is. She's terrified she'll have to go into foster care if anyone finds out she's on her own."

This news hits me like a punch to the gut. "No wonder Brittany was so worried about the bookstore closing. Her livelihood depends on it now." And maybe it's her mom who keeps disappointing her. Her father took off years ago.

"Not to mention she's still grieving for your mom. Brittany adored Zoe, but please don't let on that you know. Brittany thinks her mom will come back eventually. She has in the past."

"Okay, but keep me posted. I'll threaten her job if I have to so she'll stay with me. She shouldn't be on her own."

Renee's eyes twinkle with amusement over the rim of her mug. "That's the reason I told you. I knew you'd come to the rescue. You're a sucker for anything lost or broken."

"You're just afraid those deeply buried motherly instincts—that you deny having—almost surfaced there." Renee has vowed since high school that she'll never have kids, mostly because her childhood wasn't all that great. "Feeding Brittany and being her confidante shows your resolve is slipping."

Renee shakes her head and is stuffing her mouth with pizza when my phone dings with a text. "It's from Dylan. No activity at my house last night. He's going into his office for a few minutes, and then he'll pick me up so we can go to the storage unit together as soon as it opens."

Renee says, "Maybe the cops arrested the right person if nothing happened last night at your house."

"Or the other killer got spooked and is lying low." I still don't see how Crystal could've killed Chad alone. And if that's true, why would she protect her partner in crime?

I'M SITTING on the couch reading email while Gage and Renee are getting ready upstairs, trying not to get too excited about what we'll find in the storage unit. I say to Cooper, "Chances are my uncle will claim rights to whatever we find anyway, right, Coop?" Which just makes me sad.

A knock at the door interrupts my scrolling. Must be Dylan. Cooper is barking as I set my phone on the coffee table and open the door.

Wade is standing on the other side. "Hey, Sawyer. I was hoping I'd catch you before you left this morning. I found some crown molding on sale that's almost an exact match to your existing wood. We need to jump on it at this price." He throws a thumb over his shoulder. "I have a sample in the truck. Want to come see?"

"Yes!" We've been looking for something with a similar pattern for a long time with no luck. I feared we'd have to have it custom-made.

I close the door behind me and follow Wade to his truck. He opens the driver's door, then grabs my arm and pushes me inside. "Don't scream, or I'll hurt you." Wade picks up a gun from the floorboard and points it at me. "Slide over."

It was Wade all along?

Cooper must've slipped out behind me. He jumps in too and is in my lap by the time Wade closes the door and starts the engine. My heart is beating triple time as Wade takes off. "What do you want with me, Wade?" Maybe I can jump out at the next stop sign.

He keeps his gun pointed at me from the far side of his body. "Someone at the bank told me you and Dylan read the letter in the Admiral's box."

"Yeah, but it only had cryptic clues."

It's as if Wade is in his own world, staring blankly at the road ahead. "I would've liked to see what your mom left in the storage locker for you, but I checked the place out. Swarming with cameras. Dylan thinks he'll catch me, but I'm smarter than he is. Now that Dylan is gone from your house, we're going to go get what your mother hid there instead."

Wade must've watched my house all night long. "I haven't figured out where she hid it yet." I can barely remember the clue my mom left because I'm so scared. How am I going to get away from him? He's rolling through all the stops signs in his rush. "I recorded what was in the note on my phone. We should go back and get it."

"Nope. You better think fast, Sawyer. I'm not sticking around long enough for Dylan to figure out who really killed Chad. And if you don't find it right away, you're next."

Next?

"Did Chad know about the things my mom hid?"

"Yeah. I owed him money. Told him we could split whatever we found, but he got greedy. I snuck Methanol in his beer that afternoon that was supposed to make him die quickly. Instead, he hung on until book club."

So that's why no one saw Chad get poisoned. "Where did you get Methanol?"

"It's in windshield washer fluid."

"Oh." We're almost to my house. I don't want to be trapped inside with Wade. Maybe I can keep him talking outside in the truck to give Dylan time to find me. I can barely draw in enough air to ask, "So the golf ball through my store window was you?"

Wade frowns. "I don't know what you're talking about."

It wasn't Wade? This throws me off, but there's no time to think about that now. "Did you, Crystal, and Julie work together to kill Chad?"

Wade shakes his head as he pulls into my driveway. "Just me. I found Crystal's apartment key in Chad's things. I planted the DDT when she was in San Diego to throw off the cops. And the can in Madge's bag. I needed time for you to find what your mom hid. Figured Chad's lab results would take weeks."

"How did you even know my mother hid anything for me? I didn't even know until after Chad died."

"Your mother and the Admiral asked me for help with her computer while they were typing your note." Wade throws his truck into Park and then faces me. "I went back later and read it. Now come quietly."

Would he risk shooting me if I run? I reach for the door handle, but Wade grabs my arm. "Not that way. You're coming out my side."

Wade drags Cooper and me out along with him. My knees are so weak from fear that when I hit the concrete, I stumble, and Cooper hops out of my arms. Wade catches me before I fall, sticking his gun in my lower back as he marches me up to the front door.

"I don't have my key. It's in my purse at Renee's." Cooper is whimpering at my feet. I just want him to run, but he never leaves my side.

"I've got mine." Wade produces a key ring from his pocket. "You were way too trusting to think I wouldn't make myself a copy from the ones Ed left for you in the kitchen."

I *was* way too trusting. However, right now, all I can think about is finding something to hit Wade with so I can get away. It's probably too much to hope that Dylan will check my house cameras from his phone in time. Gage and Renee might still be getting ready and not even know I'm gone yet.

I need to save myself.

The new alarm is beeping wildly, so Wade shouts, "Turn that thing off!"

When I hesitate, because maybe the siren will alert my neighbors, Wade twists my arm harder. "Now."

I start to put my new code in when my panicked brain remembers that when Ed set up the alarm, he made me an emergency code, so I type that in. If I punch the buttons right down the middle, it'll stop the alarm and then it's supposed to make a call to the cops. But I never tested it.

I punch in the code and hold my breath.

Thankfully, the beeping stops. Will the cops get the call? Has Ed had time to set that up? He said it'd take a few days.

It's getting harder to breathe.

Wade drags me farther inside and closes the door behind us. "What did the note in the Admiral's box say?"

I can't think straight. "Something about the kitchen."

"Let's go." He pulls me down the hall while Cooper growls behind us.

There are knives in the kitchen. And heavy pots. All sorts of weapons. "Please. I have to think for a minute, Wade."

He releases me with a shove. I have to hold out my hands to stop myself from crashing into the island. My heaviest pots are beside the pantry, so I inch my way toward the cupboard. "The note said something about the advice I gave Mom about her kitchen. That I should always keep at my fingertips ingredients filled with spice and life."

He growls, "You've got five minutes. Start looking."

Spice and life. My advice about the kitchen.

I run through all the many conversations my mom and I had about the kitchen.

Wade says, "Four minutes, Sawyer."

As I desperately try to think about what advice I gave my mother, I swivel my head to take in the whole kitchen. Where could something be hidden? Behind a wall? Under a floorboard? She wouldn't hide whatever she left in a place I'd have to destroy to retrieve it, would she?

I turn back to the pantry, and it hits me. "I'd told my mom not to make the pantry deeper than her arm because things would get lost. And that's where the spices are to make food come to life!" I close my eyes and think back to the remodel plans I'd studied. Then I open the pantry and stick my arm inside. I can touch the back. The dimensions for the pantry on the plans were much deeper than the shelves currently inside.

Wade steps to the exposed side of the pantry by the back door and then moves in front of it again. "There must be a false back."

"Of course. Living with a magician, my mom had to know the power of the false compartment. There will probably be a release somewhere."

"You got one minute before I start hacking that thing up." Wade points his gun at me again. "Start looking. I need to see your hands at all times."

My hands are shaking so hard, it's difficult to move them as I slip my fingers under the pantry shelves. I could throw a can at him, but that might not be enough to help me get away. "If the Twain book is hidden back here, you don't want it, Wade."

"Why not?" he barks.

"Because my uncle said the book is signed for my great-great-grandmother. Super easy to identify. You won't be able to sell it for years." I don't know if I've just helped myself or made things worse, but by the set of his jaw, he's considering it.

Finally, he says, "We don't know for sure that's what's hidden back there. You've got thirty seconds."

I still need a distraction. "So besides getting greedy, was Crystal right about why you killed Chad? Were you that jealous of him? And about him having Julie and not you?"

"Shut up and keep looking!"

I've hit a nerve and will poke some more, while my fingers keep feeling around for a release. "Once you disappear, you'll never see her again. This was all for nothing, Wade."

"Julie will come with me. She wants out of this Podunk town as much as I do. Especially once I tell her what I did for her. I did all this for her!"

Wade is losing it. I need to poke even harder. "Julie and her kid are going to run off with you? Hide out until the cops finally find you? That's no way to live."

He shoves me with his boot. "She loves me! And I have it all planned. They'll never find us. Now stop talking and look!"

Wade shoving me must've been all Cooper could take. He jumps on Wade's leg, growling as he bites the denim.

Wade screams, "Get off!" and shakes his leg.

This is my chance.

I jump sideways and grab my French iron-clad ceramic pot that must weigh twenty pounds. Then I stand up and swing. I hit Wade's arm hard enough that the gun flies across the kitchen floor.

I need to get that gun before he does.

Both Wade and I lunge for the weapon, but his arms are longer than mine. Cooper helps out by biting Wade's wrist, but my dog has only slowed Wade down for the moment it takes to push Cooper aside.

Wade is stronger than me. The gun is probably my only chance to get away. I stretch as far as my arm will reach and get two fingers on the weapon, before Wade's hand snatches the gun from my grasp.

The only thing I have left is my pot, and it's no match for a gun.

Just as I've given up hope of getting out alive, a black boot stomps on Wade's wrist and Dylan calls out, "Police. Drop the weapon."

Thank goodness.

I roll away and try to catch my breath while Dylan and a suit-clad man wrestle Wade into a pair of cuffs. Four more cops join the party and keep Wade under control.

I'm shaking so hard, it's difficult to sit up, but with one big heave, I manage. I close my eyes and concentrate on breathing before I pass out.

Cooper climbs into my lap and licks my cheek, so I hug him tight. "Thanks, buddy. What a good boy. You probably saved my life."

Wade, with his hands behind his back, mutters, "Damn dog," before he's hauled outside by the suits.

Dylan crouches beside me. "You okay?"

The concern on his face brings tears to my eyes and clogs my throat, so I just nod as I put Cooper down.

Dylan helps me up and pulls me into his arms. "Can I hold you for a few minutes? That was way too close."

I still can't speak, so I nod against his chest. It feels nice to be in his arms. Safe.

"I'm so sorry, Sawyer."

I swallow back the lump in my throat. "It's not your fault. Thank you for getting here so fast."

He hugs me even tighter. "I got a motion alert from your cameras and watched on my phone as I ran here. It was torture." He lays a soft kiss on the top of my head. "Remind me never to make you mad when you're in the kitchen. That was a real wallop."

That makes me smile. Dylan's good at that. "My dad's collapsible knife was in my purse at Renee's, so I had to improvise." I'm so shaken, I could stay in Dylan's arms all day. And that might lead to something I'm not sure I'm ready for. He's way too tempting at the moment.

I lean away, instantly missing the solid warmth of his chest, and scoop up Cooper. "This guy is the real hero. I think a rawhide treat is in order. Don't you, Coop?"

My dog's happy tail wag says it all.

After I give Cooper a treat, I lean on the kitchen island beside Dylan again. "I should have known it was Wade all along. He's the only person Cooper was ever afraid of."

"I suspected Wade too. Especially when I saw how much money he owed Chad and how he fawned over Julie. She insists she and Wade were just friends, but Wade clearly thought they were more. We convinced Crystal to let us arrest her last night to draw him out. She had a solid alibi for when the Admiral was attacked."

"And you told her what to say to get under Wade's skin? To force him to act?"

"Yeah. We wanted him to think if Crystal had figured it out, then others might as well. We never had any hard evidence to arrest him."

I turn to my dog. "Well, I'll always listen to your instincts in the future, buddy."

Dylan gives Coop a scratch behind the ears. "Cooper *loves* me. Just sayin'." Dylan's lips tilt into a sweet grin as he leans closer to kiss me.

I tilt my chin to meet him halfway and whisper, "I'll take that under advisement."

"Sawyer?" my uncle's booming voice calls from the hallway, ruining the moment. Then the kitchen door swings open. "There you are. What did you find?"

Dylan growls, "She's fine after Wade kidnapped her. Thanks for asking."

We both glare at my bully of an uncle.

"Sorry. I'm glad you're okay, Sawyer." My uncle crosses his massive arms. "So? Did you find the book?"

I sigh and start for the pantry to keep looking for a release.

Dylan shakes his head slightly, and his eyes are saying *don't do it.*

He's right. If this pantry is anything as complicated as my dad's puzzle boxes, my uncle probably won't find the release on his own. Especially because he doesn't know what to look for. I pour myself a glass of water at the sink instead. "Nope. Guess I'll have to keep looking."

Whatever's behind the pantry can stay right where it is until I'm good and ready to find it.

CHAPTER 18

*J*t's after 1:00 p.m. by the time I finish with the police. Dylan went to Renee's and retrieved my purse and cell phone, and then he snuck me a grilled cheese sandwich from the diner on the way back because the suits took so long wrapping everything up. I just sent Dylan a text to tell him I'm on my way home.

As I poke at the swinging door to make my escape from the municipal building, it feels like it's been a month rather than just six days since Wade killed Chad. Wade and I had been alone in my house almost every day since my mom died. It creeps me out so much, I shiver. Thankfully, it's over now, and Wade is going to be locked up for a very long time.

Brittany is sitting at the bottom of the concrete steps, staring at the people milling in the park across the street, when I plop beside her. "What a crazy few days, huh?"

Startled, Brittany jumps. Then she wraps me in a tight hug. "I'm glad you're okay."

"Me too." I return the hug, happy for it. I'll take all the hugs I can get today, especially from Brittany now that I know she's scared about her mom. "Are *you* okay? It looked like you were a million miles away just now."

Brittany slowly releases me and then starts picking at her black nail polish. "Renee mentioned that she told you. About my mom and all. She promised you wouldn't tell Dylan."

"Not as long as I know you're safe." I give Brittany's shoulder a bump. "Why don't you stay with Cooper and me until your mom gets back? You can help me with his obedience training after work."

Brittany picks almost all her nail polish off during the pregnant pause while I wait for her answer.

Finally, she says, "Only if you let me help with groceries and stuff too. I'm not going to sponge off you."

"Deal. Want to go with Dylan and me to the storage unit and see what my mom left for me? We aren't going to open the bookstore today."

"Yeah." Brittany hops up from the steps. "As long as you guys don't get all flirty. It grosses me out."

"I think we can control ourselves." Smiling, I get up too and lead the way to my house, where Dylan and Cooper are waiting for me. Dylan is finally taking a much-needed day off now that Wade is in custody.

As we start up the hill, Brittany says, "I need to tell you something. Zoe had some papers drawn up that my mother signed a long time ago. In case my mom didn't come back again."

Why hadn't my mom mentioned something as big as that? "You mean like a temporary guardianship thing?"

"Sort of." Brittany shoves her hands into her black hoodie. "I was surprised Zoe never said anything to you. I kept thinking you'd find out any day, and then I wasn't sure what you'd do."

"I'll do whatever you and my mom did before." Renee had said Brittany loved my mom. Maybe this relationship has been going on longer than Renee even knows. "When was the last time you saw your mother?"

When all I get is a shrug, I say, "That long, huh? Okay. We'll ask Gage if he can help us. It'll all work out."

Brittany quickly wipes a stray tear from her eye. "That's what your mom always said, but she used a lawyer from the city to do the paperwork. Not Gage. My mother insisted on that. So, no one around here would find out and stick their big noses into our business."

"Did you live with my mom before I came back?" I hadn't been home for a few years, so I wouldn't have known. Then a horrible thought hits me. "Did you move out because of me?"

"No. I moved back to my apartment when the hospice nurses started coming so people around here wouldn't know. Before that, I stayed in your old room sometimes. Or by myself. Zoe paid my mom's rent so I could have my space. I'm not a baby."

No, but only fifteen. Probably better not to point that out right now, though. "I know you can take care of yourself, but you're not an adult. Who signed the paperwork in your life?"

"Zoe used to take me if I had to go to the doctor or dentist in the city and stuff, but I had to forge my mom's signature for school things. Your mom knew I was doing it, though."

My mother must've been Brittany's legal guardian. How could she fail to mention that to Megan or me? Maybe she intended to before she got too sick and never got around to it. The last days had gone downhill really fast. This must be one more reason my mom wants me to stay here. To take care of Brittany.

I still can't figure out how my mom paid for the lawyers and Brittany's apartment rent though.

My mother had hired a firm from the city to do her kitchen remodel. Maybe she found a way to slip Brittany's paperwork in there as well to make the trust pay for Brittany's care. Or, maybe my mom sold the Twain book to pay for it.

Disappointment fills me for a few seconds, but then quickly passes. It's just a book, and one I didn't even know existed until a few days ago. It'd be okay if my mom sold it. Brittany needed someone to look out for her. "Okay. We'll keep this between us for now. In the meantime, let's go get your things this afternoon and get you settled back in."

Now I have a whole new worry. I need to find that law firm in San Francisco and get a copy of the guardianship agreement as soon as I can. What if Brittany gets sick and requires a guardian's signature?

Brittany's voice is just above a whisper when she says, "Thanks, Sawyer."

"No worries." I throw an arm around my new ward's shoulder and draw her against me as we approach my house. "This old house is too big for just me and Coop anyway."

Dylan and Cooper are waiting for us on the porch. Bert, the one who gave me my dog, is standing right next to them. She and Dylan are the same height.

She lifts a huge hand and says, "Hi, Sawyer. I'm here for the one-week doodle well check."

"You're checking up on Cooper?" I lean down and pet my dog, who's jumping on my leg. "Like I'd be a bad dog owner or something?" I think I'm a little insulted.

I guess it's better than a social worker checking up on my parenting skills now that I'll have Brittany to care for. I'm not sure what I'm doing in that department, but a dog I think I can handle.

"No." Bert shakes her head. "Your mom wanted me to make sure you're okay with keeping Cooper. She worried it might be too much."

I narrow my eyes. "That's not what you said when you

shoved him at me. You were worried about your chakras, remember?"

Bert laughs. "I was just pulling your leg. I've known your mom for years, and I miss her. And I'll take him if he's too much. Your mom never meant to add to your burdens. She hoped Cooper would help you heal."

"He's done more than that." I pick up my dog and cuddle him against my chest. "This guy saved my life this morning. I'm keeping him."

Bert lumbers down the steps. "Doodles are hard not to love. I'll check back in a month or so, just to be sure."

I open my mouth to protest, but Bert is quicker. "Your mom asked me to check in with you too, Sawyer. Let you know I'm not only a breeder of dogs, but I was also your mom's therapist." She sweeps her arm out toward Dylan and Brittany and says, "Looks like you're surrounded by the ones your mom hoped you'd let help you. Still, you can call if you'd ever like to talk."

Wait a minute. Don't therapists know people's secrets? She might know about Brittany. "Hey, Bert? Wait up, will you?"

I hand Coop to Brittany and join Bert at the bottom of the steps. Whispering, I ask, "Do you know where I can find Brittany's paperwork?"

Bert smiles as she nods. "Find what your mom hid, and you'll figure that part out. Your mom thought it'd be better to spring all her secrets on you a few at a time. Brittany knew to call me if she needed anything in the meantime."

A few secrets at a time? "Are there any more surprises?"

"You knew your mom, Sawyer." Bert laughs and starts walking away. "What do you think?"

I think that's a big fat yes.

DYLAN IS DRIVING Brittany and me to the storage unit located outside town when Brittany leans forward from the backseat and says, "Wade really killed his best friend just to have Julie? That's so messed up."

"And because Chad wanted a bigger piece of whatever Zoe hid." Dylan's eyes cut to Brittany's in his mirror. "I've been breaking up fights between Chad and Wade for years. They kept escalating to the point where I was afraid one of them was going to hurt the other seriously. There was underlying hate."

"Why?" Brittany's brows scrunch. "Didn't Chad's family take Wade in after his parents died?"

"Yes, but Wade was always upset that Chad and his father didn't include him in their business. Treated him like the ward he was after his parents died. He thought for sure when Chad's dad died a few years later, he'd be asked to be part of their affairs, but that didn't happen either. Wade always resented that Chad lived a life Wade never did, even after he was a part of it. When Julie picked Chad over him, Wade lost it."

At the word "ward," Brittany's eyes, full of worry, cut to mine. I give her hand resting on the seat a quick squeeze, silently telling her she'll never be treated like that.

Dylan pulls up to the storage facility's front doors and parks. My uncle is sitting in his fancy car with his arms crossed, waiting for us. My sister and her family are there too, in their car. I wanted to do this together, and luckily, my sister's schedule worked out for a change. That and I promised to make dinner for everyone afterward.

Gage is here too, just in case we need some legal help.

We all get out, and, after I get hugs from my sister's kids, Collin and Alexandra run ahead into the lobby. Apparently, they think this is a fun adventure.

My stomach is housing a swarm of butterflies in anticipation of what's inside when my sister puts a hand on my arm and whispers, "Whatever we find is all yours, Sawyer. We're just here out of curiosity. And to find out about Brittany. You get that, right?"

I shake my head. "Don't commit until you see what it is first. Okay?"

My sister reluctantly nods to appease me.

A guy in his sixties is sitting behind a reception counter and smiles. "Need some help?"

"Yes." I pull out my key. "Can you point us to number 101?"

"101?" The guy's brows disappear under his baseball cap. "Are you Sawyer?"

I nod.

"Mike. Nice to meet you. I'll show you myself. My father left your mom that unit and what's inside a few years ago after he died. It's yours now as long as you need it."

"Thank you. I'm sorry about your father too, Mike." That his dad gave my mom the unit probably explains why I've never seen a monthly bill.

Mike smiles. "Right back atcha. This way."

My butterflies have turned to a horde of angry bees in my gut as we all follow Mike to what looks like a standard metal office door. It's not the same as all the other doors that slide up like a garage door that we passed in the long, tiled hallway.

Mike explains, "My father was an avid reader. Loved to talk books with your mom. They became good friends. May I?" He holds his hand out for the key, and I drop it in his palm. "He left her this from his estate." So maybe Mike is the one who was supposed to explain where the wine came from. Not a note.

My uncle's face turns red. "Zoe inherited whatever's in there?"

Mike nods, opens the door, and then stands back to let us step inside. "Except for the book."

I start to enter first, but my uncle beats me to the door and says, "That book belonged to both of us, if it's the one I think it is."

Shaking my head, refusing to argue with him in front of the kids, I follow behind. It's cold inside and filled with bottles of wine in racks stacked ten bottles high on each side. I pick up a familiar-looking bottle and show the label to Dylan.

He smiles, recognizing the name as I do from the expensive wine website. Who knows what it's all worth, but it's a lot. Half will be plenty to keep Brittany and me afloat until I can open my restaurant.

Mike has finally made his way in behind the rest and points to a case in the corner. "I helped your mom make that, Sawyer."

We all shuffle to the very end, where an ancient book sits in a glass case. Its binding is leather and very old, but in perfect shape. My nephew, Collin, squeezes by everyone and reads the title. "*The Celebrated Jumping Frog of Calaveras County*? By Mark Twain? What kind of book is that?"

My uncle says, "One worth a heck of a lot of money. Don't get too attached. We're selling it."

Mike frowns. "Zoe hoped you'd display it in the bookstore where it belongs. It's why I made that case."

I glance at my sister, who is shaking her head in a "let it go" kind of way. Megan hates drama.

Gage clears his throat. "Actually, Mayor, you and I should talk outside. It could have been excluded from the trust for a reason."

My uncle's jaw clenches, but he reluctantly follows Gage out into the hall. Once my uncle is out of earshot, I turn to Mike and ask, "Did my mom leave any paperwork? Or a note for me?"

"Not that I know of. She just said to tell you to sell the wine or keep it for your restaurant." Mike hands me back my key. "This is just a fraction of what my dad left for my brother and me. I've been selling ours little by little because we could never possibly drink it all. I'd be happy to give you my broker's name if you want it. He's done a good job for us. Your mom used him when she sold a few cases."

That's where my mom got the money for Brittany and the lawyers. "Thank you, Mike. I'll call you tomorrow about that."

He nods and makes a hasty retreat.

I say to my sister, "I'll sell it all and you can have half. Please? I insist."

Megan shakes her head. "Still not interested. But what about finding something that's supposed to explain things?" My sister's eyes cut toward Brittany, whose back is to us as she reads all the labels aloud in what sounds to me like perfect French.

I'd explained about Brittany's confession and what Bert said when I'd asked my sister to join us. "If the Twain book is here, and the wine, then that only leaves whatever is in the pantry at the house. Come on, guys. We need to go. Preferably before Uncle Frank figures out what we have."

I grab two expensive bottles of wine from the rack and shove them into my brother-in-law's hands. "Keep these for a special occasion. No arguments."

Lance looks at Megan, who shrugs, and then at his brother, Dylan, who's standing by the door watching Gage and my uncle fight. "Should I? Sawyer needs this worse than we do."

Dylan grins. "Doubt Sawyer will take no for an answer, but they're your eardrums."

Lance kisses me on the cheek. "Thank you, Sawyer."

"Thank my mom."

After I lock up and wave to Mike, we all race back to our cars, leaving Gage and my uncle still arguing in the parking lot. Dylan, Brittany, and I arrive at my house first.

I want a chance to see what's behind the pantry before my uncle arrives, so as soon as Dylan stops the car, I run to the house.

Once inside, Dylan jogs after me toward the kitchen while Brittany lets Coop out of the laundry room. I skid to a stop in front of the pantry and dive right in, throwing cans aside as fast as I can. My inner OCD freak is cringing at how long it'll take me to put all of it back in order when I'm done. Dylan and I have it mostly cleaned out when Brittany kneels beside me.

She says, "Want me to open this?"

I turn and blink at her. "You know how?"

Brittany nods. "Your mom showed me. I think I know what's behind here." Her fingers dance between the shelves, and suddenly, the front pops open, revealing shelves with two fat envelopes resting on them.

My sister's family joins us just as Brittany pulls out the two legal-size envelopes. Tears form in Brittany's eyes as she hands them over. "I've seen these a few times. These are the papers your mom had drawn up. In this envelope are the ones you need when I'm sick or whatever. The other is just a bunch of legal stuff that says Zoe adopted me."

Dylan says to a visibly disappointed Collin, who was hoping for buried treasure or some such, "Hey. I figured out Sawyer had a PlayStation a few nights ago. Want to go check it out?"

Collin's face lights up. "Yeah! Let's go!"

Dylan runs a hand down my arm as he passes by to follow our nephew to the living room. I'm grateful he's distracting Collin from any potential drama once my uncle gets here. Because there will be drama if Brittany is entitled to the trust too.

After the guys are gone, my sister says, "Do I want to know how he knows you had a PlayStation when the kids didn't even know?"

"Dylan stayed over *on the couch* to protect me the other night. He had to stay up anyway, so he played with it."

My sister grunts in disbelief while Brittany grins and says, "Never pegged you for the video-game type."

I inherited it from a former roommate right before I'd moved here. I've never even used it, but Brittany doesn't need to know that. "I'm just full of surprises." I hold out my hand for the paperwork.

Gage and my uncle join us in the kitchen too.

My uncle growls, "What'd you find, Sawyer?"

I draw a deep breath and slowly open the envelope. Inside is a stack of legal papers, and my mom left a note attached to the front. I clear my throat and read aloud, *"Taa-daa! I knew you guys would figure out the puzzle. I know I wasn't always the best mother, but somehow, I still ended up with the best daughters any mother could wish for. You raised each other at times, despite your goofy parents. So, I hope you both can find it in your hearts to help raise your new sister too. Good karma follows your spirit through all your many lives, and Brittany is a gem who needs her sisters to help her shine her brightest. Just like both of you do. Love you for eternity. Mom."*

That is so something our incredibly kind mother would do. It brings tears to my eyes.

I catch my sister's gaze, and she smiles and nods in agreement. We both understand why our mom took Brittany in. It was our mom's incredible big heart that made it easier to excuse the crazy, irresponsible things she often did.

Uncle Frank grabs the papers from my grasp and hands them to Gage. "I'm not letting a street rat get a portion of the trust. Fix this!"

Brittany holds up her palms. "I don't want anything. I should go."

"Nope." I pull Brittany beside me. "You're stuck with us. Legally. Might as well get used to it."

Megan nods. "I'm happy to have a new sister, Brittany." Megan draws Alexandra beside her. "Alex and Collin could use a cool aunt."

"Hey!" I'd take offense to that, but I'm happy to have Brittany too.

Gage hands the papers back to me. "These appear to be in order. And if so, Brittany is an equal heir to the trust."

My uncle is turning purple, he's so mad. "Not going to happen. I'll hire a lawyer from the city and fight this. Until then, no one spends another dime of the trust's money!" He stomps out of my kitchen, and after a few moments, the front door slams shut.

I smile and say, "Who wants to tell Brittany the good news? Gage?"

Gage grins. "Brittany, assuming these papers check out, you'll probably never get a lump sum of money from the trust, but you can go to any college you choose. Anywhere in the world, all expenses paid."

Brittany looks at me first and then Megan to confirm. "Anywhere I want? Even, like, Oxford?"

Megan says, "If you can get in, you can go. Please, take advantage of it. Especially because it'll piss off Uncle Frank."

Dylan appears by my side, and I ask him, "How long have you been standing there?"

He says, "Long enough," before gently pulling me out of the kitchen and to the front porch. After the front door closes behind us, he asks, "Do I want to know how Zoe ended up with Brittany?"

"Better not to ask." I stand on my tiptoes and hug Dylan. "I might actually miss solving crimes with you. Parts of it was fun. Thanks for saving me from Wade today."

When I lean away, he pulls me right back. "There's always going to be a new crime you can help me with. And we still have that golf ball to get to the bottom of. How about we leave it to be continued?" His eyes fill with hope.

As I stare into those blue eyes, remembering how much I used to love him, against my better judgment, I whisper, "Yes. To be continued."

ALSO BY TAMRA BAUMANN

It Had to Be Series:

It Had to Be Him

It Had to Be Love

It Had to Be Fate

It Had to Be Them

Heartbreaker Series:

Seeing Double

Dealing Double

Crossing Double

Matchmaker Series:

Matching Mr. Right

Perfectly Ms. Matched

Matched for Love

Truly A Match

ABOUT THE AUTHOR

Tamra Baumann is an award-winning author of light-hearted contemporary romance and cozy mystery. A reality-show junkie, she justifies her addiction by telling others she's scouting for potential character material. She adamantly denies she's actually living vicariously in their closets. Tamra resides with her real-life characters—her husband, kids, and their adorable goldendoodle in the sunny Southwest. Visit her online at: www.tamrabaumann.com